kinsey *and* me

Also by Sue Grafton

KINSEY MILLHONE MYSTERIES

A is for Alibi

B is for Burglar

C is for Corpse

D is for Deadbeat

E is for Evidence

F is for Fugitive

G is for Gumshoe

H is for Homicide

I is for Innocent

J is for Judgment

K is for Killer

L is for Lawless

M is for Malice

N is for Noose

O is for Outlaw

P is for Peril

Q is for Quarry

R is for Ricochet

S is for Silence

T is for Trespass

U is for Undertow

V is for Vengeance

A MARIAN WOOD BOOK
Published by G. P. Putnam's Sons
a member of Penguin Group (USA) Inc.
New York

kinsey *and* me

stories

sue grafton.

A MARIAN WOOD BOOK
Published by G. P. Putnam's Sons
Publishers Since 1838
Published by the Penguin Group
Penguin Group (USA) Inc., 375 Hudson Street, New York, New York 10014, USA
Penguin Group (Canada), 90 Eglinton Avenue East, Suite 700, Toronto, Ontario M4P 2Y3, Canada
(a division of Pearson Penguin Canada Inc.) · Penguin Books Ltd, 80 Strand, London WC2R 0RL, England ·
Penguin Ireland, 25 St Stephen's Green, Dublin 2, Ireland (a division of Penguin Books Ltd) · Penguin Group
(Australia), 707 Collins Street, Melbourne, Victoria 3008, Australia (a division of Pearson Australia Group
Pty Ltd) · Penguin Books India Pvt Ltd, 11 Community Centre, Panchsheel Park, New Delhi–110 017, India ·
Penguin Group (NZ), 67 Apollo Drive, Rosedale, Auckland 0632, New Zealand (a division of Pearson
New Zealand Ltd) · Penguin Books (South Africa), Rosebank Office Park, 181 Jan Smuts Avenue,
Parktown North 2193, South Africa · Penguin China, B7 Jiaming Center, 27 East Third Ring
Road North, Chaoyang District, Beijing 100020, China

Penguin Books Ltd, Registered Offices: 80 Strand, London WC2R 0RL, England

Pages 285-86 constitute an extension of this copyright page.

Library of Congress Cataloging-in-Publication Data

Grafton, Sue.
[Short stories. Selections]
Kinsey and Me : Stories / Sue Grafton.
p.   cm.
"A Marian Wood Book."
ISBN 978-0-399-16383-8
1. Detective and mystery stories, American.   I. Title.
PS3557.R13K56   2013   2012039977
813'.54—dc23

Printed in the United States of America
1   3   5   7   9   10   8   6   4   2

This book is printed on acid-free paper. ∞

Book design by Katy Riegel

This is a work of fiction. Names, characters, places, and incidents either are the product of the author's imagination or are used fictitiously, and any resemblance to actual persons, living or dead, businesses, companies, events, or locales is entirely coincidental.

For Ivan, Marian, and Molly:

With admiration, appreciation, and affection

contents

preface *xiii*

part one: kinsey

introduction *3*

between the sheets *7*

long gone *37*

the parker shotgun *61*

non sung smoke *85*

falling off the roof *107*

a poison that leaves no trace   *125*

full circle   *145*

a little missionary work   *163*

the lying game   *191*

entr'acte

An Eye for an I: Justice, Morality, the Nature of the
Hard-boiled Private Investigator, and
All That Existential Stuff   *199*

part two
. . . and me

introduction   *207*

a woman capable of anything   *211*

that's not an easy way to go   *217*

lost people   *225*

clue   *229*

night visit, corridor a   233

april 24, 1960   239

the closet   245

maple hill   249

a portable life   257

the quarrel   263

jessie   271

death review   275

a letter from my father   279

preface

A MYSTERY SHORT STORY is a marvel of ingenuity. The writer works on a small canvas, word-painting with the equivalent of a brush with three hairs. In the space of twenty or so manuscript pages, the writer must establish the credentials and personality of the detective (Kinsey Millhone in this case), as well as the time period and the physical setting. Usually, there's a murder or a missing person, whose disappearance is a matter of concern. Lesser crimes, such as burglary, theft, embezzlement, or fraud, may provide the spark for the story line, but as a rule, murder is the glue that holds the pieces in place.

In short order, the writer has to lay out the nature of the crime and introduce two or three viable suspects (or *persons of interest* as they're referred to these days). With a few deft strokes, the writer must further create suspense and generate a modicum of action while demonstrating how the detective organizes the subsequent inquiry and arrives at a working theory, which is then tested for accuracy. A touch of humor is a nice addition to the mix, lightening the mood and allowing the reader momentary relief from the tensions implicit in the process. In the end, the resolution must satisfy the conditions set forth at the beginning.

While the mystery novelist has room to develop subplots and peripheral characters, as well as the leisure to flesh out the private life of the protagonist, in the short story such indulgences are stripped away. The subtleties of the artfully disguised clue and the placing of road signs pointing the reader in the wrong direction may be present in the short story, but pared to a minimum.

The crime story, the mystery story, and the detective story are related forms that differ in the following ways. A crime story dramatizes the planning, commission, or aftermath of a crime without introducing any element of mystery. The reader is invited along for the ride, a witness to events and fully apprised of what's going on. Here, the reader functions as a voyeur, caught up in the action and subject to its rewards or consequences. The mystery story, on the other hand, proposes a puzzle with a crime at its center, but doesn't rely on the ratiocinations of a sleuth to drive the plot toward its conclusions. Instead, the reader serves in that role, observing, analyzing, and drawing inferences from the tantalizing questions the writer has proposed.

The detective story is governed by a special set of laws, many of which were laid out by S. S. Van Dine in an essay on the subject written in 1928. Not all of the strictures still apply, but many of the rules of the game are as critical today as they were back then. For starters, a detective story has to have a detective and, by definition, the detective must detect. The reader *must* be made privy to all of the information the detective uncovers in the course of an investigation. Of primary importance is the necessity for fair play. The clues have to be plainly stated though the detective's intellectual leaps needn't be entirely spelled out. The culprit has to be a visible entity in the body of the tale. In other words, the killer can't be someone who pops out of nowhere in the last paragraph.

Generally speaking, the killer can't be a maniac or a stone-cold crazoid operating without a rational plan. The point of a mystery is to figure out *whodunit* and the "who" has to be a visible player, though the means and methods might not be obvious. The killer can't be a professional hit man whose sole motivation is financial and who therefore has no relationship with the victim at all. The crime must have its roots in the past or present reality of the victim.

In a first-person narrative, the detective cannot also be cast as the killer because this would undermine the fundamental trust between the writer and the reader. The "I" who tells the story is presumed to be revealing all, not reporting objective events while neatly sidestepping his own complicity. The solution to the puzzle and the explanation for the crime have to be natural and logical. No ghosts, no Ouija boards, and no Divine Intervention. There are other, lesser axioms and if you're curious, you can look them up on the Internet the same way I did. The principles in play are what make the detective story challenging. The best practitioners are masters of their craft and experts at sleight of hand, performing their literary magic tricks with a grace and delicacy that make the illusions seem real.

For me, the mystery short story is appealing for two reasons.

One, I can utilize ideas that are clever, but too quirky or slight to support the extended trajectory of the novel. And two, I can complete a manuscript in two weeks as opposed to the longer gestation and delivery time required of a novel. The short story allows me to shift gears. Like an invitation to go outside and play, the shorter form offers a refreshing change of pace.

The Kinsey Millhone stories, which constitute the first section of this book, appeared in various magazines and crime anthologies over a five-year period that began in 1986. The single exception, "The Lying Game," I wrote in response to an invitation from Lands' End to submit a short story for the fortieth-anniversary catalogue. As a rule, I don't write to order, and I can't obligingly create a short story in response to even the kindest of requests. In this instance, Roz Chast and Garrison Keillor had agreed to contribute. Aside from the fact that I'm a huge fan of both humorists, there was something about the combination of writerly personalities and styles that appealed to my Dark Side. I went straight to a Lands' End catalogue and leafed through, looking for an item of clothing that had some magic attached. I got as far as Outerwear, and when I read the description of the Squall Parka I knew I'd found my inspiration. In 1991, these stories, with the exception of "The Lying Game," were brought together in a collection called *Kinsey and Me*, which was privately published by my husband, Steven Humphrey, through his company, Bench Press. The print run consisted of three hundred hardcover copies, which I numbered and signed, and twenty-six hand-bound copies that I lettered and signed. Some of these were sold and some were given as gifts to family and friends.

THE STORIES IN the second section of the book I wrote in the ten years following my mother's death. At the remove of some fifty years, I still find myself reluctant to lift the veil on a period of my life that was chaotic and confused. Looking back, I can see that I was rudderless and floundering, that in attempting to save myself, I hurt others. For this, I am deeply apologetic. I wish now that I'd been more giving, more gracious, less self-absorbed, and certainly less irresponsible than I was. Maturity would have been a big help, but that didn't come until later. Astoundingly, out of these same struggles I've been gifted with three incredible children, a husband whom I adore, and four granddaughters, whose energy and goodness fill my world with light. I've also been given friends who've encouraged me to this telling with more generosity and understanding than I've sometimes accorded myself.

I wish life could be edited as deftly as prose. It would be nice to go back and write a better story, correcting weaknesses and follies in the light of what I now know. What I've noticed though is that any attempt to trim out the dark matter takes away some of the good that was also buried in the muck. The past is a package deal and I don't believe there's a way to tell some of the truth without telling most. Wisdom comes at a price, and I have paid dearly for mine.

part one

kinsey

introduction

KINSEY MILLHONE ENTERED my life, like an apparition, sometime in 1977. I was living in Columbus, Ohio, at the time, writing movies for television while my husband attended Ohio State, working on his Ph.D. She arrived by degrees, insinuating herself with all the cunning of a stray cat who knew long before I did that she was here to stay. The name came first. The "Kinsey" I spotted in a copy of *The Hollywood Reporter* in the little column announcing births. A couple in Hollywood had named their infant daughter Kinsey and the name leapt out at me. "Millhone" was probably the product of a finger stroll through the telephone book or a random matching process, wherein I tried various syllables and rhythms until I found one that suited me.

I should note that the novels are set in the 1980s because of the decision I made at the time to have Kinsey age one year for every two and a half books. In *A is for Alibi*, she's thirty-two years old.

Thirty years later, in *V is for Vengeance*, she's thirty-eight. My only other choice was to have her age one year for every book, which would mean that if I kept her in real time, she'd be middle-aged by now and less likely to live with such reckless abandon. Since her life proceeds at such a measured pace, I am, myself, caught in a time warp. One obvious consequence of this same decision is that many of the technological advancements in the forensic sciences and most certainly innovations in communications are nowhere in evidence. No Internet, no cell phones, little DNA testing. This means she's forced to do her sleuthing the old-fashioned way, which better suits her personal style and the needs of the narrative.

I originally decided to write about a hard-boiled private eye because those are the books I was raised on. My father, C. W. Grafton, was a municipal bond attorney all his life, but he also wrote and published three mystery novels: *The Rat Began to Gnaw the Rope*, *The Rope Began to Hang the Butcher*, and *Beyond a Reasonable Doubt*. Because of him, I developed a real passion for the genre. I elected to write about a female protagonist at the outset because I'm female (hot news, huh?) and I figured it was my one area of expertise. When I started work on *A is for Alibi*, I wasn't even sure what a private investigator did. In the course of writing that first book, I began the long (and continuing) task of educating myself. I read books on forensics, toxicology, burglary and theft, homicide, arson, anatomy, and poisonous plants, among many others. My personal library has grown since I began writing about Kinsey and I now have quite a storehouse of information at my fingertips.

The cases I write about are invented, though some owe their inspiration to tidbits gleaned from the crime section of my local newspaper, which I clip from almost daily. I like looking at the dark side of human nature, trying to understand what makes people kill each other instead of going into therapy. In my soul, I'm a real law-and-order type and I don't want people to get away with murder. In a mystery novel there is justice and I like that a lot.

Kinsey is my alter ego—the person I might have been had I not married young and had children. The '68 VW she drove (until *G is for Gumshoe*) was a car I owned some years ago. In *H is for Homicide*, she acquires the 1974 VW that sat in my driveway until I donated it as a raffle item for a local theater group. The lucky ticket holder "won" the car for her ten-dollar purchase. It was pale blue with only one minor ding in the left rear fender. I didn't mind Kinsey using the car, but with her driving record, I refused to put her on my insurance policy.

What's stimulating about her presence in my life is that since she can know only what I know, I have to do a great deal of research and this allows me, in essence, to lead two lives—hers and mine. Because of her, I've taken a women's self-defense class and a class in criminal law. I've also made the acquaintance of doctors, lawyers, P. I.'s, cops, coroners, and all manner of experts. I own both of her handguns and, in fact, I learned to shoot so that I'd know what it feels like. I own the all-purpose dress she refers to in the books. Like Kinsey, I've been married and divorced twice (though I'm currently married to husband number three and intend to remain so for life). The process of writing informs both her life and mine.

While our biographies are different, our sensibilities are the same. As I've said on previous occasions, I think of us as one soul in two bodies and she got the good one. The particulars of her history usually come to me in the moment of writing. Often I feel she's peering over my shoulder, whispering, nudging me, and making bawdy remarks. The humor comes from her, and the acid observations—also whatever tenderness seeps into the page. She is a marvel for which I take only partial credit, though she probably claims *all* the credit for me. It amuses me that I invented someone who has gone on to support me. It amuses her, I'm sure, that she will live in this world long after I am gone. I trust that you will enjoy her companionship as I have.

Sue Grafton

between the sheets

I SQUINTED AT THE woman sitting across the desk from me. I could have sworn she'd just told me there was a dead man in her daughter's bed, which seemed like a strange thing to say, accompanied, as it was, by a pleasant smile and carefully modulated tone. Maybe I'd misunderstood.

It was nine o'clock in the morning, some ordinary day of the week. I was, I confess, hungover—a rare occurrence in my life. I do not drink often or much, but the night before I'd been at a birthday party for my landlord, Henry Pitts, who'd just turned eighty-two. Apparently the celebration had gotten out of hand because here I was, feeling fuzzy-headed and faintly nauseated, trying to look like an especially smart and capable private investigator, which is what I am when I'm in good form.

My name is Kinsey Millhone. I'm thirty-two years old, divorced, a licensed P.I., running my own small agency in a town ninety-five miles north of Los Angeles. The woman had told me her name was Emily Culpepper and that much made sense. She was very small, one of those women who at any age will be thought "cute," God forbid. She had short dark hair and a sweet face and she looked like a perfect suburban housewife. She was wearing a pale blue blouse with a Peter Pan collar, a heather-colored Shetland sweater with grosgrain ribbon down the front, a heather tweed skirt, hose, and Capezios with a dainty heel. I guessed her to be roughly my age.

I reached for my legal pad and a pencil as though prepared to take important notes. "Excuse me, Mrs. Culpepper, but could I ask you to repeat that?"

The pleasant smile became fixed. She leaned forward. "Are you recording this?" she said with alarm. "I mean, can this be used against me in court?"

"I'm just trying to understand what you're talking about," I replied. "I *thought* you just told me there was a dead man in your daughter's bed. Is that correct?"

She nodded solemnly, her eyes huge.

I wrote down, *Dead man in daughter's bed,* but I wasn't really sure what to ask next. So many questions crowd about when someone says something like that. "Do you know the man?"

"Oh, yes. It's Gerald," she said.

I noted the name. "Your husband?"

"My lover," she said. "I'm divorced."

"And where is your daughter at this point?"

"She's with him. My husband. But she's probably on her way home. He really isn't supposed to take her on weekdays. It says so in my decree, but he's been out of town and I thought it was all right. Just this once."

"I'm sure it is," I said, hoping to reassure her on this one small point. "And when did you notice"—I checked my notes—"Gerald?"

"This morning at about six. Well, closer to ten of, actually."

"What kind of dead is he?"

"What?"

"I'm wondering if you noticed the cause of death."

"Oh. Yes, I did. He was shot."

I waited for her to go on, but she didn't. "Where?"

She pointed to her heart.

I made another brief note. This was like pulling teeth. "And you're sure he was dead?"

"I'm not positive," she replied uneasily. "But he was cold. And stiff. And he didn't breathe at all."

"That should cover it," I said. "What about the weapon?"

"A gun."

"You saw it?"

"It was right on the bed beside him."

"Do you happen to know the make?" I thought the technicalities would throw her, but she perked right up.

"Well, it's a little High Standard two-shot derringer, a .22, with dual barrels and double action, so it's safety-engineered. I mean, it can't fire accidentally, even if it's dropped. And let's see. It's polished nickel with black grips and it's just about that wide," she said, holding her thumb and index finger about an inch apart.

I was staring at her. "The gun is yours?"

"Of course. I just bought it last week. That's why I was so upset when I realized he'd been shot with it. And right in Althea's bed. She's only four, but she's big for her age. She takes after my ex-husband's side of the family."

I really didn't think we'd exhausted the matter of Gerald quite yet. "Why did you buy a gun?"

"It was on sale. Half off."

"Is that what you told the police?" She paled and I didn't like this new expression on her face. "You did call the police, didn't you? I mean, when you discovered that Gerald was dead?"

"Actually, I didn't. I know I should have, but I didn't think anyone would believe me because we quarreled last night and I walked out. I never lose my temper, but I just blew my stack. I stood there and screamed at him. It was awful. I told him I'd kill him. I actually said that. Then I burst into tears and ran out the door and drove around all night."

"Did anyone hear you make this threat?"

"Just the neighbors on both sides."

I had a strong desire to groan, but I repressed the impulse. "I see. And what did you do besides drive around all night? Did you talk to anyone? Can anyone verify your whereabouts for the time you were gone?"

"I don't think so. I just drove. I was trying to work up the nerve to kick him out. We've been living together for about six months, and it's been heaven. Just wonderful. I can't think when I've been happier."

"Usually people don't get killed when things are that good," I pointed out.

"I know, then I found out he'd been cheating on me with a

woman right in the same apartment building, which is what made me see red. I was a basket case. I really was. Can you believe it? The man has borrowed thousands of dollars from me and then to find out he was f— Well, doing you-know-what with Caroline."

"And you knew nothing about it until last night?"

"No, no. I found out about Caroline weeks ago. I won't even tell you about the scene I had with her. It was horrible. She was so hysterical, she moved out. I don't know where she went, but good riddance."

"Had Gerald ever done this before?"

"Cheat? I'm not sure. I suppose so. Actually, he has. I know he's been involved with dozens of women. Gerald was a bit of a Don Juan. He cheated incessantly from what he said, but I never thought he'd do it to me."

"What was the attraction?" I asked. I'm always curious about women who fall in love with bounders and cads.

"Gerald is—"

"Was," I reminded her.

"Yes. Well, he was very good-looking and so . . . I don't know . . . tenderhearted. It's hard to explain, but he was very loving and sentimental. Such a romantic. I adored him. Really."

She seemed on the verge of tears and I allowed her a few moments to compose herself.

"What did you quarrel about last night?"

"I don't even remember," she said. "We went out to have a drink and one thing led to another. We got into some silly argument at the bar and next thing you know, the whole subject of his past came up—this woman Lorraine he was crazy about years ago,

Ann-Marie, Trish, Lynn. He kept talking about how wonderful they were. He got ugly and so did I. We came back to the apartment and things just went from bad to worse. I had to get out of there so I left. When I came back this morning, I thought he was gone. Then I noticed Althea's bedroom door was ajar and there he was. Right in her bed, like Goldilocks."

"What was he doing in her room?"

"Well, I'd locked him out of mine. He kept banging on the bedroom door, insisting that I let him in, but I refused. I told him if he so much as set foot in there again, I'd blow his ba— I indicated I'd injure him where it counts. Anyway, it looks like he took a glass and a bottle of bourbon into her room and drank 'til he passed out. I waited until I could hear him snoring and then I unlocked my bedroom door and slipped out the front. When I came back this morning, I could see he was still stretched out on Althea's bed. I stood in the doorway and told him he'd have to move out. I thought he was listening to me, of course, just pretending to be asleep, but when I finished and he didn't say a word, I got furious and started shaking him. That's when I realized he was dead, when I pulled the covers down and saw all the blood."

I was taking notes as fast as I could and I didn't realize she'd stopped. When the silence stretched, I glanced up at her. She was beginning to dissolve, her mouth trembling, eyes brimming with tears. "Take your time," I murmured.

"Well," she said. She fumbled in her handbag for a tissue and dabbed at her eyes. She blew her nose and took a deep breath. "Anyway, when I saw the gun on the bed, I just did the first thing that occurred to me."

I could feel my heart sink. "What was that?"

"I picked it up."

"Mrs. Culpepper, you shouldn't have done that. Now your fingerprints are *on* the gun."

"I know. That's why I put it right back down and left. My goodness, I was so upset."

"I can imagine," I said. "What next?"

"Well, I got in my car and drove around some more and then I stopped and looked up your number in the phone book and came here."

"Why me?" I said, trying not to sound plaintive.

"You're a woman. I thought you'd understand. I'll pay you anything if you'll help me straighten this out. I mean, if you could explain it all to the police . . ." She twisted the tissue, looking at me helplessly.

My eyeballs were starting to bulge with pain. I wanted an Alka-Seltzer in the worst kind of way. I slid my desk drawer open a crack and spied a packet. I wondered what would happen if I opened the foil and slipped an Alka-Seltzer onto my tongue like a Necco wafer. I've heard it kills you to do that, but I'm not sure it's true. The rumor circulated through my grade school one year, along with the yarn about the mouse tail that showed up in a bottle of soda pop. I've been uneasy about pop bottles ever since, but who knows how stories like that get started.

I tried to bring my battered intelligence back to the matter at hand. I knew I was secretly hoping to avoid dealing with Emily Culpepper's problem, which was a whopper.

"Emily . . . May I call you Emily?"

"Please do. And I'll call you Kinsey, if that's all right."

"Perfect," I said. "I think what we should do at this point is deposit you in the offices of a friend of mine, an attorney right here in the building. While you're bringing her up to date, I'll take your keys and go over to your place and check this out and then I'll call the cops. They'll want to talk to you, of course, but at least they'll be forced to do it in the presence of legal counsel."

I made a quick call to Hermione, apprising her of the situation, and then I walked Emily Culpepper across the hall and left her there, taking her house keys with me as I headed down the back stairs to the municipal lot where my VW was parked.

IT WAS "WINTER" in Santa Teresa, which is to say California at its best. The day was sunny, the town lush and green, the ocean churning away like a washing machine on the gentle cycle. While most of the country endured rain, sleet, hail, and snow, we were in shirtsleeves and shorts playing volleyball at the beach. At least, some people were. I was on my way out to Emily Culpepper's apartment building, reciting to myself a litany of the troubles she had brought down on herself. Not only had Gerald been shot with her little derringer, but she'd picked the damn thing up, thus (probably) smudging any latent prints and superimposing a clear set of her own. And then, instead of calling the cops right away, which at least would have made her look like a conscientious citizen, she'd run! The whole situation was so damning, I wondered if she was setting me up, providing herself with an elaborate (though preposterous)

alibi of sorts. Maybe she'd actually killed him and had cooked up this bizarre tale to cover her tracks. Her behavior throughout had been so dumb, it might almost pass for smart.

The address she'd given me was on a shady side street not far from downtown Santa Teresa. There were twenty apartments altogether, ten down, ten up, arranged in a square. The building was done in that mock Spanish style so prevalent out here: red tile roof, whitewashed stucco walls, arches, and a central courtyard with a fountain in the center. Emily's apartment was number two, on the ground floor, right next to the manager's. I scanned the premises. There wasn't a soul in sight, so I took out the keys she'd given me and unlocked her front door, feeling guilty somehow and very tense. Dead bodies aren't fun and I wasn't sure quite what was in store.

My heart was thudding and I could feel a drop of sweat trickle down the small of my back. She'd described the layout for me, but I still took a few moments to orient myself. The room I'd stepped into was a combination living room–dining room, with a kitchen counter jutting out to my right and the kitchen beyond. Everything was done in greens and golds, with comfortable-looking upholstered furniture. There were a few toys scattered through the room, but for the most part the apartment was clean and orderly.

I crossed the living room. To the left, there was a short hallway with a bathroom visible at the end and a bedroom on either side. Emily had indicated that her bedroom was on the left, Althea's on the right. Both doors were closed. I found myself tiptoeing down the hall and then I stood for a moment outside Althea's room. I placed a tissue over the knob to preserve any prints, and then I opened the door.

I peered around the frame, being careful not to touch anything. A quick glimpse showed pale pink walls, toy shelves, stuffed
animals on the window ledge, a child-sized flouncy white cano-
pied bed.

And no body.

I pulled my head back into the hallway and stared at the door
with puzzlement. Was this the right room?

I opened the other bedroom door and stuck my head in briefly.
Everything looked fine. No evidence of a body anywhere. Emily's
room was just as tidy as her daughter's. Maybe Emily Culpepper had
flipped her tiny lid. I went back into Althea's room, feeling utterly
perplexed. What was going on? The bed looked absolutely untouched,
the coverlet a pristine white, the pillows plump. Cautiously, I pulled
the spread down and examined the linens under it. No sign of blood.
Under the fitted sheet, there was a rubber sheet, apparently to pro-
tect the mattress from any bedwetting misdemeanors on Althea's
part. I peeled back the rubber sheet. The mattress itself showed no
evidence of blood or bullet holes. I remade the bed, smoothing the
coverlet back into place, rearranging the ruffled throw pillows
on top.

I backed out of the bedroom, mentally scratching my head. I
found the telephone, which I'd seen on the kitchen wall. Emily had
written a phone number in pencil beside the phone. I covered the
receiver with a tissue and picked it up. The line was dead.

"May I help you?"

I jumped a foot. The woman was standing just to my right, her
expression dark with suspicion. She was in her forties, with a faded

prettiness, spoiled now by the deep lines that pulled at her mouth and tugged at the corners of her eyes.

"Oh God, you scared me to death!" I gasped.

"So I see."

"Hey, I know how it looks, but honestly, Emily Culpepper gave me her house keys and asked me to come over here to check on something for her."

"And what might that be?" she asked.

"I'm a private investigator. I've got identification right here."

I opened my handbag and took out the photostat of my license with that awful picture of me. "I'm Kinsey Millhone," I said. I pointed to the name on my ID and then gave her a chance to study it for a moment. I was hoping she'd remark that the picture didn't look a thing like me, but she never said a word. She returned the ID grudgingly. "You still haven't said what you're doing."

"Are you a neighbor of Emily's?"

"I'm the building manager. Pat Norman."

"Do you know Emily's friend Gerald?"

"Gerry? Well, yes. I know him." She still seemed suspicious, as though I might, at any minute, pull out a rubber snake and toss it at her as a joke.

"Maybe you know what's going on, then," I said. "Emily says she quarreled with him last night and left in a snit. When she came home this morning, she found him in her daughter's room, shot to death."

"Dead!" she said, startled. "Good heavens, why would she do that? I can't believe it. That's not like Emily at all."

"Well, it seems to be a little bit more complicated than that," I went on. "I can't find the body and her phone is dead. Do you mind if I borrow yours?"

I FOLLOWED PAT NORMAN into her apartment. She showed me the phone and I called Hermione, uncomfortably aware that Pat was eavesdropping shamelessly as I reported the details. Hermione said she'd collect Emily and the two of them would be over in ten minutes.

While I waited, Pat offered me some coffee. I accepted, looking around idly while she got out the cups and saucers. Her apartment was done up in much the same manner as Emily's. The layout was different, but the carpet was the same and the wallpaper in the kitchen was identical, right down to the telephone number penciled on the wall by the phone. Pat's taste ran to framed photographs of herself with celebrities, signed with various extravagant sentiments. I didn't recognize any of the signatures, but I supposed I should be impressed. "Quite a collection," I remarked. I never said of what.

"I was on the LPGA tour when I was younger," she said.

"How long have you managed this place?"

"Two years."

"What about Emily? How long has she lived here?"

"Ever since she and that husband of hers broke up. Ten months, I'd guess. Gerald moved in soon afterwards." She hesitated. "I have to be honest and tell you that I did hear them quarrel last night. I could hardly help it with her place right next to mine. I don't for a minute believe she'd hurt him, but she did make threats—not that she meant them. Given his behavior, who could blame her if she did?"

"Do you know what they quarreled about?"

"Women, I'm sure. I heard he was quite a philanderer. He was the sort who borrowed money and then disappeared."

"Did you hear anything unusual once she left?"

"I can't say that I did."

"What about Caroline? The one he was supposedly having an affair with?"

" 'Supposedly' my behind. He fooled around with her for months before Emily found out. I knew the two of them were going at it hot and heavy, but I kept my mouth shut. It was none of my business and I kept out of it."

"Did he borrow money from Caroline?"

"I have no idea. She had the apartment two doors down from Emily's. She only left last week. Short notice, too. Very inconsiderate." She glanced down at her watch. "Fortunately, I'm showing the place this afternoon. I hope to have it rented before the month is out."

There was a knock at the door and she went out to answer it. I half expected to see Hermione and Emily, but it was a short person, who said, "Is my mommy here?"

Pat shot me a look, suddenly taking on that special, silly tone adults use with kids. "No, she's not, Althea. Why don't you come on in. Is your daddy with you?"

"He's in the car."

Ordinarily, I don't take to children. I'm an only child myself, raised by a maiden aunt who thought most kids were a nuisance, sometimes including me. But Althea had a strange appeal. Her sturdy four-year-old body was topped by an ancient face. I knew exactly what she'd look like as an adult. Her cheeks were plump and she wore plastic glasses with pink frames, the lenses so thick they made her gray eyes seem huge. She had mild brown hair, straight as a stick, caught up in pink barrettes that were already sliding off. She wore a Polly Flinders dress, smocked across the front, with short puffed sleeves biting into her plump upper arms. She seemed poised and humorless and I could imagine her, later in life, evolving into one of those mysterious women to whom men gravitate. In some terribly bossy, mundane way, she would break all their hearts and never quite understand their pain.

"I suppose I should go get him," Pat said to me in a lowered tone. I watched Althea's gaze shift from Pat to me.

"Hi, I'm Kinsey," I said to Althea.

She said, "Hello."

Pat hurried off to the parking lot to tell Mr. Culpepper what was going on.

Althea regarded me with the solemnity of a cat. She sat herself on an upholstered chair, scooting way back until her legs stuck straight out. "Who are you?"

"I'm a private investigator," I said. "Do you know what that is?"

She nodded, pushing her glasses back on her nose.

I assumed her knowledge of private investigators came from TV and I was reasonably sure I didn't look like one, which might explain why she was staring.

"I didn't wet the bed," she announced.

"I'm sure you didn't."

She studied me until she was satisfied that she was no longer a suspect. "Where do you live?"

"Over by the beach," I said.

"Why did you come here?"

"Your mom asked me to."

"What for?"

"Just to look around and talk to Pat, things like that."

She looked at her shoes, which were patent leather with a T-strap. "Know what?"

"What?"

"Chicken butt," she said, and then a small, shy smile played across her face.

I laughed, as much at the look on her face as the joke, which I'd told myself when I was her age. "What's your daddy's name?"

"David. He's nicer than Gerald."

"I'll bet."

She had to lean forward then and pick at her shoe. She sat back, wagging her feet back and forth. "Where's my mother?"

"On her way home, I expect," I said.

Silence. Althea made some mouth noises like horses clopping. Then she sighed, resting her head on one hand. "Do you wet your bed?"

"Not lately."

"Me neither because only babies wet the bed and I'm big."

She fell silent. Apparently, we'd exhausted the subject.

I could hear the murmur of voices and Pat returned in the company of a man who introduced himself as David Culpepper. He was big, with a mustache, beard, and bushy head of hair. Wide shoulders, narrow hips, and biceps that suggested he lifted weights. He wore boots, blue jeans, and a flannel shirt that made him look like he should be accompanied by Babe the Blue Ox. "Pat filled me in," he said. "Is Emily here yet?"

"She's on her way," I said.

Without even thinking about it, we all looked at Althea, aware of the fact that whatever was happening, she should be spared any tacky revelations.

Pat, talking now like Minnie Mouse, said, "Althea, sweetheart, do you want to go outside and play on the swings?"

"I already *did* that."

"Althea," her father said warningly.

Althea sighed and got up, moving toward the front door with an injured air. As soon as she'd disappeared, David Culpepper turned to me.

"What is this?"

"You know as much as we do, at this point," I said. "Your wife swears that at six this morning, Gerald was dead as a doornail in Althea's bed. I can't find a trace of him."

"But my God," he said, "why would Emily say such a thing if it weren't true?"

"Uh, I hope you'll excuse me," Pat said. "I've got an apartment to show and I'd just as soon wait outside. Let me know if you need anything." She took a set of keys from the counter and moved out into the courtyard.

"Maybe you should see Althea's room yourself," I said to David.

"I'd like that."

Emily's apartment was still open and we moved through the living room to Althea's bedroom, which was just as bare of bodies as it had been when I first checked. David went through the same procedure I had, pulling back the counterpane and the top sheet to the bedding underneath.

"Was Gerald responsible for the breakup of your marriage?" I asked, watching as he remade the bed.

"I guess you could say that."

"What else could you say?"

"I don't know that it's any of your business."

"Wait and tell the cops, then," I said.

He sighed. "Emily had worked before Althea was born, but she stayed home after that. Apparently, she was getting restless. Or that's what she claims now. Once Althea started preschool, Emily had too much time on her hands. She started spending her afternoons at the country club. I thought she was having a ball. Hell, I wouldn't mind a schedule like that myself. She played tennis, golf, bridge. She met Gerald."

He left the rest unsaid, but the implications were clear. Her relationship with Gerald must have started out as recreational sex, developing into an affair with more serious overtones.

"What sort of work do you do?" I asked.

"I'm a building contractor. It's pretty basic stuff," he said, almost apologetically. "I guess I didn't come across as romantic—a man of the world. I sure never had any leisure time. I busted my nuts just trying to get the bills paid."

"From what Emily says, Gerald was a skunk. He cheated, he borrowed money. Why would she put up with that?"

"Ask her," he said. "The guy was a jerk. Try paying alimony and child support when you know the money's goin' to the guy who's diddling your wife."

"David, how dare you!"

Both of us turned. Emily Culpepper was standing in the doorway, her color high. Behind her, I saw Hermione Santoni, the criminal attorney whose office is just across the hall from mine. Hermione is almost six feet tall, with black curly hair and violet eyes—all of which David Culpepper took in at a glance. I made introductions all around and went through the whole explanation again.

"But he was right there!" Emily was saying. "I swear to God he was."

"What about your room? Maybe we should take another look," I said.

Uneasily, the four of us edged into the room like cartoon characters, bumping into each other, exchanging wary looks. There was still no body. David checked the closet and Emily got down on her hands and knees to look under the bed.

She opened the bed table drawer. "Well, here's my gun," she said, reaching for it.

"Don't pick it up!" I snapped at her. "Just leave the damn thing where it is."

Startled, Emily withdrew her hand. "Sorry," she murmured.

"Let's just find Gerald."

Hermione peeked in the clothes hamper. In the interests of thoroughness, I backtracked, checking Althea's room and the hall linen closet, noting with interest how tidy it was. I can't ever make my sheets lie flat and I usually have the towels all shoved together in a bunch. Emily's towels were color coded and her sheets were starched and pressed flat. She even had a nice empty space left over for the set coming back from the laundry. I wondered if she ironed men's underwear for them. She seemed like the type.

I was just returning to the bedroom when we heard Pat scream. It was a doozy, like something out of a butcher-knife movie only more prolonged. I was out of the apartment like a shot. I spotted her standing in the courtyard, two doors away, face white, mouth working helplessly. She pointed and I pushed past her into the empty apartment, which apparently had belonged to Caroline. Pat followed on my heels.

There was a body sprawled on the floor in the living room. I hoped it was Gerald and not someone else.

"It's him," Pat said. "Oh my God and he's dead just like she said he was. I thought I'd open the apartment to let it air before the people showed up to have a look. The door was unlocked so I walked right in and there he was." She burst into tears.

I couldn't figure out how he'd gotten here. Was it possible that he was still alive when Emily had seen him this morning? Could he have *crawled* all this way? That couldn't be the case or he'd have left a trail of blood. Emily had said when she found his body, he was already cold. I bent over the body briefly, puzzled by what appeared to be a soft pile of white powder near the dead man's right hand. It looked like soap powder and the granules adhering to his right index finger suggested that he'd tried to leave a message of some kind. A word had been spelled out almost invisibly on the surface of the spilled soap.

"What is that?" David said, coming up behind me.

"I don't know," I said. "It looks like M-A-F-I-A."

"Jesus, a Mafia hit?" he said, anxiously.

"Oh, don't be ridiculous!" Pat murmured, blowing her nose. "What would they want with him?"

I moved into the kitchenette. The detergent box itself was on the floor near the sink, empty by the look of it. It was one of those one-load sizes, dispensed from machines in commercial laundromats. I left it where it was, figuring the crime scene fellows would want to dust it for prints.

By now, of course, Emily Culpepper had joined us, along with Hermione and a couple I'd never seen before. The four of them clustered just outside the door and I saw the woman lean over and whisper to Hermione.

"Is this the one for rent?"

Hermione nodded, putting a finger to her lips. I guess she hoped to discourage conversation so she could hear what was going on inside.

The woman's voice dropped. "The ad said there were built-ins. Do you know if the refrigerator is frost-free?" Maybe she thought Hermione was agenting the place.

Hermione shook her head. "I just got here," she whispered. "There's a body in the living room."

"The former occupant?" the woman asked.

"Someone else," Hermione said.

The woman nodded, as if this were not an unusual occurrence in the course of a housing search. She conveyed the news to hubby and he lifted up on tiptoe, trying to get a better view.

"Look," David said, "I'm going back to Pat's and call the police.

Don't touch a thing." We all stared at him. The place was empty except for Gerald and none of us wanted to touch *him*.

Pat began to sob again quietly. Emily put a comforting arm around her and drew her out into the courtyard, where she helped her sit down on the edge of the fountain. The prospective tenants decided to have a little look around and I saw them disappear into the apartment. I perched on the fountain rim on the other side of Pat, patting at Emily ineffectually. Hermione paced up and down the courtyard, smoking a cigarette.

Emily leaned forward and caught my eye. "Well, at least now you know I'm not nuts," she said. "I did find him this morning. I just can't understand how he ended up down here."

"You're sure he was dead when you saw him," I said, quizzing her on the point for the second time.

"Well, I couldn't swear to it."

"What about this Mafia business? Do you have any reason to believe he was tied to the Mob?" I couldn't believe I was saying shit like this—the Mob—like Gerald had been "fingered" for betraying some crime boss. Ludicrous. The whole business felt like bad TV.

Pat clutched my arm, digging her nails in painfully. "I just remembered. Caroline called two days ago and said she'd be dropping by. She wanted to pick up the refund on her cleaning deposit because she didn't leave a forwarding address."

"Wow," I said. "Uh, so what?"

"What if she came back?"

"Last night?" I said.

Pat nodded vigorously. "Maybe she overheard Emily threaten

him. She could have waited 'til Emily drove off and then gone in there herself."

"Did she know about the gun?"

"Everybody knew about that," Pat said.

Emily seemed skeptical. "I did leave my front door unlocked, but it still doesn't make any sense. If *she* killed him, why move the body to her own apartment? Why not leave it in mine?"

"And why cut your telephone line?" I said. "The thing is, we really don't know what the scheme consisted of. Maybe you interrupted the killer."

Emily spoke up. "Wait a minute. Suppose what he wrote are the first few letters of the murderer's *name*."

I could see us all mouthing "Mafia," trying to imagine what the name might be.

David came striding back across the courtyard. "The police are on their way," he said.

"Uh, me too, gang," Hermione interjected. "I've got a meeting in ten minutes. I have to get back to the office."

"But what am I supposed to do?" Emily said. "What if I'm grilled and carted off to jail?"

"I'll be back in an hour. Just keep your mouth shut. Tell them I'm your attorney and I've told you not to say a word unless I'm present."

"Can I do that?" Emily asked. "I mean, is that legitimate?"

"That's what the Miranda decision was about, dear," Hermione said with more patience than I might have mustered at that point.

I gave her a quick word of thanks and watched her head off toward the street where her car was parked.

There was something about this setup that nudged at me. It was one of those situations I was sure had a simple explanation if I could only make the mental leap. I felt a tug and looked down to find Althea standing next to me, slipping her hand into mine. She was apparently attracted to me in the same way cats unerringly select the lap of someone who's ailurophobic. (That's a fear of cats, folks.) I was flattered, I'll admit, but uncertain what I'd done to warrant such trust.

Pat became aware of her at just about the same time I did.

"Oh look, everybody. Here's Althea," Pat chirped, sounding like she'd just had a hit of helium.

"We'll go for a walk," I said in a normal tone. I was afraid if I hung around, I'd start talking like her.

Althea and I headed out to the alley and strolled up and down, passing the rear entrance to the courtyard now and then. I could see that two uniformed policemen had arrived and once I spotted the prospective tenants checking out the laundry room. The crime scene investigators must have been delayed because for thirty minutes, everybody just stood around. One officer took a report and the second secured the area with tape, posting signs that said CRIME SCENE—NO ADMITTANCE. Althea, meanwhile, was entirely too quiet for my taste.

"Aren't you curious about all this?" I asked, finally.

She shook her head solemnly. "Because we didn't come here before, when I played."

"What'd you do?"

"Just nothing."

"That sounds boring," I said. "Wonder why you did that."

"Just because," she said.

"That's your story and you're sticking to it, right?" I said in jest. I looked down at that earnest little face, the fat cheeks, the glasses, the huge gray eyes. This was no laughing matter to the child and I knew I shouldn't make light.

"Gerald's dead," she remarked.

"Looks that way," I said, wishing I knew what the hell was going on.

I thought about the man shot to death in her room, the empty apartment two doors away. Emily must have stumbled onto the murder scene before the body could be moved. But why kill him there? And why move him somewhere else? And why weren't there any traces of him in Althea's bed? I thought about the detergent on the rug with the letters spelling . . . What? It was all so perplexing. The answer seemed to tease, the solution hovering just out of sight. I stood still for a moment, questions stirring at the back of my brain.

"Let's go see if we can use Pat's phone," I said to Althea. She trotted beside me obediently. We walked back toward the courtyard, past the laundry room.

"Hang on," I said. I popped my head in the door. Sure enough, there was a machine on the wall, dispensing small detergent boxes like the one on Caroline's floor. Well, at least I was pretty sure where *that* came from.

We approached the fountain, where Pat and Emily still sat, waiting for a homicide detective to arrive, along with the medical examiner, photographers, and assorted crime scene specialists.

"Can I use your phone?" I said casually to Pat. She nodded.

What I was suddenly curious about was the telephone number I'd seen penciled on the wall by both Emily's phone and Pat's. Why both places? Aside from their living in the same building, what did those two have in common? I wondered if the answer to this whole puzzle was hidden somewhere in that seven-digit code.

I went into Pat's apartment, crossing to the phone. I checked the number and then dialed. The line rang twice and then someone picked up. A singsong voice said, "At the sound of the tone, General Telephone time will be twelve o'clock, exactly." I burst out laughing and Althea looked at me.

"What's so funny?" she said.

"Skip it. I just made a fool of myself," I said.

As I started toward the door, I caught sight of Pat's photographs and experienced one of those remarkable mental earthquakes that jolt all the pieces into place. Maybe the right question here wasn't *why* but *who*. "Althea, was Gerald a *golf* pro?"

She nodded.

"Hey, kiddo," I said, "we just cracked this case."

Althea looked more worried than thrilled.

By the time we reached the courtyard, Lieutenant Dolan had arrived and was consulting with the uniformed police officers while David, Emily, and Pat looked on. He seemed startled to see me, but not necessarily displeased. Dolan is assistant division commander for Crimes Against Persons, handling the homicide detail for the STPD. He's in his fifties, a baggy-faced man with a keen intellect. While he finds himself annoyed with me much of the time, he knows I respect him and he knows I won't tread on his turf. Having spent two years as a cop myself, I know better than to withhold information or tamper with evidence.

"How did you get involved in this?" he asked.

I gave him a condensed version of the entire sequence of events, starting with Emily's appearance in my office. When I finished, he shoved his hands down in his pockets and rocked back on his heels. "I suppose you have the whole thing wrapped up," he said, facetiously.

"Actually, I do," I said. "Want me to demonstrate?"

"It's your show."

I took Althea by the hand and returned to Emily's apartment, the whole group trooping after us into Althea's room. I was beginning to feel a bit like Hercule Poirot, but I had to talk my way through this one. I waited until everyone was assembled, including the apartment hunters, who lurked at the rear, peering around surreptitiously. Maybe she'd be arrested and they could have dibs on this place.

"Let's go back to the beginning," I said. "Emily was convinced that Gerald was killed in Althea's bed, but when I got here, the body was gone and there wasn't any sign that a murder had been committed.

"I went to Pat's apartment to use the phone and that's when Althea showed up with her father. Emily had let David take her overnight and she was just being returned. Or so they led us to believe. The truth is, David had brought her back earlier. He found Gerald's body and realized how bad things looked for Emily—"

"Wait a minute," Dolan said. "What makes you so sure the body was here in the first place? You only have Mrs. Culpepper's word for it, right?"

"Well, yes, but it turns out to be true."

"Where's your proof?" Dolan asked. I could see that he was interested, but unconvinced.

My heart did a flip-flop, but I proceeded as if I were sure of myself. Secretly, I thought, Shit, why didn't I verify this first? I didn't need to make a fool of myself publicly.

I stripped the bed. As before, the sheets were clean as a whistle and the mattress looked like it had never been touched, let alone used as target practice by someone with a grudge. David flexed his fingers nervously. Emily reached down protectively and pulled Althea close.

I said, "Now, let's turn the mattress over."

The two uniformed officers gave the mattress a tug, lifting and turning it in one smooth motion. On the flip side, down in the lower right quadrant was a puncture in the ticking and a smear of dark red. "I think if you dig down in there, you'll find the .22 slug that killed him."

"But what about the soap powder and the cut in the telephone line?" Pat asked.

"That was all embellishment," I said. "David was doing what he could to divert suspicion from his ex-wife, so he went through the whole routine. Moved the body, turned the mattress, changed the sheets."

"Him?" Emily said with surprise, as if she'd never known him to change a sheet in his life.

"Oh sure. I noticed a set was missing from the linen closet and I also knew that Althea was feeling anxious about something. He'd sent her next door to play, but she'd seen him stripping off the sheets. She was worried she'd be accused of wetting the bed."

Althea was looking from face to face. She must have sensed her daddy was still in trouble somehow.

I went on. "David cautioned her not to tell anyone they'd been here and that's just what she did. She told me they hadn't been here. I thought it was an odd thing to say until I realized she'd taken him literally." I paused, looking at her. "You tried to do what your daddy told you, didn't you?"

Althea nodded, her mouth beginning to pucker, eyes filling with tears. David swooped her up in his arms and hugged her. "You did fine, sweetie. It's all right."

"I'd like to hear the rest of this," Dolan said.

"Well, after he moved the body, he started setting up false clues. He bought detergent and spilled it on the rug. He took Gerald's finger and wrote in the soap, all of this because he hoped to persuade us the man was killed by someone else. David must have borrowed all those corny devices from old *Hawaii Five-O* reruns."

"Up yours!" he snapped. "You can't prove a word of this."

"I think I can," I said equably.

"David killed Gerald?" Emily said, blinking those big innocent eyes.

I shook my head. "It was Pat," I replied. "Patricia."

Everyone turned simultaneously and stared, except for the couple in the rear.

"Who?" the hubby asked the wife.

"Me?!" Pat said. "Well, that's ridiculous. Why would I do such a thing?"

"You'll have to tell us that yourself," I said. "I suspect you fell in love with him years ago, when you played the Haig and Haig Mixed Team Tournament back in 'sixty-six. You told me yourself you were on the LPGA circuit back then. You still have the photograph of the two of you taken at the tournament, which he inscribed 'To My Darling Trish, with All the Love in My Heart, Gerry.' I spotted it the first time I used your phone, but of course at that point I hadn't seen Gerald yet. When I went back again, I recognized him and I also remembered what Emily had said about an ex-girlfriend of his named Trish."

Dolan looked over at her. "You want an attorney present before you make a response?"

"Oh, what difference does it make," she said impatiently. "The son of a bitch is dead and that's all I care about. I'd hoped to push the blame off on someone else, but then David came along and made a mess of it. 'Mafia!' I couldn't believe my eyes."

"Serves you right," David said. "You tried to frame Emily."

"Oh, poo. She could have pleaded temporary insanity. No jury's going to want to hang a little thing like her," she said.

"But why did you kill him?" Emily said, aghast. "I don't understand."

"To save fools like you, if nothing else," Pat said. "You have no idea what he did to me. I was twenty-two and as green as they come. That bastard took me for every dime I had and then ran off with some tart with a lower handicap. He broke my heart, ruined my backswing, and wrecked my career. And then, to have him come waltzing into my life again after all these years! It was too much! The worst of it was that he didn't even recognize me! Hadn't the faintest idea who I was. After everything I'd suffered, I was nothing to him. Not even a fond memory. I knew right then I'd get even with him if it was the last thing I ever did."

The hubby in the back said, "Hear! Hear!" and clapped until his wife gave him a nudge.

The party broke up after that. Pat was handcuffed and taken away and everybody else spent a good fifteen minutes reliving events. Emily asked David to stay for a while, touched that he'd tried to save her. Belatedly, I noticed that my head was starting to pound all over again, so I excused myself. Althea trailed after me, watching every move I made. She planted herself on the sidewalk while I got in my car and then rolled the window down on the passenger side, beckoning to her. She sidled over to the car.

"Are you okay?" I asked.

She nodded and then spoke up, her tone shy. "When I grow up, I want to be like you."

"Good plan," I said. "I'll tell you what. You come around to my office twenty years from now and we'll form a partnership."

"Okay," she said gravely and we sealed it with a handshake.

long gone

SEPTEMBER IN SANTA TERESA. I've never known anyone yet who doesn't suffer a certain restlessness when autumn rolls around. It's the season of new school clothes, fresh notebooks, and finely sharpened pencils without any teeth marks in the wood. We're all eight years old again and anything is possible. The new year should never begin on January 1. It begins in the fall and continues as long as our saddle oxfords remain unscuffed and our lunch boxes have no dents.

My name is Kinsey Millhone. I'm female, thirty-two, twice divorced, "doing business as" Kinsey Millhone Investigations in a little town ninety-five miles north of Los Angeles. Mine isn't a walk-in trade like a beauty salon. Most of my clients find themselves in a bind and then seek my services, hoping I can offer a solution for a mere thirty bucks an hour, plus expenses. Robert Ackerman's message was waiting on my answering machine that Monday morning at nine when I got in.

"Hello. My name is Robert Ackerman and I wonder if you could give me a call. My wife is missing and I'm worried sick. I was hoping you could help me out." In the background, I could hear whiny children, my favorite kind. He repeated his name and gave me a telephone number. I made a pot of coffee before I called him back.

A little person answered the phone. There was a murmured child-sized hello and then I heard a lot of heavy breathing close to the mouthpiece.

"Hi," I said. "Can I speak to your daddy?"

"Yes." Long silence.

"Today?" I added.

The receiver was clunked down on a tabletop and I could hear the clatter of footsteps in a room that sounded as if it didn't have any carpeting. In due course, Robert Ackerman picked up the phone.

"Lucy?"

"It's Kinsey Millhone, Mr. Ackerman. I just got your message on my answering machine. Can you tell me what's going on?"

"Oh wow, yeah—"

He was interrupted by a piercing shriek that sounded like one of those policeman's whistles you use to discourage obscene phone callers. I didn't jerk back quite in time. Shit, that hurt.

I listened patiently while he dealt with the errant child.

"Sorry," he said when he came back on the line. "Look, is there any way you could come out to the house? I've got my hands full and I just can't get away."

I took his address and brief directions, then headed out to my car.

ROBERT AND THE MISSING Mrs. Ackerman lived in a housing tract that looked like it was built in the forties, before anyone ever dreamed up the notion of family rooms, country kitchens, and his-'n'-hers solar spas. What we had here was a basic drywall box, cramped living room with a dining L, a kitchen, and one bathroom sandwiched between two nine-by-twelve-foot bedrooms. When Robert answered the door I could just about see the whole place at a glance. The only thing the builders had been lavish with was the hardwood floors, which, in this case, was unfortunate. Little children had banged and scraped these floors and had brought in some kind of foot grit that I sensed before I was even asked to step inside.

Robert, though harried, had a boyish appeal—a man in his early thirties perhaps, lean and handsome, with dark eyes and dark hair that came to a pixie point in the middle of his forehead. He was wearing chinos and a plain white T-shirt. He had a baby, maybe eight months old, propped on his hip like a grocery bag. Another child clung to his right leg, while a third rode his tricycle at various walls and doorways, making quite loud sounds with his mouth.

"Hi, come on in," Robert said. "We can talk out in the backyard while the kids play." His smile was sweet.

I followed him through the tiny disorganized house and out to the backyard, where he set the baby down in a sandpile framed with two-by-fours. The second child held on to Robert's belt loops and stuck a thumb in its mouth, staring at me while the tricycle child tried to ride off the edge of the porch. I'm not fond of children. I'm really not. Especially the kind who wear hard brown shoes. Like dogs, these infants sensed my distaste and kept their distance, eyeing me with a mixture of rancor and disdain.

The backyard was scruffy, fenced in, and littered with the fifty-pound sacks the sand had come in. Robert gave the children homemade-style cookies out of a cardboard box and shooed them away. In fifteen minutes the sugar would probably turn them into lunatics. I gave my watch a quick glance, hoping to be gone by then.

"You want a lawn chair?"

"No, this is fine," I said and settled on the grass. There wasn't a lawn chair in sight, but the offer was nice anyway.

He perched on the edge of the sandbox and ran a distracted hand across his head. "God, I'm sorry everything is such a mess, but Lucy hasn't been here for two days. She didn't come home from work on Friday and I've been a wreck ever since."

"I take it you notified the police."

"Sure. Friday night. She never showed up at the babysitter's house to pick the kids up. I finally got a call here at seven asking where she was. I figured she'd just stopped off at the grocery store or something, so I went ahead and picked 'em up and brought 'em home. By ten o'clock when I hadn't heard from her, I knew something was wrong. I called her boss at home and he said as far as he knew she'd left work at five as usual, so that's when I called the police."

"You filed a missing persons report?"

"I can do that today. With an adult, you have to wait seventy-two hours, and even then, there's not much they can do."

"What else did they suggest?"

"The usual stuff, I guess. I mean, I called everyone we know. I talked to her mom in Bakersfield and this friend of hers at work. Nobody has any idea where she is. I'm scared something's happened to her."

"You've checked with hospitals in the area, I take it."

"Sure. That's the first thing I did."

"Did she give you any indication that anything was wrong?"

"Not a word."

"Was she depressed or behaving oddly?"

"Well, she was kind of restless the past couple of months. She always seemed to get excited around this time of year. She said it reminded her of her old elementary school days." He shrugged. "I hated mine."

"But she's never disappeared like this before."

"Oh, heck no. I just mentioned her mood because you asked. I don't think it amounted to anything."

"Does she have any problems with alcohol or drugs?"

"Lucy isn't really like that," he said. "She's petite and kind of quiet. A homebody, I guess you'd say."

"What about your relationship? Do the two of you get along okay?"

"As far as I'm concerned, we do. I mean, once in a while we get into it, but never anything serious."

"What are your disagreements about?"

He smiled ruefully. "Money, mostly. With three kids, we never seem to have enough. I mean, I'm crazy about big families, but it's tough financially. I always wanted four or five, but she says three is plenty, especially with the oldest not in school yet. We fight about that some—having more kids."

"You both work?"

"We have to. Just to make ends meet. She has a job in an escrow company downtown, and I work for the phone company."

"Doing what?"

"Installer," he said.

"Has there been any hint of someone else in her life?"

He sighed, plucking at the grass between his feet. "In a way, I wish I could say yes. I'd like to think maybe she just got fed up or something and checked into a motel for the weekend. Something like that."

"But you don't think she did."

"Un-uhn, and I'm going crazy with anxiety. Somebody's got to find out where she is."

"Mr. Ackerman—"

"You can call me Rob," he said.

Clients always say that. I mean, unless their names are something else.

"Rob," I said, "the police are truly your best bet in a situation like this. I'm just one person. They've got a vast machinery they can put to work and it won't cost you a cent."

"You charge a lot, huh?"

"Thirty bucks an hour plus expenses."

He thought about that for a moment, then gave me a searching look. "Could you maybe put in ten hours? I got three hundred bucks we were saving for a trip to the San Diego Zoo."

I pretended to think about it, but the truth was, I knew I couldn't say no to that boyish face. Anyway, the kids were starting to whine and I wanted to get out of there. I waived the retainer and said I'd send him an itemized bill when the ten hours were up. I figured I could put a contract in the mail and reduce my contact with the short persons who were crowding around him now, begging for more sweets. I asked for a recent photograph of Lucy, but all he could come up with was a two-year-old snapshot of her with the two older kids. She looked beleaguered even then, and that was before the third baby came along. I thought about quiet little Lucy Ackerman, whose three strapping sons had legs the size of my arms. If I were she, I know where I'd be. Long gone.

Lucy Ackerman was employed as an escrow officer for a small company on State Street not far from my office. It was a modest establishment of white walls, rust-and-brown-plaid furniture, with burnt-orange carpets. There were Gauguin reproductions all around, and a live plant on every desk. I introduced myself first to the office manager, a Mrs. Merriman, who was in her sixties, had tall hair, and wore lace-up boots with stiletto heels. She looked like a woman who'd trade all her pension monies for a head-to-toe body tuck.

I said, "Robert Ackerman has asked me to see if I can locate his wife."

"Well, the poor man. I heard about that," she said with her mouth. Her eyes said, "Fat chance!"

"Do you have any idea where she might be?"

"I think you'd better talk to Mr. Sotherland." She had turned all prim and officious, but my guess was she knew something and was just dying to be asked. I intended to accommodate her as soon as I'd talked to him. The protocol in small offices, I've found, is ironclad.

Gavin Sotherland got up from his swivel chair and stretched a big hand across the desk to shake mine. The other member of the office force, Barbara Hemdahl, the bookkeeper, got up from her chair simultaneously and excused herself. Mr. Sotherland watched her depart and then motioned me into the same seat. I sank into leather still hot from Barbara Hemdahl's backside, a curiously intimate effect. I made a mental note to find out what she knew, and then I looked, with interest, at the company vice president. I picked up all these names and job titles because his was cast in stand-up bronze letters on his desk, and the two women both had white plastic name tags affixed to their breasts, like nurses. As nearly as I could tell, there were only four of them in the office, including Lucy Ackerman, and I couldn't understand how they could fail to identify each other on sight. Maybe all the badges were for customers who couldn't be trusted to tell one from the other without the proper IDs.

Gavin Sotherland was large, an ex-jock to all appearances, maybe forty-five years old, with a heavy head of blond hair thinning slightly at the crown. He had a slight paunch, a slight stoop to his shoulders, and a grip that was damp with sweat. He had his coat off, and his once-starched white shirt was limp and wrinkled, his beige gabardine pants heavily creased across the lap. Altogether, he looked like a man who'd just crossed a continent by rail. Still, I was forced to credit him with good looks, even if he had let himself go to seed.

"Nice to meet you, Miss Millhone. I'm so glad you're here." His voice was deep and rumbling, with confidence-inspiring undertones. On the other hand, I didn't like the look in his eyes. He could have been a con man, for all I knew. "I understand Mrs. Ackerman never got home Friday night," he said.

"That's what I'm told," I replied. "Can you tell me anything about her day here?"

He studied me briefly. "Well, now, I'm going to have to be honest with you. Our bookkeeper has come across some discrepancies in the accounts. It looks like Lucy Ackerman has just walked off with half a million dollars entrusted to us."

"How'd she manage that?"

I was picturing Lucy Ackerman, free of those truck-busting kids, lying on a beach in Rio, slurping some kind of rum drink out of a coconut.

Mr. Sotherland looked pained. "In the most straightforward manner imaginable," he said. "It looks like she opened a new bank account at a branch in Montebello and deposited ten checks that should have gone into other accounts. Last Friday, she withdrew over five hundred thousand dollars in cash, claiming we were closing out a big real estate deal. We found the passbook in her bottom drawer." He tossed the booklet across the desk to me and I picked it up. The word void had been punched into the pages in a series of holes. A quick glance showed ten deposits at intervals dating back over the past three months and a zero balance as of last Friday's date.

"Didn't anybody else double-check this stuff?"

"We'd just undergone our annual audit in June. Everything was fine. We trusted this woman implicitly and had every reason to."

"You discovered the loss this morning?"

"Yes, ma'am, but I'll admit I was suspicious Friday night when Robert Ackerman called me at home. It was completely unlike that woman to disappear without a word. She's worked here eight years and she's been punctual and conscientious since the day she walked in."

"Well, punctual at any rate," I said. "Have you notified the police?"

"I was just about to do that. I'll have to alert the Department of Corporations, too. God, I can't believe she did this to us. I'll be fired. They'll probably shut this entire office down."

"Would you mind if I had a quick look around?"

"To what end?"

"There's always a chance we can figure out where she went. If we move fast enough, maybe we can catch her before she gets away with it."

"Well, I doubt that," he said. "The last anybody saw her was Friday afternoon. That's two full days. She could be anywhere by now."

"Mr. Sotherland, her husband has already authorized three hundred dollars' worth of my time. Why not take advantage of it?"

He stared at me. "Won't the police object?"

"Probably. But I don't intend to get in anybody's way, and whatever I find out, I'll turn over to them. They may not be able to get a fraud detective out here until late morning, anyway. If I get a line on her, it'll make you look good to the company *and* to the cops."

He gave a sigh of resignation and waved his hand. "Hell, I don't care. Do what you want."

When I left his office, he was putting the call through to the police department.

I SAT BRIEFLY at Lucy's desk, which was neat and well organized. Her drawers contained the usual office supplies, no personal items at all. There was a calendar on her desktop, one of those loose-leaf affairs with a page for each day. I checked back through the past couple of months. The only personal notation was for an appointment at the Women's Health Center August 2 and a second visit last Friday afternoon. It must have been a busy day for Lucy, what with a doctor's appointment and ripping off her company for half a million bucks. I made a note of the address she'd penciled in at the time of her first visit. The other two women in the office were keeping an eye on me, I noticed, though both pretended to be occupied with paperwork.

When I finished my search, I got up and crossed the room to Mrs. Merriman's desk. "Is there any way I can make a copy of the passbook for that account Mrs. Ackerman opened?"

"Well, yes, if Mr. Sotherland approves," she said.

"I'm also wondering where she kept her coat and purse during the day."

"In the back. We each have a locker in the storage room."

"I'd like to take a look at that, too."

I waited patiently while she cleared both matters with her boss, and then I accompanied her to the rear. There was a door that opened onto the parking lot. To the left of it was a small restroom and, on the right, there was a storage room that housed four connecting upright metal lockers, the copy machine, and numerous shelves neatly stacked with office supplies. Each shoulder-high locker was marked with a name. Lucy Ackerman's was still securely padlocked. There was something about the blank look of that locker that seemed ominous somehow. I looked at the lock, fairly itching to have a crack at it with my little set of key picks, but I didn't want to push my luck with the cops on the way.

"I'd like for someone to let me know what's in that locker when it's finally opened," I remarked while Mrs. Merriman ran off the copy of the passbook pages for me.

"This, too," I said, handing her a carbon of the withdrawal slip Lucy'd been required to sign in receipt of the cash. It had been folded and tucked into the back of the booklet. "You have any theories about where she went?"

Mrs. Merriman's mouth pursed piously, as though she were debating with herself about how much she might say.

"I wouldn't want to be accused of talking out of school," she ventured.

"Mrs. Merriman, it does look like a crime's been committed," I suggested. "The police are going to ask you the same thing when they get here."

"Oh. Well, in that case, I suppose it's all right. I mean, I don't have the faintest idea where she is, but I do think she's been acting oddly the past few months."

"Like what?"

"She seemed secretive. Smug. Like she knew something the rest of us didn't know about."

"That certainly turned out to be the case," I said.

"Oh, I didn't mean it was related to that," she said hesitantly. "I think she was having an affair."

That got my attention. "An affair? With whom?"

She paused for a moment, touching at one of the hairpins that supported her ornate hairdo. She allowed her gaze to stray back toward Mr. Sotherland's office. I turned and looked in that direction too.

"Really?" I said. No wonder he was in a sweat, I thought.

"I couldn't swear to it," she murmured, "but his marriage has been rocky for years, and I gather she hasn't been that happy herself. She has those beastly little boys, you know, and a husband who seems determined to spawn more. She and Mr. Sotherland—Gavie, she calls him—have . . . well, I'm sure they've been together. Whether it's connected to this matter of the missing money, I wouldn't presume to guess." Having said as much, she was suddenly uneasy. "You won't repeat what I've said to the police, I hope."

"Absolutely not," I said. "Unless they ask, of course."

"Oh. Of course."

"By the way, is there a company travel agent?"

"Right next door," she replied.

I HAD A BRIEF chat with the bookkeeper, who added nothing to the general picture of Lucy Ackerman's last few days at work. I retrieved my VW from the parking lot and headed over to the health center eight blocks away, wondering what Lucy had been up to. I was guessing birth control and probably the permanent sort. If she was having an affair (and determined not to get pregnant again in any event), it would seem logical, but I hadn't any idea how to verify the fact. Medical personnel are notoriously stingy with information like that.

I parked in front of the clinic and grabbed my clipboard from the backseat. I have a supply of all-purpose forms for occasions like this. They look like a cross between a job application and an insurance claim. I filled one out now in Lucy's name and forged her signature at the bottom where it said "authorization to release information." As a model, I used the Xerox copy of the withdrawal slip she'd tucked in her passbook. I'll admit my methods would be considered unorthodox, nay illegal, in the eyes of law-enforcement officers everywhere, but I reasoned that the information I was seeking would never actually be used in court, and therefore it couldn't matter *that* much how it was obtained.

I went into the clinic, noting gratefully the near-empty waiting room. I approached the counter and took out my wallet with my California Fidelity ID. I do occasional insurance investigations for CF in exchange for office space. They once made the mistake of issuing me a company identification card with my picture right on it that I've been flashing around quite shamelessly ever since.

I had a choice of three female clerks and, after a brief assessment, I made eye contact with the oldest of them. In places like this, the younger employees usually have no authority at all and are, thus, impossible to con. People without authority will often simply stand there, reciting the rules like mynah birds. Having no power, they also seem to take a vicious satisfaction in forcing others to comply.

The woman approached the counter on her side, looking at me expectantly. I showed her my CF ID and made the form on the clipboard conspicuous, as though I had nothing to hide.

"Hi. My name is Kinsey Millhone," I said. "I wonder if you can give me some help. Your name is what?"

She seemed wary of the request, as though her name had magical powers that might be taken from her by force. "Lillian Vincent," she said reluctantly. "What sort of help did you need?"

"Lucy Ackerman has applied for some insurance benefits and we need verification of the claim. You'll want a copy of the release form for your files, of course."

I passed the forged paper to her and then busied myself with my clipboard as though it were all perfectly matter-of-fact.

She was instantly alert. "What is this?"

I gave her a look. "Oh, sorry. She's applying for maternity leave and we need her due date."

"Maternity leave?"

"Isn't she a patient here?"

Lillian Vincent looked at me. "Just a moment," she said, and moved away from the desk with the form in hand. She went to a file cabinet and extracted a chart, returning to the counter. She pushed it over to me. "The woman has had a tubal ligation," she said, her manner crisp.

I blinked, smiling slightly as though she were making a joke. "There must be some mistake."

"Lucy Ackerman must have made it then if she thinks she can pull this off." She opened the chart and tapped significantly at the August 2 date. "She was just in here Friday for a final checkup and a medical release. She's sterile."

I looked at the chart. Sure enough, that's what it said. I raised my eyebrows and then shook my head slightly. "God. Well. I guess I better have a copy of that."

"I should think so," the woman said and ran one off for me on the desktop dry copier. She placed it on the counter and watched as I tucked it onto my clipboard.

She said, "I don't know how they think they can get away with it."

"People love to cheat," I replied.

It was nearly noon by the time I got back to the travel agency next door to the place where Lucy Ackerman had worked. It didn't take any time at all to unearth the reservations she'd made two weeks before. Buenos Aires, first class on Pan Am. For one. She'd picked up the ticket Friday afternoon just before the agency closed for the weekend.

The travel agent rested his elbows on the counter and looked at me with interest, hoping to hear all the gory details, I'm sure. "I heard about that business next door," he said. He was young, maybe twenty-four, with a pug nose, auburn hair, and a gap between his teeth. He'd make the perfect costar on a wholesome family TV show.

"How'd she pay for the ticket?"

"Cash," he said. "I mean, who'd have thunk?"

"Did she say anything in particular at the time?"

"Not really. She seemed jazzed and we joked some about Montezuma's revenge and stuff like that. I knew she was married and I was asking her all about who was keeping the kids and what her old man was going to do while she was gone. God, I never in a million *years* guessed she was pulling off a scam like that, you know?"

"Did you ask why she was going to Argentina by herself?"

"Well, yeah, and she said it was a surprise." He shrugged. "It didn't really make sense, but she was laughing like a kid, and I thought I just didn't get the joke."

I asked for a copy of the itinerary, such as it was. She had paid for a round-trip ticket, but there were no reservations coming back. Maybe she intended to cash in the return ticket once she got down there. I tucked the travel docs onto my clipboard along with the copy of her medical forms. Something about this whole deal had begun to chafe, but I couldn't figure out quite why.

"Thanks for your help," I said, heading toward the door.

"No problem. I guess the other guy didn't get it either," he remarked.

I paused, mid-stride, turning back. "Get what?"

"The joke. I heard 'em next door and they were fighting like cats and dogs. He was pissed."

"Really," I said. I stared at him. "What time was this?"

"Five-fifteen. Something like that. They were closed and so were we, but Dad wanted me to stick around for a while until the cleaning crew got here. He owns this place, which is how I got in the business myself. These new guys were starting and he wanted me to make sure they understood what to do."

"Are you going to be here for a while?"

"Sure."

"Good. The police may want to hear about this."

I went back into the escrow office with mental alarm bells clanging away like crazy. Both Barbara Hemdahl and Mrs. Merriman had opted to eat lunch in. Or maybe the cops had ordered them to stay where they were. The bookkeeper sat at her desk with a sandwich, apple, and a carton of milk neatly arranged in front of her, while Mrs. Merriman picked at something in a plastic container she must have brought in from a fast-food place.

"How's it going?" I asked.

Barbara Hemdahl spoke up from her side of the room. "The detectives went off for a search warrant so they can get in all the lockers back there, collecting evidence."

"Only one of 'em is locked," I pointed out.

She shrugged. "I guess they can't even peek without the paperwork."

Mrs. Merriman spoke up then, her expression tinged with guilt. "Actually, they asked the rest of us if we'd open our lockers voluntarily, so of course we did."

Mrs. Merriman and Barbara Hemdahl exchanged a look.

"And?"

Mrs. Merriman colored slightly. "There was an overnight case in Mr. Sotherland's locker and I guess the things in it were hers."

"Is it still back there?"

"Well, yes, but they left a uniformed officer on guard so nobody'd walk off with it. They've got everything spread out on the copy machine."

I went through the rear of the office, peering into the storage room. I knew the guy on duty and he didn't object to my doing a visual survey of the items, as long as I didn't touch anything. The overnight case had been packed with all the personal belongings women like to keep on hand in case the rest of the luggage gets sent to Mexicali by mistake. I spotted a toothbrush and toothpaste, slippers, a filmy nightie, prescription drugs, hairbrush, extra eyeglasses in a case. I spotted a round plastic container, slightly convex, about the size of a compact, tucked under a change of underwear.

Gavin Sotherland was still sitting at his desk when I stopped by his office. His skin tone was gray and his shirt was hanging out, a big ring of sweat under each arm. He was smoking a cigarette with the air of a man who's quit the habit and has taken it up again under duress. A second uniformed officer was standing just inside the door to my right.

I leaned against the frame, but Gavin scarcely looked up.

I said, "You knew what she was doing, but you thought she'd take you with her when she left."

His smile was bitter. "Life is full of surprises," he said.

I WAS GOING TO have to tell Robert Ackerman what I'd discovered, and I dreaded it. As a stalling maneuver, just to demonstrate what a good girl I was, I drove over to the police station first and dropped off the data I'd collected, filling them in on the theory I'd come up with. They didn't exactly pin a medal on me, but they weren't as pissed off as I thought they'd be, given the number of penal codes I'd violated in the process. They were even moderately courteous, which is unusual in their treatment of me. Unfortunately, none of it took that long and before I knew it, I was standing at the Ackermans' front door again.

I rang the bell and waited, bad jokes running through my head. Well, there's good news and bad news, Robert. The good news is we've wrapped it up with hours to spare so you won't have to pay me the full three hundred dollars we agreed to. The bad news is your wife's a thief, she's probably dead, and we're just getting out a warrant now, because we think we know where the body's stashed.

The door opened and Robert was standing there with a finger to his lips. "The kids are down for their naps," he whispered.

I nodded elaborately, pantomiming my understanding, as though the silence he'd imposed required this special behavior on my part.

He motioned me in and together we tiptoed through the house and out to the backyard, where we continued to talk in low tones. I wasn't sure which bedroom the little rug rats slept in, and I didn't want to be responsible for waking them.

Half a day of playing papa to the boys had left Robert looking disheveled and sorely in need of relief.

"I didn't expect you back this soon," he whispered.

I found myself whispering too, feeling anxious at the sense of secrecy. It reminded me of grade school somehow, the smell of autumn hanging in the air, the two of us perched on the edge of the sandbox like little kids, conspiring. I didn't want to break his heart, but what was I to do?

"I think we've got it wrapped up," I said.

He looked at me for a moment, apparently guessing from my expression that the news wasn't good. "Is she okay?"

"We don't think so," I said. And then I told him what I'd learned, starting with the embezzlement and the relationship with Gavin, taking it right through to the quarrel the travel agent had heard. Robert was way ahead of me.

"She's dead, isn't she?"

"We don't know it for a fact, but we suspect as much."

He nodded, tears welling up. He wrapped his arms around his knees and propped his chin on his fists. He looked so young. I wanted to reach out and touch him. "She was really having an affair?" he asked plaintively.

"You must have suspected as much," I said. "You said she was restless and excited for months. Didn't that give you a clue?"

He shrugged one shoulder, using the sleeve of his T-shirt to dash at the tears trickling down his cheeks. "I don't know," he said. "I guess."

"And then you stopped by the office Friday afternoon and found her getting ready to leave the country. That's when you killed her, isn't it?"

He froze, staring at me. At first, I thought he'd deny it, but maybe he realized there wasn't any point. He nodded mutely.

"And then you hired me to make it look good, right?"

He made a kind of squeaking sound in the back of his throat, and sobbed once, his voice reduced to a whisper again. "She shouldn't have done it—betrayed us like that. We loved her so much."

"Have you got the money here?"

He nodded, looking miserable. "I wasn't going to pay your fee out of that," he said incongruously. "We really did have a little fund so we could go to San Diego one day."

"I'm sorry things didn't work out," I said.

"I didn't do so bad, though, did I? I mean, I could have gotten away with it, don't you think?"

I'd been talking about the trip to the zoo. He thought I was referring to his murdering his wife. Talk about poor communication. God.

"Well, you nearly pulled it off," I said. Shit, I was sitting there trying to make the guy feel good.

He looked at me piteously, eyes red and flooded, his mouth trembling. "But where did I slip up? What did I do wrong?"

"You put her diaphragm in the overnight case you packed. You thought you'd shift suspicion onto Gavin Sotherland, but you didn't realize she'd had her tubes tied."

A momentary rage flashed through his eyes and then flickered out. I suspected that her voluntary sterilization was more insulting to him than the affair with her boss.

"Jesus, I don't know what she saw in him," he breathed. "He's such a pig."

"Well," I said, "if it's any comfort to you, she wasn't going to take *him* either. She just wanted freedom, you know?"

He pulled out a handkerchief and blew his nose, trying to compose himself. He mopped his eyes, shivering with tension. "How can you prove it, though, without a body? Do you know where she is?"

"I think we do," I said softly. "The sandbox, Robert. Right under us."

He seemed to shrink. "Oh, God," he whispered. "Oh, God, don't turn me in. I'll give you the money, I don't give a damn. Just let me stay here with my kids. The little guys need me. I did it for them. I swear I did. You don't have to tell the cops, do you?"

I shook my head and opened my shirt collar, showing him the mike. "I don't have to tell a soul," I said, and then I looked over toward the side yard.

For once, I was glad to see Lieutenant Dolan amble into view.

the parker shotgun

THE CHRISTMAS HOLIDAYS had come and gone, and the new year was under way. January, in California, is as good as it gets—cool, clear, and green, with a sky the color of wisteria and a surf that thunders like a volley of gunfire in a distant field. My name is Kinsey Millhone. I'm a private investigator, licensed, bonded, insured; white, female, age thirty-two, unmarried, and physically fit. That Monday morning, I was sitting in my office with my feet up, wondering what life would bring, when a woman walked in and tossed a photograph on my desk. My introduction to the Parker shotgun began with a graphic view of its apparent effect when fired at a formerly nice-looking man at close range. His face was still largely intact, but he had no use now for a pocket comb. With effort, I kept my expression neutral as I glanced up at her.

"Somebody killed my husband."

"I can see that," I said.

She snatched the picture back and stared at it as though she might have missed some telling detail. Her face suffused with pink, and she blinked back tears. "Jesus. Rudd was killed five months ago, and the cops have done shit. I'm so sick of getting the runaround I could scream."

She sat down abruptly and pressed a hand to her mouth, trying to compose herself. She was in her late twenties, with a gaudy prettiness. Her hair was an odd shade of brown, like Cherry Coke, worn shoulder length and straight. Her eyes were large, a lush mink brown; her mouth was full. Her complexion was all warm tones, tanned, and clear. She didn't seem to be wearing makeup, but she was still as vivid as a magazine illustration, a good four-color run on slick paper. She was seven months pregnant by the look of her; not voluminous yet, but rotund. When she was calmer, she identified herself as Lisa Osterling.

"That's a crime lab photo. How'd you come by it?" I said when the preliminaries were disposed of.

She fumbled in her handbag for a tissue and blew her nose. "I have my little ways," she said morosely. "Actually I know the photographer and I stole a print. I'm going to have it blown up and hung on the wall just so I won't forget. The police are hoping I'll drop the whole thing, but I got news for *them*." Her mouth was starting to tremble again, and a tear splashed onto her skirt as though my ceiling had a leak.

"What's the story?" I said. "The cops in this town are usually pretty good." I got up and filled a paper cup with water from my Sparkletts dispenser, passing it over to her.

She murmured a thank-you and drank it down, staring into the bottom of the cup as she spoke. "Rudd was a cocaine dealer until a month or so before he died. They haven't said as much, but I know they've written him off as some kind of small-time punk. What do they care? They'd like to think he was killed in a drug deal—a double cross or something like that. He wasn't, though. He'd given it all up because of this."

She glanced down at the swell of her belly. She was wearing a kelly green T-shirt with an arrow down the front. The word oops! was written across her breasts in machine embroidery.

"What's your theory?" I asked. Already I was leaning toward the official police version of events. Drug dealing isn't synonymous with longevity. There's too much money involved and too many amateurs getting into the act. This was Santa Teresa—ninety-five miles north of the big time in L.A., but there are still standards to maintain. A shotgun blast is the underworld equivalent of a bad annual review.

"I don't have a theory. I just don't like theirs. I want you to look into it so I can clear Rudd's name before the baby comes."

I shrugged. "I'll do what I can, but I can't guarantee the results. How are you going to feel if the cops are right?"

She stood up, giving me a flat look. "I don't know why Rudd died, but it had nothing to do with drugs," she said. She opened her handbag and extracted a roll of bills the size of a wad of socks. "What do you charge?"

"Thirty bucks an hour plus expenses."

She peeled off several hundred-dollar bills and laid them on the desk.

I got out a contract.

MY SECOND ENCOUNTER with the Parker shotgun came in the form of a dealer's appraisal slip that I discovered when I was nosing through Rudd Osterling's private possessions an hour later at the house. The address she'd given me was on the Bluffs, a residential area on the west side of town, overlooking the Pacific. It should have been an elegant neighborhood, but the ocean generated too much fog and too much corrosive salt air. The houses were small and had a temporary feel to them, as though the occupants intended to move on when the month was up. No one seemed to get around to painting the trim, and the yards looked like they were kept by people who spent all day at the beach. I followed her in my car, reviewing the information she'd given me as I urged my ancient VW up Capilla Hill and took a right on Presipio.

The late Rudd Osterling had been in Santa Teresa since the sixties, when he migrated to the West Coast in search of sunshine, good surf, good dope, and casual sex. Lisa told me he'd lived in vans and communes, working variously as a roofer, tree trimmer, bean picker, fry cook, and forklift operator—never with any noticeable ambition or success. He'd started dealing cocaine two years earlier, apparently netting more money than he was accustomed to. Then he'd met and married Lisa, and she'd been determined to see him clean up his act. According to her, he'd retired from the drug trade and was just in the process of setting himself up in a landscape maintenance business when someone blew the top of his head off.

I pulled into the driveway behind her, glancing at the frame-

and-stucco bungalow with its patchy grass and dilapidated fence. It looked like one of those households where there's always something under construction, probably without permits and not up to code. In this case, a foundation had been laid for an addition to the garage, but the weeds were already growing up through cracks in the concrete. A wooden outbuilding had been dismantled, the old lumber tossed in an unsightly pile. Closer to the house, there were stacks of cheap pecan wood paneling, sun-bleached in places and warped along one edge. It was all hapless and depressing, but she scarcely looked at it.

I followed her into the house.

"We were just getting the house fixed up when he died," she remarked.

"When did you buy the place?" I was manufacturing small talk, trying to cover my distaste at the sight of the old linoleum counter, where a line of ants stretched from a crust of toast and jelly all the way out the back door.

"We didn't really. This was my mother's. She and my stepdad moved back to the Midwest last year."

"What about Rudd? Did he have any family out here?"

"They're all in Connecticut, I think, real la-di-da. His parents are dead, and his sisters wouldn't even come out to the funeral."

"Did he have a lot of friends?"

"All cocaine dealers have friends."

"Enemies?"

"Not that I ever heard about."

"Who was his supplier?"

"I don't know that."

"No disputes? Suits pending? Quarrels with the neighbors? Family arguments about the inheritance?"

She gave me a no on all four counts.

I had told her I wanted to go through his personal belongings, so she showed me into the tiny back bedroom, where he'd set up a card table and some cardboard file boxes. A real entrepreneur. I began to search while she leaned against the door frame, watching.

I said, "Tell me about what was going on the week he died." I was sorting through canceled checks in a Nike shoe box. Most were written to the neighborhood supermarket, utilities, telephone company.

She moved to the desk chair and sat down. "I can't tell you much because I was at work. I do alterations and repairs at a dry cleaner's up at Presipio Mall. Rudd would stop in now and then when he was out running around. He'd picked up a few jobs already, but he really wasn't doing the gardening full-time. He was trying to get all his old business squared away. Some kid owed him money. I remember that."

"He sold cocaine on *credit*?"

She shrugged. "Maybe it was grass or pills. Somehow the kid owed him a bundle. That's all I know."

"I don't suppose he kept any records."

"Un-uhn. It was all in his head. He was too paranoid to put anything down in black and white."

The file boxes were jammed with old letters, tax returns, receipts. It all looked like junk to me.

"What about the day he was killed? Were you at work then?"

She shook her head. "It was a Saturday. I was off work, but I'd gone to the market. I was out maybe an hour and a half, and when I got home, police cars were parked in front, and the paramedics were here. Neighbors were standing out on the street." She stopped talking, and I was left to imagine the rest.

"Had he been expecting anyone?"

"If he was, he never said anything to me. He was in the garage, doing I don't know what. Chauncey, next door, heard the shotgun go off, but by the time he got here to investigate, whoever did it was gone."

I got up and moved toward the hallway. "Is this the bedroom down here?"

"Right. I haven't gotten rid of his stuff yet. I guess I'll have to eventually. I'm going to use his office for the nursery."

I moved into the master bedroom and went through his hanging clothes. "Did the police find anything?"

"They didn't look. Well, one guy came through and poked around some. About five minutes' worth."

I began to check through the drawers she indicated were his. Nothing remarkable came to light. On top of the chest was one of those brass-and-walnut caddies, where Rudd apparently kept his watch, keys, loose change. Almost idly, I picked it up. Under it there was a folded slip of paper. It was a partially completed appraisal form from a gun shop out in Colgate, a township to the north of us. "What's a Parker?" I said when I'd glanced at it. She peered over the slip.

"Oh. That's probably the appraisal on the shotgun he got."

"The one he was killed with?"

"Well, I don't know. They never found the weapon, but the homicide detective said they couldn't run it through ballistics, anyway—or whatever it is they do."

"Why'd he have it appraised in the first place?"

"He was taking it in trade for a big drug debt, and he needed to know if it was worth it."

"Was this the kid you mentioned before or someone else?"

"The same one, I think. At first, Rudd intended to turn around and sell the gun, but then he found out it was a collector's item so he decided to keep it. The gun dealer called a couple of times after Rudd died, but it was gone by then."

"And you told the cops all this stuff?"

"Sure. They couldn't have cared less."

I doubted that, but I tucked the slip in my pocket anyway. I'd check it out and then talk to Dolan in Homicide.

THE GUN SHOP was located on a narrow side street in Colgate, just off the main thoroughfare. Colgate looks like it's made up of hardware stores, U-Haul rentals, and plant nurseries—places that seem to have half their merchandise outside, surrounded by chain-link fence. The gun shop had been set up in someone's front parlor in a dinky white frame house. There were some glass counters filled with gun paraphernalia, but no guns in sight.

The man who came out of the back room was in his fifties, with a narrow face and graying hair, gray eyes made luminous by rimless glasses. He wore a dress shirt with the sleeves rolled up and a long gray apron tied around his waist. He had perfect teeth, but when he talked I could see the rim of pink where his upper plate was fit, and it spoiled the effect. Still, I had to give him credit for a certain level of good looks, maybe a seven on a scale of ten. Not bad for a man his age. "Yes, ma'am," he said. He had a trace of an accent, Virginia, I thought.

"Are you Avery Lamb?"

"That's right. What can I help you with?"

"I'm not sure. I'm wondering what you can tell me about this appraisal you did." I handed him the slip.

He glanced down and then looked up at me. "Where did you get this?"

"Rudd Osterling's widow," I said.

"She told me she didn't have the gun."

"That's right."

His manner was a combination of confusion and wariness. "What's your connection to the matter?"

I took out a business card and gave it to him. "She hired me to look into Rudd's death. I thought the shotgun might be relevant since he was killed with one."

He shook his head. "I don't know what's going on. This is the second time it's disappeared."

"Meaning what?"

"Some woman brought it in to have it appraised back in June. I made an offer on it then, but before we could work out a deal, she claimed the gun was stolen."

"I take it you had some doubts about that."

"Sure I did. I don't think she ever filed a police report, and I suspect she knew damn well who took it but didn't intend to pursue it. Next thing I knew, this Osterling fellow brought the same gun in. It had a beavertail forend and an English grip. There was no mistaking it."

"Wasn't that a bit of a coincidence? His bringing the gun in to you?"

"Not really. I'm one of the few master gunsmiths in this area. All he had to do was ask around the same way she did."

"Did you tell her the gun had showed up?"

He shrugged with his mouth and a lift of his brows. "Before I could talk to her, he was dead and the Parker was gone again."

I checked the date on the slip. "That was in August?"

"That's right, and I haven't seen the gun since."

"Did he tell you how he acquired it?"

"Said he took it in trade. I told him this other woman showed up with it first, but he didn't seem to care about that."

"How much was the Parker worth?"

He hesitated, weighing his words. "I offered him six thousand."

"But what's its value out in the marketplace?"

"Depends on what people are willing to pay."

I tried to control the little surge of impatience he had sparked. I could tell he'd jumped into his crafty negotiator's mode, unwilling to tip his hand in case the gun showed up and he could nick it off cheap. "Look," I said, "I'm asking you in confidence. This won't go any further unless it becomes a police matter, and then neither one of us will have a choice. Right now, the gun's missing anyway, so what difference does it make?"

He didn't seem entirely convinced, but he got my point. He cleared his throat with obvious embarrassment. "Ninety-six."

I stared at him. "Thousand dollars?"

He nodded.

"Jesus. That's a lot for a gun, isn't it?"

His voice dropped. "Ms. Millhone, that gun is priceless. It's an A-1 Special 28-gauge with a two-barrel set. There were only two of them made."

"But why so much?"

"For one thing, the Parker's a beautifully crafted shotgun. There are different grades, of course, but this one was exceptional. Fine wood. Some of the most incredible scrollwork you'll ever see. Parker had an Italian working for him back then who'd spend sometimes five thousand hours on the engraving alone. The company went out of business around 1942, so there aren't any more to be had."

"You said there were two. Where's the other one, or would you know?"

"Only what I've heard. A dealer in Ohio bought the one at auction a couple years back for ninety-six. I understand some fella down in Texas has it now, part of a collection of Parkers. The gun Rudd Osterling brought in has been missing for years. I don't think he knew what he had on his hands."

"And you didn't tell him."

Lamb shifted his gaze. "I told him enough," he said carefully. "I can't help it if the man didn't do his homework."

"How'd you know it was the missing Parker?"

"The serial number matched, and so did everything else. It wasn't a fake, either. I examined the gun under heavy magnification, checking for fill-in welds and traces of markings that might have been overstamped. After I checked it out, I showed it to a buddy of mine, a big gun buff, and he recognized it, too."

"Who else knew about it besides you and this friend?"

"Whoever Rudd Osterling got it from, I guess."

"I'll want the woman's name and address if you've still got it. Maybe she knows how the gun fell into Rudd's hands."

Again he hesitated for a moment, and then he shrugged. "I don't see why not." He made a note on a piece of scratch paper and pushed it across the counter to me. "I'd like to know if the gun shows up," he said.

"Sure, as long as Mrs. Osterling doesn't object."

I didn't have any other questions for the moment. I moved toward the door, then glanced back at him. "How could Rudd have sold the gun if it was stolen property? Wouldn't he have needed a bill of sale for it? Some proof of ownership?"

Avery Lamb's face was devoid of expression. "Not necessarily. If an avid collector got hold of that gun, it would sink out of sight, and that's the last you'd ever see of it. He'd keep it in his basement and never show it to a soul. It'd be enough if he knew he had it. You don't need a bill of sale for that."

I SAT OUT IN my car and made some notes while the information was fresh. Then I checked the address Lamb had given me, and I could feel the adrenaline stir. It was right back in Rudd's neighborhood.

The woman's name was Jackie Barnett. The address was two streets over from the Osterling house and just about parallel—a big corner lot planted with avocado trees and bracketed with palms. The house itself was yellow stucco with flaking brown shutters and a yard that needed mowing. The mailbox read SQUIRES, but the house number seemed to match. There was a basketball hoop nailed up above the two-car garage and a dismantled motorcycle in the driveway.

I parked my car and got out. As I approached the house, I saw an old man in a wheelchair planted in the side yard like a lawn ornament. He was parchment pale, with baby-fine white hair and rheumy eyes. The left half of his face had been disconnected by a stroke, and his left arm and hand rested uselessly in his lap. I caught sight of a woman peering through the window, apparently drawn by the sound of my car door slamming shut. I crossed the yard, moving toward the front porch. She opened the door before I had a chance to knock.

"You must be Kinsey Millhone. I just got off the phone with Avery. He said you'd be stopping by."

"That was quick. I didn't realize he'd be calling ahead. Saves me an explanation. I take it you're Jackie Barnett."

"That's right. Come in if you like. I just have to check on him," she said, indicating the man in the yard.

"Your father?"

She shot me a look. "Husband," she said. I watched her cross the grass toward the old man, grateful for a chance to recover from my gaffe. I could see now that she was older than she'd first appeared. She must have been in her fifties—at that stage where women wear too much makeup and dye their hair too bold a shade of blond. She was buxom, clearly overweight, but lush. In a seventeenth-century painting, she'd have been depicted supine, her plump naked body draped in sheer white. Standing over her, something with a goat's rear end would be poised for assault. Both would look coy but excited at the prospects. The old man was beyond the pleasures of the flesh, yet the noises he made—garbled and indistinguishable because of the stroke—had the same intimate quality as sounds uttered in the throes of passion, a disquieting effect.

I looked away from him, thinking of Avery Lamb instead. He hadn't actually told me the woman was a stranger to him, but he'd certainly implied as much. I wondered now what their relationship consisted of.

Jackie spoke to the old man briefly, adjusting his lap robe. Then she came back and we went inside.

"Is your name Barnett or Squires?" I asked.

"Technically it's Squires, but I still use Barnett for the most part," she said. She seemed angry, and I thought at first the rage was directed at me. She caught my look. "I'm sorry," she said, "but I've about had it with him. Have you ever dealt with a stroke victim?"

"I understand it's difficult."

"It's impossible! I know I sound hard-hearted, but he was always short-tempered and now he's frustrated on top of that. Self-centered, demanding. Nothing suits him. Nothing. I put him out in the yard sometimes just so I won't have to fool with him. Have a seat, hon."

I sat. "How long has he been sick?"

"He had the first stroke in June. He's been in and out of the hospital ever since."

"What's the story on the gun you took out to Avery's shop?"

"Oh, that's right. He said you were looking into some fellow's death. He lived right here on the Bluffs, too, didn't he?"

"Over on Whitmore."

"That was terrible. I read about it in the papers, but I never did hear the end of it. What went on?"

"I wasn't given the details," I said briefly. "Actually, I'm trying to track down a shotgun that belonged to him. Avery Lamb says it was the same gun you brought in."

She had automatically proceeded to get out two cups and saucers, so her answer was delayed until she'd poured coffee for us both. She passed a cup over to me, and then she sat down, stirring milk into hers. She glanced at me self-consciously. "I just took that gun to spite *him*," she said with a nod toward the yard. "I've been married to Bill for six years and miserable for every one of them. It was my own damn fault. I'd been divorced for ages and I was doing fine, but somehow when I hit fifty, I got in a panic. Afraid of growing old alone, I guess. I ran into Bill, and he looked like a catch. He was retired, but he had loads of money, or so he said. He promised me the moon. Said we'd travel. Said he'd buy me clothes and a car and I don't know what all. Turns out he's a penny-pinching miser with a mean mouth and a quick fist. At least he can't do that anymore." She paused to shake her head, staring down at her coffee cup.

"The gun was his?"

"Well, yes, it was. He has a collection of shotguns. I swear he took better care of them than he did of me. I just despise guns. I was always after him to get rid of them. Makes me nervous to have them in the house. Anyway, when he got sick, it turned out he had insurance, but it only paid eighty percent. I was afraid his whole life savings would go up in smoke. I figured he'd go on for years, using up all the money, and then I'd be stuck with his debts when he died. So

I just picked up one of the guns and took it out to that gun place to sell. I was going to buy me some clothes."

"What made you change your mind?"

"Well, I didn't think it'd be worth but eight or nine hundred dollars. Then Avery said he'd give me six thousand for it, so I had to guess it was worth at least twice that. I got nervous and thought I better put it back."

"How soon after that did the gun disappear?"

"Oh, gee, I don't know. I didn't pay much attention until Bill got out of the hospital the second time. He's the one who noticed it was gone," she said. "Of course, he raised pluperfect hell. You should have seen him. He had a conniption fit for two days, and then he had another stroke and had to be hospitalized all over again. Served him right if you ask me. At least I had Labor Day weekend to myself. I needed it."

"Do you have any idea who might have taken the gun?"

She gave me a long, candid look. Her eyes were very blue and couldn't have appeared more guileless. "Not the faintest."

I let her practice her wide-eyed stare for a moment, and then I laid out a little bait just to see what she'd do. "God, that's too bad," I said. "I'm assuming you reported it to the police."

I could see her debate briefly before she replied. Yes or no. Check one. "Well, of course," she said.

She was one of those liars who blush from lack of practice.

I kept my tone of voice mild. "What about the insurance? Did you put in a claim?"

She looked at me blankly, and I had the feeling I'd taken her by surprise on that one. She said, "You know, it never even occurred to me. But of course he probably would have it insured, wouldn't he?"

"Sure, if the gun's worth that much. What company is he with?"

"I don't remember offhand. I'd have to look it up."

"I'd do that if I were you," I said. "You can file a claim, and then all you have to do is give the agent the case number."

"Case number?"

"The police will give you that from their report."

She stirred restlessly, glancing at her watch. "Oh, lordy, I'm going to have to give him his medicine. Was there anything else you wanted to ask while you were here?" Now that she'd told me a fib or two, she was anxious to get rid of me so she could assess the situation. Avery Lamb had told me she never reported it to the cops. I wondered if she'd call him up now to compare notes.

"Could I take a quick look at his collection?" I said, getting up.

"I suppose that'd be all right. It's in here," she said. She moved toward a small paneled den, and I followed, stepping around a suitcase near the door.

A rack of six guns was enclosed in a glass-fronted cabinet. All of them were beautifully engraved, with fine wood stocks, and I wondered how a priceless Parker could really be distinguished. Both the cabinet and the rack were locked, and there were no empty slots. "Did he keep the Parker in here?"

She shook her head. "The Parker had its own case." She hauled out a handsome wood case from behind the couch and opened it for me, demonstrating its emptiness as though she might be setting up a magic trick. Actually, there was a set of barrels in the box, but nothing else.

I glanced around. There was a shotgun propped in one corner, and I picked it up, checking the manufacturer's imprint on the frame. L. C. Smith. Too bad. For a moment I'd thought it might be the missing Parker. I'm always hoping for the obvious. I set the Smith back in the corner with regret.

"Well, I guess that'll do," I said. "Thanks for the coffee."

"No trouble. I wish I could be more help." She started easing me toward the door.

I held out my hand. "Nice meeting you," I said. "Thanks again for your time."

She gave my hand a perfunctory shake. "That's all right. Sorry I'm in such a rush, but you know how it is when you have someone sick."

Next thing I knew, the door was closing at my back and I was heading toward my car, wondering what she was up to.

I'd just reached the driveway when a white Corvette came roaring down the street and rumbled into the drive. The kid at the wheel flipped the ignition key and cantilevered himself up onto the seat top. "Hi. You know if my mom's here?"

"Who, Jackie? Sure," I said, taking a flier. "You must be Doug."

He looked puzzled. "No, Eric. Do I know you?"

I shook my head. "I'm just a friend passing through."

He hopped out of the Corvette. I moved on toward my car, keeping an eye on him as he headed toward the house. He looked about seventeen, blond, blue-eyed, with good cheekbones, a moody, sensual mouth, lean surfer's body. I pictured him in a few years, hanging out in resort hotels, picking up women three times his age. He'd do well. So would they.

Jackie had apparently heard him pull in, and she came out onto the porch, intercepting him with a quick look at me. She put her arm through his, and the two moved into the house. I looked over at the old man. He was making noises again, plucking aimlessly at his bad hand with his good one. I felt a mental jolt, like an interior tremor shifting the ground under me. I was beginning to get it.

I DROVE THE TWO blocks to Lisa Osterling's. She was in the back-yard, stretched out on a chaise in a sunsuit that made her belly look like a watermelon in a laundry bag. Her face and arms were rosy, and her tanned legs glistened with tanning oil. As I crossed the grass, she raised a hand to her eyes, shading her face from the winter sunlight so she could look at me. "I didn't expect to see you back so soon."

"I have a question," I said, "and then I need to use your phone. Did Rudd know a kid named Eric Barnett?"

"I'm not sure. What's he look like?"

I gave her a quick rundown, including a description of the white Corvette. I could see the recognition in her face as she sat up.

"Oh, him. Sure. He was over here two or three times a week. I just never knew his name. Rudd said he lived around here some-where and stopped by to borrow tools so he could work on his motorcycle. Is he the one who owed Rudd the money?"

"Well, I don't know how we're going to prove it, but I suspect he was."

"You think he killed him?"

"I can't answer that yet, but I'm working on it. Is the phone in here?" I was moving toward the kitchen. She struggled to her feet and followed me into the house. There was a wall phone near the back door. I tucked the receiver against my shoulder, pulling the appraisal slip out of my pocket. I dialed Avery Lamb's gun shop. The phone rang twice.

Somebody picked up on the other end. "Gun shop."

"Mr. Lamb?"

"This is Orville Lamb. Did you want me or my brother, Avery?"

"Avery, actually. I have a quick question for him."

"Well, he left a short while ago, and I'm not sure when he'll be back. Is it something I can help you with?"

"Maybe so," I said. "If you had a priceless shotgun—say, an Ithaca or a Parker, one of the classics—would you shoot a gun like that?"

"You could," he said dubiously, "but it wouldn't be a good idea, especially if it was in mint condition to begin with. You wouldn't want to take a chance on lowering the value. Now, if it'd been in use previously, I don't guess it would matter much, but still I wouldn't advise it—just speaking for myself. Is this a gun of yours?"

But I'd hung up. Lisa was right behind me, her expression anxious. "I've got to go in a minute," I said, "but here's what I think went on. Eric Barnett's stepfather has a collection of fine shotguns, one of which turns out to be very, very valuable. The old man was hospitalized, and Eric's mother decided to hock one of the guns in order to do a little something for herself before he'd blown every asset he had on his medical bills. She had no idea the gun she chose was worth so much, but the gun dealer recognized it as the find of a lifetime. I don't know whether he told her that or not, but when she realized it was more valuable than she thought, she lost her nerve and put it back."

"Was that the same gun Rudd took in trade?"

"Exactly. My guess is that she mentioned it to her son, who saw a chance to square his drug debt. He offered Rudd the shotgun in trade, and Rudd decided he'd better get the gun appraised, so he took it out to the same place. The gun dealer recognized it when he brought it in."

She stared at me. "Rudd was killed over the gun itself, wasn't he?" she said.

"I think so, yes. It might have been an accident. Maybe there was a struggle and the gun went off."

She closed her eyes and nodded. "Okay. Oh, wow. That feels better. I can live with that." Her eyes came open, and she smiled painfully. "Now what?"

"I have one more hunch to check out, and then I think we'll know what's what."

She reached over and squeezed my arm. "Thanks."

"Yeah, well, it's not over yet, but we're getting there."

WHEN I GOT back to Jackie Barnett's, the white Corvette was still in the driveway, but the old man in the wheelchair had apparently been moved into the house. I knocked, and after an interval, Eric opened the door, his expression altering only slightly when he saw me.

I said, "Hello again. Can I talk to your mom?"

"Well, not really. She's gone right now."

"Did she and Avery go off together?"

"Who?"

I smiled briefly. "You can drop the bullshit, Eric. I saw the suit-case in the hall when I was here the first time. Are they gone for good or just for a quick jaunt?"

"They said they'd be back by the end of the week," he mumbled. It was clear he looked a lot slicker than he really was. I almost felt bad that he was so far outclassed.

"Do you mind if I talk to your stepfather?"

He flushed. "She doesn't want him upset."

"I won't upset him."

He shifted uneasily, trying to decide what to do with me.

I thought I'd help him out. "Could I just make a suggestion here? According to the California penal code, grand theft is committed when the real or personal property taken is of a value exceeding two hundred dollars. Now that includes domestic fowl, avocados, olives, citrus, nuts, and artichokes. Also shotguns, and it's punishable by imprisonment in the county jail or state prison for not more than one year. I don't think you'd care for it."

He stepped away from the door and let me in.

The old man was huddled in his wheelchair in the den. The rheumy eyes came up to meet mine, but there was no recognition in them. Or maybe there was recognition but no interest. I hunkered beside his wheelchair. "Is your hearing okay?"

He began to pluck aimlessly at his pant leg with his good hand, looking away from me. I've seen dogs with the same expression when they've done potty on the rug and know you've got a roll of newspaper tucked behind your back.

"Want me to tell you what I think happened?" I didn't really need to wait. He couldn't answer in any mode that I could interpret. "I think when you came home from the hospital the first time and found out the gun was gone, the shit hit the fan. You must have figured out that Eric took it. He'd probably taken other things if he'd been doing cocaine for long. You probably hounded him until you found out what he'd done with it, and then you went over to Rudd's to get it. Maybe you took the L. C. Smith with you the first time, or maybe you came back for it when he refused to return the Parker. In either case, you blew his head off and then came back across the neighbors' yards. And then you had another stroke."

I became aware of Eric in the doorway behind me. I glanced back at him. "You want to talk about this stuff?" I asked.

"Did he kill Rudd?"

"I think so," I said. I stared at the old man.

His face had taken on a canny stubbornness, and what was I going to do? I'd have to talk to Lieutenant Dolan about the situation, but the cops would probably never find any real proof, and even if they did, what could they do to him? He'd be lucky if he lived out the year.

"Rudd was a nice guy," Eric said.

"God, Eric. You *all* must have guessed what happened," I said snappishly.

He had the good grace to color up at that, and then he left the room. I stood up. To save myself, I couldn't work up any righteous anger at the pitiful remainder of a human being hunched in front of me. I crossed to the gun cabinet.

The Parker shotgun was in the rack, three slots down, looking like the other classic shotguns in the case. The old man would die, and Jackie would inherit it from his estate. Then she'd marry Avery and they'd all have what they wanted. I stood there for a moment, and then I started looking through the desk drawers until I found the keys. I unlocked the cabinet and then unlocked the rack. I substituted the L. C. Smith for the Parker and then locked the whole business up again. The old man was whimpering, but he never looked at me, and Eric was nowhere in sight when I left.

The last I saw of the Parker shotgun, Lisa Osterling was holding it somewhat awkwardly across her bulky midriff. I'd talk to Lieutenant Dolan all right, but I wasn't going to tell him everything. Sometimes justice is served in other ways.

non sung smoke

THE DAY WAS an odd one, brooding and chill, sunlight alternating with an erratic wind that was being pushed toward California in advance of a tropical storm called Bo. It was late September in Santa Teresa. Instead of the usual Indian summer, we were caught up in vague presentiments of the long, gray winter to come. I found myself pulling sweaters out of my bottom drawer and I went to the office smelling of mothballs and last year's cologne.

I spent the morning caught up in routine paperwork, which usually leaves me feeling productive, but this was the end of a dull week and I was so bored I would have taken on just about anything. The young woman showed up just before lunch, announcing herself with a tentative tap on my office door. She couldn't have been more than twenty, with a sultry, pornographic face and a tumble of long dark hair. She was wearing an outfit that suggested she hadn't gone home the night before unless, of course, she simply favored low-cut sequined cocktail dresses at noon. Her spike heels were a dyed-to-match green and her legs were bare. She moved over to my desk with an air of uncertainty, like someone just learning to roller-skate.

"Hi, how are you? Have a seat," I said.

She sank into a chair. "Thanks. I'm Mona Starling. I guess you're Kinsey Millhone, huh?"

"Yes, that's right."

"Are you really a private detective?"

"Licensed and bonded," I said.

"Are you single?"

I did a combination nod and shrug that I hoped would cover two divorces and my current happily *un*married state.

"Great," she said, "then you'll understand. God, I can't believe I'm really doing this. I've never hired a detective, but I don't know what else to do."

"What's going on?"

She blushed, maybe from nervousness, maybe from embarrassment, but the heightened coloring only made her green eyes more vivid. She shifted in her seat, the sequins on her dress winking merrily. Something about her posture made me downgrade her age. She looked barely old enough to drive.

"I hope you don't think this is dumb. I . . . uh, ran into this guy last night and we really hit it off. He told me his name was Gage. I don't know if that's true or not. Sometimes guys make up names, you know, like if they're married or maybe not sure they want to see you again. Anyway, we had a terrific time, only he left without telling me how to get in touch. I was just wondering how much it might cost to find out who he is."

"How do you know he won't get in touch with you?"

"Well, he might. I mean, I'll give him a couple of days, of course. All I'm asking for is his name and address. Just in case."

"I take it you'll want his phone number, too."

She laughed uneasily. "Well, yeah."

"What if he doesn't want to renew the acquaintance?"

"Oh, I wouldn't bother him if he felt that way. I know it looks like a pickup, but it really wasn't. For me, at any rate. I don't want him to think it was casual on my part."

"I take it you were . . . ah, *intimate*," I said.

"Un-uhn, we just balled, but it was incredible and I'd really like to see him again."

Reluctantly, I pulled out a legal pad and made a note. "Where'd you meet this man?"

"I ran into him at Mooter's. He talked like he hung out there a lot. The music was so loud we were having to shout, so after a while we went to the bar next door, where it was quiet. We talked for hours. I know what you're going to say. Like why don't I let well enough alone or something, but I just can't."

"Why not go back to Mooter's and ask around?"

"Well, I would, but I, uh, have this boyfriend who's really jealous and he'd figure it out. If I even look at another guy, he has this incredible ESP reaction. He's spooky sometimes."

"How'd you get away with it last night?"

"He was working, so I was on my own," she said. "Say you'll help me, okay? Please? I've been cruising around all night looking for his car. He lives somewhere in Montebello, I'm almost sure."

"I can probably find him, Mona, but my services aren't cheap."

"I don't care," she said. "That's fine. I have money. Just tell me how much."

I debated briefly and finally asked her for fifty bucks. I didn't have the heart to charge my usual rates. I didn't really want her business, but it was better than typing up file notes for the case I'd just done. She put a fifty-dollar bill on my desk and I wrote out a receipt, bypassing my standard contract. As young as she was, I wasn't sure it'd be binding anyway.

I jotted down a description of the man named Gage. He sounded like every stud on the prowl I've ever seen. Early thirties, five-foot-ten, good build, dark hair, dark mustache, great smile, and a dimple in his chin. I was prepared to keep writing, but that was the extent of it. For all of their alleged hours of conversation, she knew precious little about him. I quizzed her at length about hobbies, interests, what sort of work he did. The only real information she could give me was that he drove an old silver Jaguar, which is where they "got it on" (her parlance, not mine) the first time. The second time was at her place. After that, he apparently disappeared like a puff of smoke. Real soul mates, these two. I didn't want to tell her what an old story it was. In Santa Teresa, the eligible men are so much in demand they can do anything they want. I took her address and telephone number and said I'd get back to her. As soon as she left, I picked up my handbag and car keys. I had a few personal errands to run and figured I'd tuck her business in when I was finished with my own.

Mooter's is one of a number of bars on the Santa Teresa singles' circuit. By night, it's crowded and impossibly noisy. Happy hour features well drinks for fifty cents and the bartender rings a gong for every five-dollar tip. The tables are small, jammed together around a dance floor the size of a boxing ring. The walls are covered with caricatures of celebrities, possibly purchased from some other bar, as they seem to be signed and dedicated to someone named Stan, whom nobody's ever heard of. An ex-husband of mine played jazz piano there once upon a time, but I hadn't been in for years.

I arrived that afternoon at two, just in time to watch the place being opened up. Two men, day drinkers by the look of them, edged in ahead of me and took up what I surmised were habitual perches at one end of the bar. They were exchanging the kind of pleasantries that suggest daily contact of no particular depth. The man who let us in apparently doubled as bartender and bouncer. He was in his thirties, with curly blond hair, and a T-shirt reading BOUNCER stretched across an impressively muscular chest. His arms were so big I thought he might rip his sleeves out when he flexed.

I found an empty stool at the far end of the bar and waited while he made a couple of martinis for the two men who'd come in with me. A waitress appeared for work, taking off her coat as she moved through the bar to the kitchen area.

The bartender then ambled in my direction with an inquiring look.

"I'll have a wine spritzer," I said.

A skinny guy with a guitar case came into the bar behind me. When the bartender saw him, he grinned.

"Hey, how's it goin'? How's Fresno?"

They shook hands and the guy took a stool two down from mine. "Hot. And dull, but Mary Jane's was fine. We really packed 'em in."

"Smirnoff on the rocks?"

"Nah, not today. Gimme a beer instead. Bud'll do."

The bartender pulled one for him and set his drink on the bar at the same time I got mine. I wondered what it must be like to hang out all day in saloons, nursing beers, shooting the shit with idlers and ne'er-do-wells. The waitress came out of the kitchen, tying an apron around her waist. She took a sandwich order from the guys at the far end of the bar. The other fellow and I both declined when she asked if we were interested in lunch. She began to busy herself with napkins and flatware.

The bartender caught my eye. "You want to run a tab?"

I shook my head. "This is fine," I said. "I'm trying to get in touch with a guy who was in here last night."

"Good luck. The place was a zoo."

"Apparently, he's a regular. I thought you might identify him from a description."

"What's he done?"

"Not a thing. From what I was told, he picked up a young lady and ran out on her afterward. She wants to get in touch with him, that's all."

He stood and looked at me. "You're a private detective."

"That's right."

He and the other fellow exchanged a look.

The fellow said, "Help the woman. This is great."

The bartender shrugged. "Sure, why not? What's he look like?"

The waitress paused, listening in on the conversation with interest.

I mentioned the first name and description Mona'd given me. "The only other thing I know about him is he drives an old silver Jaguar."

"Gage Vesca," the other fellow said promptly.

The bartender said, "Yeah, that's him."

"You know how I might get in touch?"

The other fellow shook his head and the bartender shrugged. "All I know is he's a jerk. The guy's got a vanity license plate reads STALYUN if that tells you anything. Besides that, he just got married a couple months back. He's bad news. Better warn your client. He'll screw anything that moves."

"I'll pass the word. Thanks." I put a five-dollar bill on the bar and hopped down off the stool, leaving the spritzer untouched.

"Hey, who's the babe?" the bartender asked.

"Can't tell you that," I said, as I picked up my bag.

The waitress spoke up. "Well, I know which one she's talking about. That girl in the green-sequined dress."

I WENT BACK TO my office and checked the telephone book. No listing for Vescas of any kind. Directory Assistance didn't have him either, so I put in a call to a friend of mine at the DMV who plugged the license plate into the computer. The name Gage Vesca came up, with an address in Montebello. I used my crisscross directory for a match and came up with the phone number, which I dialed just to see if it was good. As soon as the maid said "Vesca residence," I hung up.

I put in a call to Mona Starling and gave her what I had, including the warning about his marital status and his character references, which were poor. She didn't seem to care. After that, I figured if she pursued him, it was her lookout—and his. She thanked me profusely before she rang off, relief audible in her voice.

That was Saturday.

Monday morning, I opened my front door, picked up the paper, and caught the headlines about Gage Vesca's death.

"Shit!"

He'd been shot in the head at close range sometime between two and six A.M. on Sunday, then crammed into the trunk of his Jaguar and left in the long-term parking lot at the airport. Maybe somebody hoped the body wouldn't be discovered for days. Time enough to set up an alibi or pull a disappearing act. As it was, the trunk had popped open and a passerby had spotted him. My hands were starting to shake. What kind of chump had I been?

I tried Mona Starling's number and got a busy signal. I threw some clothes on, grabbed my car keys, and headed over to the Frontage Road address she'd given me. As I chirped to a stop out front, a Yellow Cab pulled away from the curb with a lone passenger. I checked the house number. A duplex. I figured the odds were even that I'd just watched Mona split. She must have seen the headlines about the same time I did.

I took off again, craning for a glimpse of the taxi somewhere ahead. Beyond the next intersection, there was a freeway on-ramp.

I caught a flash of yellow and pursued it. By keeping my foot to the floor and judiciously changing lanes, I managed to slide in right behind the taxi as it took the airport exit. By the time the cab deposited Mona at the curb out in front, I was squealing into the short-term lot with the parking ticket held between my teeth. I shoved it in my handbag and ran.

The airport at Santa Teresa only has five gates, and it didn't take much detecting to figure out which one was correct. United was announcing a final boarding call for a flight to San Francisco. I used the fifty bucks Mona'd paid me to snag a seat and a boarding pass from a startled reservations clerk and then I headed for the gate. I had no luggage and nothing on me to set off the security alarm as I whipped through. I flashed my ticket, opened the double doors, and raced across the tarmac for the plane, taking the portable boarding stairs two at a time. The flight attendant pulled the door shut behind me. I was in.

I spotted Mona eight rows back in a window seat on the left-hand side, her face turned away from me. This time she was wearing jeans and an oversized shirt. The aisle seat was occupied, but the middle was empty. The plane was still sitting on the runway, engines revving, as I bumped across some guy's knees, saying, "'Scuse me, pardon me," and popped in beside Ms. Starling. She turned a blanched face toward me and a little cry escaped. "What are you doing here?"

"See if you can guess."

"I didn't do it," she whispered hoarsely.

"Yeah, right. I bet. That's probably why you got on a plane the minute the story broke," I said.

"That's *not* what happened."

"The hell it's not!"

The man on my left leaned forward and looked at us quizzically.

"The fellow she picked up Friday night got killed," I said, conversationally. I pointed my index finger at my head like a gun and fired. He decided to mind his own business, which suited me. Mona got to her feet and tried to squeeze past. All I had to do was extend my knees and she was trapped. Other people were taking an interest by now. She did a quick survey of the situation, rolled her eyes, and sat down again. "Let's get off the plane. I'll explain in a minute. Just don't make a scene," she said, the color high in her cheeks.

"Hey, let's not cause you any embarrassment," I said. "A man was murdered. That's all we're talking about."

"I know he's dead," she hissed, "but I'm innocent. I swear to God."

We got up together and bumped and thumped across the man's knees, heading down the aisle toward the door. The flight attendant was peeved, but she let us deplane.

WE WENT UPSTAIRS to the airport bar and found a little table at the rear. When the waitress came, I shook my head, but Mona ordered a Pink Squirrel. The waitress had questions about her age, but I had to question her taste. A Pink Squirrel? Mona had pulled her wallet out and the waitress scrutinized her California driver's license, checking Mona's face against the stamp-sized color photograph, apparently satisfied at the match. As she passed the wallet back to

Mona, I snagged it and peeked at the license myself. She was twenty-one by a month. The address was the same one she'd given me. The waitress disappeared and Mona snatched her wallet, shoving it down in her purse again.

"What was that for?" she said sulkily.

"Just checking. You want to tell me what's going on?"

She picked up a packet of airport matches and began to bend the cover back and forth. "I lied to you."

"This comes as no surprise," I said. "What's the truth?"

"Well, I did pick him up, but we didn't screw. I just told you that because I couldn't think of any other reason I'd want his home address."

"Why *did* you want it?"

She broke off eye contact. "He stole something and I had to get it back."

I stared at her. "Let me take a flier," I said. "It had to be something illegal or you'd have told me about it right up front. Or reported it to the cops. So it must be dope. Was it coke or grass?"

She was wide-eyed. "Grass, but how did you know?"

"Just tell me the rest," I replied with a shake of my head. I love the young. They're always amazed that we know anything.

Mona glanced up to my right.

The waitress was approaching with her tray. She set an airport cocktail napkin on the table and placed the Pink Squirrel on it. "That'll be three-fifty."

Mona took five ones from her billfold and waved her off. She sipped at the drink and shivered. The concoction was the same pink as bubble gum, which made me shiver a bit as well. She licked her lips. "My boyfriend got a lid of this really incredible grass. 'Non Sung Smoke' it's called, from the town of Non Sung in Thailand."

"Never heard of it," I said. "Not that I'm any connoisseur."

"Well, me neither, but he paid like two thousand dollars for it and he'd only smoked one joint. The guy he got it from said half a hit would put you away so we weren't going to smoke it every day. Just special occasions."

"Pretty high-class stuff at those rates."

"The best."

"And you told Gage."

"Well, yeah," she said reluctantly. "We met and we started talking. He said he needed to score some pot so I mentioned it. I wasn't going to sell him ours. I just thought he might try it and then if he was interested, maybe we could get some for him. When we got to my place, I went in the john while he rolled a joint, and when I came out, he was gone and so was the dope. I had to take a cab back to Mooter's to pick up my car. I was in such a panic. I knew if Jimmy found out he'd have a fit!"

"He's your boyfriend?"

"Right," she said, looking down at her lap. She began to blink rapidly and she put a trembling hand to her lips.

I gave her a verbal nudge, just to head off the tears. "Then what? After I gave you the phone number, you got in touch with Gage?"

She nodded mutely, then took a deep breath. "I had to wait 'til Jimmy went off to work and then I called. Gage said—"

"Wait a minute. He answered the phone?"

"Un-uhn. She did. His wife, but I made sure she'd hung up the extension and then I talked so he only had to answer yes and no. I told him I knew he fucking stole the dope and I wanted it back like right then. I just screamed. I told him if he didn't get that shit back to me, he'd be sorry. He said he'd meet me in the parking lot at Mooter's after closing time."

"That was Saturday night?"

She nodded.

"All right. Then what?"

"That's all there was," she said. "I met him there at two-fifteen and he handed over the dope. I didn't even tell him what a shitheel he was. I just snatched the Baggie, got back in my car, and came home. When I saw the headlines this morning, I thought I'd die!"

"Who else was aware of all this?"

"No one as far as I know."

"Didn't your boyfriend think it was odd you went out at two-fifteen?"

She shook her head. "I was back before he got home."

"Didn't he realize the dope had disappeared?"

"No, because I put it back before he even looked for it. He couldn't have known."

"What about Mooter's? Was there anyone else in the parking lot?"

"Not that I saw."

"No one coming or going from the bar?"

"Just the guy who runs the place."

"What about Mrs. Vesca? Could she have followed him?"

"Well, I asked him if she overheard my call and he said no. But she could have followed, I guess. I don't know what kind of car she drives, but she could have been parked on a side street."

"Aside from that, how could anyone connect you to Vesca's death? I don't understand why you decided to run."

Her voice dropped to a whisper. "My fingerprints have to be on that car. I was just in it three nights ago."

I studied the look in her eyes and I could feel my heart sink. "You have a record," I said.

"I was picked up for shoplifting last year. But that's the only trouble I was ever in. Honestly."

"I think you ought to go to the cops with this. It's far better to be up front with them than to come up with lame excuses after they track you down, which I suspect they will."

"Oh, God, I'll die."

"No, you won't. You'll feel better. Now do what I say and I'll check the rest of it from my end."

"You will?"

"Of course!" I snapped. "If I hadn't found the guy for you, he might be okay. How do you think I feel?"

I FOLLOWED THE MAID through the Vescas' house to the pool area at the rear, where one of the cabanas had been fitted out as a personal gym. There were seven weight machines bolted to the floor, which was padded with rubber matting. Mirrors lined three walls and sunlight streamed in the fourth. Katherine Vesca, in a hot-pink leotard and silver tights, was working on her abs, an unnecessary expenditure of energy from what I could see. She was thin as a snake. Her ash-blond hair was kept off her face by a band of pink chiffon and her gray eyes were cold. She blotted sweat from her neck as she glanced at my business card. "You're connected with the police?"

"Actually, I'm not, but I'm hoping you'll answer some questions anyway."

"Why should I?"

"I'm trying to get a line on your husband's killer just like they are."

"Why not leave it up to them?"

"I have some information they don't have yet. I thought I'd see what else I could add before I pass on the facts."

"The facts?"

"About his activities the last two days of his life."

She gave me a chilly smile and crossed to the leg-press machine. She moved the pin down to the 180-pound mark, then seated herself and started to do reps. "Fire away," she said.

"I understand a phone call came in sometime on Saturday," I said.

"That's right. A woman called. He went out to meet her quite late that night and he didn't come back. I never saw him again."

"Do you know what the call was about?"

"Sorry. He never said."

"Weren't you curious?"

"When I married Gage, I agreed that I wouldn't be 'curious' about anything he did."

"And he wasn't curious about you?"

"We had an open relationship. At his insistence, I might add. He was free to do anything he liked."

"And you didn't object?"

"Sometimes, but those were his terms and I agreed."

"What sort of work did he do?"

"He didn't. Neither of us worked. I have a business here in town and I derive income from that, among other things."

"Do you know if he was caught up in anything? A quarrel? Some kind of personal feud?"

"If so, he never mentioned it," she said. "He was not well liked, but I couldn't say he had enemies."

"Do you have a theory about who killed him?"

She finished ten reps and rested. "I wish I did."

"When's the funeral?" I asked.

"Tomorrow morning at ten. You're welcome to come. Then maybe there'll be two of us."

She gave me the name of the funeral home and I made a note.

"One more thing," I said. "What sort of business are you in? Could that be relevant?"

"I don't see how. I have a bar. Called Mooter's. It's managed by my brother, Ace."

WHEN I WALKED in, he was washing beer mugs behind the bar, running each in turn across a rotating brush, then through a hot water rinse. To his right was a mounting pyramid of drying mugs, still radiating heat. Today he wore a bulging T-shirt imprinted with a slogan that read ONE NIGHT OF BAD SEX IS STILL BETTER THAN A GOOD DAY AT WORK. He fixed a look on my face, smiling pleasantly. "How's it going?"

I perched on a bar stool. "Not bad," I said. "You're Ace?"

"That's me. And you're the lady P.I. I don't think you told me your name."

"Kinsey Millhone. I'm assuming you heard about Vesca's death?"

"Yeah, Jesus. Poor guy. Looks like somebody really cleaned his clock. Hope it wasn't the little gal he dumped the other night."

"That's always a possibility."

"You want a spritzer?"

"Sure," I said. "You have a good memory."

"For drinks," he said. "That's my job." He got out the jug wine and poured some in a glass, adding soda from the hose. He added a twist of lime and put the drink in front of me. "On the house."

"Thanks," I said. I took a sip. "How come you never said he was your brother-in-law?"

"How'd you find out about that?" he asked mildly.

"I talked to your sister. She mentioned it."

He shrugged. "Didn't seem pertinent."

I was puzzled by his attitude. He wasn't acting like a man with anything to hide. "Did you see him Saturday?"

"Saw his car at closing time. That was Sunday morning, actually. What's that got to do with it?"

"He must have been killed about then. The paper said sometime between two and six."

"I locked up here shortly after two. My buddy stopped by and picked me up right out front. I was in a poker game by two thirty-five, at a private club."

"You have witnesses?"

"Just the fifty other people in the place. I guess I could have shot the guy before my buddy showed up, but why would I do that? I had no ax to grind with him. I wasn't crazy about him, but I wouldn't plug the guy. My sister adored him. Why break her heart?"

Good question, I thought.

I RETURNED TO MY office and sat down, tilting back in my swivel chair with my feet on the desk. I kept thinking Gage's death must be connected to the Non Sung Smoke, but I couldn't figure out quite how. I made a call to the Vesca house and was put on hold while the maid went to fetch Miss Katherine. She clicked on. "Yes?"

"Hello, Mrs. Vesca. This is Kinsey Millhone."

"Oh, hello. Sorry if I sounded abrupt. What can I do for you?"

"Just a question I forgot to ask you earlier. Did Gage ever mention something called Non Sung Smoke?"

"I don't think so. What is it?"

"A high-grade marijuana from Thailand. Two thousand bucks a lid. Apparently, he helped himself to somebody's stash on Friday night."

"Well, he did have some grass, but it couldn't be the same. He said it was junk. He was incensed that somebody hyped it to him."

"Really," I said, but it was more to myself than to her.

I headed down to the parking lot and retrieved my car. A dim understanding was beginning to form.

⁂

I KNOCKED AT THE door of the duplex on Frontage Road. Mona answered, looking puzzled when she caught sight of me.

"Did you talk to the cops?" I asked.

"Not yet. I was just on my way. Why? What's up?"

"It occurred to me I might have misunderstood something you said to me. Friday night when you went out, you told me your boyfriend Jimmy was at work. How come you had the nerve to stay out all night?"

"He was out of town," she said. "He got back Saturday afternoon about five."

"Couldn't he have arrived in Santa Teresa earlier that day?"

She shrugged. "I suppose so."

"What about Saturday when you met Gage in Mooter's parking lot? Was he working again?"

"Well, yes. He had a gig here in town. He got home about three," she said in the same bewildered tone.

"He's a musician, isn't he?" I said.

"Wait a minute. What *is* this? What's it got to do with him?"

"A lot," he said from behind me. A choking arm slid around my neck and I was jerked half off my feet. I hung on, trying to ease the pressure on my windpipe. I could manage to breathe if I stood on tiptoe, but I couldn't do much else. Something hard was jammed into my ribs and I didn't think it was Jimmy's fountain pen. Mona was astonished.

"Jimmy! What the hell are you doing?" she yelped.

"Back up, bitch. Step back and let us in," he said between clenched teeth. I hung on, struggling, as he half lifted, half shoved me toward the threshold. He dragged me into the apartment and kicked the door shut. He pushed me down on the couch and stood there with his gun pointed right between my eyes. Hey, I was comfy. I wasn't going anyplace.

When I saw his face, of course, my suspicions were confirmed. Jimmy was the fellow with the guitar case who'd sat next to me at Mooter's bar when I first went in. He wasn't a big guy—maybe five-eight, weighing in at 155—but he'd caught me by surprise. He was edgy and he had a crazy look in his eyes. I've noticed that in a pinch like this, my mind either goes completely blank or begins to compute at lightning speeds. I found myself staring at his gun, which was staring disconcertingly at me. It looked like a little Colt .32, a semiautomatic, almost a double for mine—locked at that moment in a briefcase in the backseat of my car. I bypassed the regrets and got straight to the point. Before being fired the first time, a semiautomatic has to be manually cocked, a maneuver that can be accomplished only with two hands. I couldn't remember hearing the sound of the slide being yanked before the nose of the gun was shoved into the small of my back. I wondered briefly if, in his haste to act, he hadn't had time to cock the gun.

"Hello, Jimmy," I said. "Nice seeing you again. Why don't you tell Mona about your run-in with Gage?"

"*You* killed Gage?" she said, staring at him with disbelief.

"That's right, Mona, and I'm going to kill you, too. Just as soon as I figure out what to do with her." He kept his eyes on me, making sure I didn't move.

"But why? What did I do?" she gasped.

"Don't give me that," he said. "You balled the guy! Cattin' around in that green-sequined dress with your tits hangin' out and you pick up a scumbag like him! I told you I'd kill you if you ever did that to me."

"But I didn't. I swear it. All I did was bring him back here to try a hit of pot. Next thing I knew he'd stolen the whole lid."

"Bullshit!"

"No, it's not!"

I said, "She's telling the truth, Jimmy. That's why she hired me."

Confused, he shot a look at her. "You never slept with him?"

"Jesus Christ, of course not. The guy was a creep! I'm not *that* low class!"

Jimmy's hand began to tremble and his gaze darted back and forth between her face and mine. "Then why'd you meet him again the next night?"

"To get the grass back. What else could I do? I didn't want you to know I'd been stiffed for two thousand dollars' worth of pot."

He stared at her, transfixed, and that's when I charged. I flew at him, head down, butting straight into his midriff, my momentum taking us both down in a heap. The gun skittered off across the floor. Mona leapt on him and punched him in the gut, using her body to hold him down while I scrambled over to the Colt. I snatched it up. Silly me. The sucker had been cocked the whole time. I was lucky I hadn't had my head blown off.

I could hear him yelling, "Jesus Christ, all right! Get off. I'm done." And then he lay there, winded. I kept the gun pointed steadily at body parts he treasured while Mona called the cops.

He rolled over on his side and sat up. I moved back a step. The wild look had left his eyes and he was starting to weep, still gasping and out of breath. "Oh, Jesus. I can't believe it."

Mona turned to him with a withering look. "It's too late for an attack of conscience, Jimmy."

He shook his head. "You don't know the half of it, babe. You're not the one who got stiffed for the dope. I was."

She looked at him blankly. "Meaning what?"

"I paid two grand for garbage. That dope was crap. I didn't want to tell you I got taken so I invented some bullshit about Non Sung Smoke. There's no such thing. I made it up."

It took an instant for the irony to penetrate. She sank down beside him. "Why didn't you trust me? Why didn't you just tell me the truth?"

His expression was bleak. "Why didn't you?"

The question hung between them like a cobweb, wavering in the autumn light.

By the time the cops came, they were huddled on the floor together, clinging to each other in despair.

The sight of them was almost enough to cure me of the lies I tell.

But not quite.

falling off the roof

It was six a.m. and I was jogging on the bike path at the beach, trotting three miles in behalf of my sagging rear end. I'm thirty-two years old, five-six, weighing in at 118, so you wouldn't think I'd have to concern myself with such things, but I'm a private eye by trade, and I'm single on top of that. Sometimes I end up running for my life, so it will never do to get out of shape.

I had just hit my stride. My breathing was audible but not labored, my shoes chunking rhythmically as the asphalt sped away underneath my feet. What worried me was the sound of someone running behind me, and gaining too. I glanced back casually and felt adrenaline shoot through my heart, jolting it into a jackhammer pace. A man in a black sweat suit was closing ground. I picked up speed, quickly assessing the situation. There wasn't another soul in sight. No other joggers. None of the usual bums sleeping on the grass.

I veered off toward the street, figuring that with luck a car would pass.

"Hey!" the man said sharply.

I ran on, mentally rehearsing every self-defense move I'd ever been taught.

"Wait up," he called. "Aren't you Kinsey Millhone?"

I slowed my pace. "That's right. Who are you?"

His stride was longer than mine, and it didn't take him long to catch up. "Harry Grissom," he said. "I need a private detective."

"Most people try me at the office first," I snapped. "You scared me half to death!"

"Sorry. The kid at the skate-rental shack told me I could find you out here. This seemed like a good place to talk."

I knew Gus from a case I'd worked, and I liked him a lot. I could feel myself become more charitable. "How do you know Gus?"

"I own some property on Granita. He rents a cottage."

"Why do you need me?"

"My brother Don was killed in a fall from his roof. The police said it was an accident, but I think he was pushed."

"Oh, really? By whom?"

"My sister-in-law."

By now we were jogging side by side at a healthy clip. He was a good-looking fellow, maybe thirty-five, with dark, bushy hair, a dark mustache, and a runner's body, long and lean. He said he was a chiropractor by profession, with a passion for skiing and a modest talent as a painter. I think he told me all this to persuade me of his solid character and the sincerity of his concern about his brother's fatal accident.

"When was he killed?" I asked.

"Six months ago."

"How long had they been married?"

"Thirteen years. Don and Susie met at college, Don's junior year. They were wrong for each other, but you couldn't tell them that. They had a stormy two-year courtship. Finally they ran off and got married. It was all downhill from there."

"What was the problem?"

"For starters, they had nothing in common. On top of that, both of them were hotheaded, stubborn, immature."

"Any kids?" I asked.

"Amy, who's eight, and a little boy, Todd, who's five."

"Go on."

"Well, the two of them fought like cats and dogs, and then suddenly things smoothed out. Susie was a doll and everything seemed fine. Don and I talked about it a couple of times. He wasn't sure what was going on, but of course he was pleased. He thought their troubles were over."

"And you agreed?"

Harry shrugged. "Well, yeah. On the surface, everything seemed fine. I had my doubts. It wasn't like she got into therapy or was 'born again.' There was definitely a change, but it didn't seem attached to anything. I thought she might be having an affair, but I never said so to him. Nobody really wants to hear that stuff, and I didn't have any proof."

"What are you saying? That she took a lover and then arranged an 'accident' to get her husband out of the way?"

"Sure, why not?"

"Divorce isn't that hard to come by in California. Murder seems like a radical way to get rid of an unwanted spouse."

"Divorce doesn't pay benefits."

"He was well insured?"

"A hundred and twenty-five thousand in whole life, with a double-indemnity clause in case of accidental death. The lady netted herself a quarter million bucks. Plus she gets all that sympathy. Divorced, she'd have had a fight on her hands and probably come out a loser. Believe me, I'm single. Half the women I date are divorced, and they all tell the same tale. Divorce is the pits. Why should Susie go through the hassle when all she had to do was give him a push?"

"Had she been physically abusive to him over the years?"

"Well, no, but she did threaten him."

"Really," I said. "When was this?"

"Late June. July. Sometime in there, when the conflict was at its worst. I can't even remember now what they were arguing about, but she said she'd kill him. I was standing right there. Next thing I knew, sure enough, he was dead."

"Come on, Harry. Lots of people say things like that in the heat of an argument. It doesn't make them killers."

"In this case it does."

"I need more than your word for it, but tell me what you want."

The gaze he turned on me was cold, his tone dead. "Find a way to nail her. I'll pay you anything you ask."

I agreed to check into it—not for the money but for the look on his face. The man was in pain.

That afternoon he stopped by my office, signed a standard contract, and gave me a fifteen-hundred-dollar advance.

The next day I went to work.

He'd given me the few newspaper clippings about Don Grissom's death: SANTA TERESA RESIDENT DIES IN FALL FROM ROOF. According to the paper, Don had climbed up to inspect for leaks after a heavy rain had sent water pouring through the ceiling in the guest bathroom. The accompanying copy of the police report indicated that to all appearances, Mr. Grissom had lost his footing on the rain-slick red tile and tumbled two stories in a fall that broke his neck. The coroner had determined that the death was accidental. Harry Grissom said the coroner was a fool.

I made a note of the Grissoms' address and presented myself at the doorstep with a clipboard in hand. While a cop is required by statute to identify herself (or himself) as a law-enforcement officer, a private investigator is free to impersonate anyone, which is what makes my job so much fun. I'm a law-abiding little bun in most instances, but I've been known to tell lies at the drop of a hat. The fib I cooked up for Susie Grissom wasn't far from the truth, and I sounded so sincere that I half believed it myself.

"Mrs. Grissom?" I said when she opened the door.

"Yes, that's right," she said cautiously. She was in her early thirties, with mild brown hair pulled up in a clip, brown eyes, freckles, no makeup, dressed in jeans and a T-shirt.

I held up the clipboard. "I'm from California Fidelity Insurance," I said. Now that much was true. I had worked for CF once upon a time and did occasional investigations for them now in exchange for downtown office space.

"Yes?"

I could tell from the look on her face that "insurance" was the magic word. If what Harry said was true and she'd just collected two hundred and fifty thousand dollars, I could see how the subject might still fascinate. "Your husband had a policy with us," I said. "Our regional office just informed us that he's . . . uh, deceased."

Her face clouded properly. "That's right. He died September fourth in a fall from the roof. What sort of policy?"

"I don't have the details, but it was probably coverage he converted from a plan at work. Was he employed at some point by a large company?"

I could see a spark of recognition. Almost everybody has worked for a large company at some point.

"Well, he did work for Raytheon briefly in 1981, but I thought he let that policy drop."

"Apparently not," I said. "I'll need some data, if you don't object. Just so we can process the claim."

"Claim?"

"Automatic payment in the case of accidental death."

She invited me in.

Now, it's not like I'm psychic, but I have to say this: From the moment I set eyes on this lady, I knew she was guilty. I've seen enough widows and orphans in my day to know what real grief looks like, and this wasn't it. This was pseudo-grief, counterfeit grief, or some reasonable facsimile, but it wasn't real sorrow.

We sat in the living room and I quizzed her at length. Once I mentioned the face value of the policy—let's be generous, I thought, fifty grand—she was as cooperative as she could be. I sat and took notes and cooed and mewed. She played her part to perfection—tears in her eyes, nose all red.

"That must have been terrible," I murmured. "You were out that day and came home to find him dead?"

She nodded mutely, then blew her nose. "I'd been to a meeting of my mystery book club," she said. "I couldn't think what was going on at the house. Police cars out front. An ambulance and everything. Then I found out he was dead. . . ."

"Awful," I said. "What a shock for the kids. How are they taking this?"

"They don't really understand much. I've done the best I could."

I was wondering how I could corroborate her alibi. I assumed the cops had done that, but I wasn't sure. "I think this is all I need for now." I got up, and she walked me to the door. "Actually," I added, "I'm a mystery fan myself."

"Oh, really?" she said, her manner brightening some. "Which authors do you like?"

Oh, shoot. Faked out, I thought. "Oh, golly, so many. Uh, Smith, and White . . ."

"Teri? Oh, she's wonderful. As a matter of fact, we're doing women writers this month. Would you like to come?"

"I'd love it," I said. "What a treat."

Which is how I ended up at a meeting of the Santa Teresa Mystery Readers—STMR as they called themselves. I was wearing my all-purpose dress with low heels and panty hose, thinking that's what suburban housewives probably wore. For the first and only time in my life, I found myself overdressed, though everyone was very nice and pretended not to notice. We had tea and cookies and laughed and chatted about writers I'd never heard of. I kept saying things like "Oh, the ending on that one scared me half to death!" or "I thought the plot line was a bit convoluted, didn't you?" I lied so well, I worried I'd be elected to office, but all that happened was that I was invited back the next month.

"I'll have Jenny give you the program for the year," Susie said. "In case you want to catch up."

The club secretary rustled up a copy of the calendar for me, listing dates and places of meetings and the books that had been discussed. We sat and sipped our tea while I tried a casual imitation of the women I could see. I'm not good at this stuff. I don't bake or do civic work. I don't know how to make small talk or sit with my legs crossed. I studied the program. As soon as Susie stepped away, I lowered my voice, leaning toward Jenny, who was probably fifty-five. She wore a matching tweedy skirt and sweater and a strand of real pearls. "This September meeting. Isn't that when Susie's husband was killed?"

She nodded. "We felt awful," the woman said. "She was in charge of refreshments that day."

"You were at the meeting?"

"Oh, yes. We had a guest speaker from the police department, and Susie had such a nice time talking to him. Afterward, of course, I worked with her in the kitchen while she was putting cookies out. All the time he was dead and she had no idea."

I shook my head. "God, I bet she fell apart. Were they very close?"

"Well, of course," she said, looking at me with interest. "How did you meet Susie? Have you known her long?"

"Well, no, but I feel I know her pretty well," I said modestly.

The woman sitting to my left had apparently been listening, and she broke in. "What sort of work do you do, Kinsey?"

"Insurance," I replied.

"Is that right? Well, the name just seems so familiar somehow. Did I see it in the news by any chance?"

"Oh, heavens. Not me," I said. I'd only been mentioned about six weeks before in connection with a homicide. "Is there a little-girls' room around here?"

I saw the two women exchange a look. Maybe I'd gotten the vocabulary wrong. "A powder room?" I amended.

"Of course. Right down the hall."

I lingered until I heard the group breaking up, and then I slipped away. The next day I canvassed Susie's neighbors.

The first was a woman in her forties, overweight, prematurely graying hair, a Mrs. Hill, according to the information I'd picked up from the city directory. "I'm from California Fidelity," I said. "We're checking into a claim for Mrs. Grissom next door. Could you answer some questions? She's authorized this." I held up a form with Susie's signature, which I'd recently faked.

"I suppose so," Mrs. Hill said reluctantly. "What exactly did you want?"

I went through a series of questions. How well did she know the Grissoms? Was she home on the day of his accident? She was singularly uninformative, the sort who answered each query without editorial comment. When it was clear she had nothing to offer, I thanked her and excused myself, moving on.

The house on the other side of the Grissoms' was dark.

I scanned the area, and on impulse tried the house directly behind the Grissoms', across an alleyway. The woman who answered the door was in her eighties and anxious for company.

"I'm from an insurance company here in town. I'm doing a report about your neighbors, the Grissoms. Your name is?"

"Mrs. Peterson. He crossed over, you know, in a fall from the roof. Not that she gives a hoot."

"Is that right," I said. Before I got my first question out, she was telling everything she knew.

"Well, you know, they quarreled so frightfully," she said, and rolled her eyes, hand against her cheek in a comic imitation of scandalized sensibilities.

"Nooo. I had no idea," I said in disbelief. "Did you happen to be home at the time he fell?"

"Oh, honey, I'm always home. I don't go anywhere now that Teddy's dead."

"Your husband?"

"My dog. I just seemed to lose heart once he passed away. At any rate, I was sitting in my little den upstairs, by the window where the light is good. I was doing cross-stitch, which can ruin your eyesight, even with glasses as good as these new bifocals of mine. . . ." She took them off and held them to the light, then put them back on again.

"You have a view of the Grissoms' house from up there?" I cut in, trying to keep her on track.

"Oh, yes. The view is perfect. Come on upstairs and you can see for yourself."

I shrugged to myself and followed her dutifully, wondering if this was going to be another dead end. People who spend too much time alone will sometimes talk your ear off. She seemed all right, alert and well oriented. For all I knew, though, she might be the neighborhood crackpot. We reached a small den at the rear of the house, and she showed me the window, which looked right out at the Grissoms' house at a distance of perhaps one hundred yards.

"Did you happen to notice him working on the roof?" I asked.

"Certainly. I watched him for an hour," she replied matter-of-factly.

I held my breath, almost afraid to prompt her.

She frowned. "I thought it was real odd he'd get up there in the rain," she remarked. "Why would anybody do that?"

"I heard there was a leak," I said.

"But that doesn't explain what that redheaded woman was doing up there too."

I could feel the hair rise on the back of my neck. "What redhead?"

"Well, I don't know who she was."

"But she was actually on the roof?"

"She crawled right out the attic window," she said comfortably.

"Mrs. Peterson, did you mention this to the police?"

"They never asked. I didn't want to cause trouble, so I kept my mouth shut. I thought if they were curious, they'd come around just like you. Now, you know, the whole thing's died down, and I don't think anybody even suspects."

"Suspects what?"

"That she pushed him."

"Mrs. Grissom did?"

"Not her. The redhead. She slipped around the far side of the chimney, where he was removing the tile. She gave him a push, and off he tumbled. Never made a sound. Too surprised, I guess."

"And you saw all this?"

"As plain as day."

"Across both yards with the sky overcast?" I said skeptically.

"Yes, indeed. I had my little opera glasses trained on the roof."

"Opera glasses?" I felt like I was suffering from echolalia, but I was so astonished, I couldn't manage much else.

"I watch everybody with those," she said, as if I should have known. She showed me the binoculars and I had a peep myself. Wow, the chimney looked like it was two feet away.

"What happened then?"

"Well, the woman crawled back in the window and drove off. She had a little white Mercedes with a scratch down the side. She was parked in the alley right out back. That's the last I saw of her."

"Did you catch the license number?"

"Not from this angle. I'm up too high."

"Why didn't you call the police at the time?"

"Oh, no. Not me. No, ma'am. If that woman had any idea what I'd seen, I'd be next on the list. I may be old, but I'm not dumb! And don't think I'll repeat this story to the police, because I won't. They should have asked me all this when it happened. I'd have told 'em then. I'm not going to do it now that she's feeling safe and has her story down pat. Absolutely not."

At that point she decided she'd said enough, and I couldn't get another word out of her, coax as I might.

I went straight over to the police station and had a chat with Lieutenant Dolan in Homicide. He listened attentively, but his attitude was plain. He was not unwilling to reopen the matter, if I'd just bring him a shred of proof. The cops in Santa Teresa take a dim view of hearsay evidence, especially in a case where they've already decided no crime was committed. Proving murder, and then proving insurance was the motive, is exceedingly difficult. If I could give him corroborating evidence, he'd see what he could do. Otherwise all we had was Mrs. Peterson's word for what went on, and at this point she might well deny everything. It was frustrating, but there was nothing he could do.

I went back to the office.

As I stood in the corridor, searching through my handbag for my keys, I heard someone call my name. "Well, Kinsey! Isn't this a surprise!"

I looked up to see the secretary of the book club coming down the hall. She was really quite an elegant little woman, hair perfectly coiffed, nails freshly done. I wondered if she'd spot the KINSEY MILLHONE INVESTIGATIONS in big brass letters on my door. Automatically I eased myself toward the California Fidelity offices next door, hoping to redirect her attention. I hadn't exactly lied to the ladies, but I hadn't really told them the truth, either, and I didn't want Susie Grissom to find out what I was really up to.

"Hello, Jenny. What are you doing here?"

"I've just been to the dentist upstairs," she said, glancing at the California Fidelity logo. "Is this the company where you work? Well, isn't that nice. I'm just so pleased I ran into you. We've scheduled a special meeting tomorrow night, and we were hoping you could come, but nobody had your home phone. Here, I'll just make a quick note of the address and the time. It's at my house, and everybody's bringing cookies, so don't you forget." She jotted the information on a scrap of paper and handed it to me.

"What's the occasion?"

She lowered her voice. "We're having a speaker, and the subject is murder. Won't that be fun?"

Actually I thought it would.

What I pondered for the rest of the day was the notion of that redhead on the roof. Of course, the woman might have been Susie Grissom in a wig, despite everybody's swearing she was at the meeting of the mystery book club. It might have been somebody else, too, but in that case, how did the redhead know he'd be up there? How did she know the house would be empty and the setup so perfect? And how'd she get in? More important, what was her motive? On the surface, Susie Grissom had everything to gain, and until now, I'd been dead certain she'd done it. Now I wasn't sure what to think. Had she had an accomplice?

I called Harry Grissom at his office. "Did your brother have a girlfriend, by any chance? A redhead?"

"What?" he said, outraged. "Of course not! Who—?"

"Knock it off, Harry. Nobody said that. I'm on the track of something else."

"Well, what's the redhead got to do with it?"

"I'm not sure. I don't want to go into detail at the moment, but somebody's linked a redhead with the circumstances of your brother's death. I just wondered who it could have been. Did he ever mention anyone with red hair? A coworker? An old flame? Some friend of Susie's?"

Harry considered briefly. "I don't think so," he said. "At least, not that I ever heard about."

"Who else might have benefited?"

"No one. Believe me, I checked out every possible angle before I came to you. Why don't you tell me what's going on? Maybe I can help."

"Let me try one thing first, and then we'll have a chat."

After work the next day I stopped at the bakery and bought some cookies, which I arranged on a plate when I got home. I put a dab of jam in the center of each, lightly sifted on some powdered sugar, and covered the plate with plastic wrap. Looked homemade to me. At ten to seven I put on some clean blue jeans, a sweater, and my tennis shoes, grabbed the plate of cookies, my handbag, and Jenny's address. She lived close to the heart of town, not that far from my office.

There were so many cars in the area, I had to park a block away. Jenny's driveway was crammed, and I had to guess that most of the women had already assembled. I'd forgotten to ask who the speaker was. It might have been Lieutenant Dolan for all I knew. I rang the bell, standing on the porch while I waited for someone to let me in. The car parked right at the end of the walk was a little white Mercedes with a scratch down the side. I'd been staring at it idly for thirty seconds before the significance hit me. The front door opened right at that moment, and I gave a little jump, nearly dropping my plate. Jenny greeted me cheerfully and ushered me in.

"Nice little Mercedes," I said. "Whose is it?"

"Mine," a voice said behind me. I turned and found myself shaking hands with the redhead who was standing there.

"I'm Shannon," she said. "Ooo, cold hands."

I remembered then that we didn't have a dentist in our building, and I wondered what had really brought Jenny there the day before.

In the living room I could see fifteen or twenty women all seated on folding chairs. Several turned to look at me, their faces blank and curious and dead. My stomach gave a sudden squeeze, and I knew I was in trouble. We were playing an elaborate game and I was "it."

"Uh, Jenny. Do you mind if I go to the potty real quick? I got a bladder the size of a walnut," I said.

"Surely. Right down here," Jenny murmured as she led the way. "Now you hurry back. I'm just putting out refreshments."

"I won't be a sec," I said. I eased the bathroom door shut behind me and flipped the lock. It was broken, of course—probably jammed. I tried the bathroom window, but it wouldn't budge. Call it precognition, intuition—anything you like. I knew as surely as I was standing there that the women of the Santa Teresa Mystery Readers had all pitched in. Susie Grissom had a problem, and they'd helped her out, providing her a surrogate killer and an alibi. I wondered how many other little domestic conflicts they'd resolved the same way. Meddlesome mothers-in-law, sassy stepkids. Tragic home accidents that everybody felt so bad about. Or maybe Don Grissom was the first, and they were waiting to see if they'd gotten away with it.

I was ice cold, and under my sweater I could feel sweat trickle down my side. Heart pounding, I flushed the toilet and washed my hands, trying to maintain an outward semblance of calm. They had to know I was a private eye, and they probably guessed I was sniffing at the traces of Don Grissom's death. Did they realize that I'd already figured out what was going on? My only hope was to play dumb and wait for a chance to escape.

As I came out of the bathroom Jenny was just passing with a large cut-glass bowl of punch. How about right now? I thought.

"Careful," she sang.

"Oh, I will be," I sang back.

I shoved her so hard, the punch flew back in her face, the rim of the bowl banging into her mouth, ice flying everywhere. She yelped, going down, taking two other women with her, in a heap. The redhead grabbed me, but I kicked her in the shin, then decked her with a punch that caught her on the jaw. I pulled a side table over, took off toward the kitchen, and yanked open the back door. Behind me, I could hear shrieks and the clatter of heels. I leapt off the porch and tore around the side of the house. In two bounds I scrambled up the neighbor's fence and dropped into the next yard. I took two more fences in succession, heading through another yard and out to the street beyond.

It was fully dark by then, but the streetlights were on and I could see well enough. I glanced back in time to see two women drop over the fence behind me, toting baseball bats. They meant business! Even at a distance of half a block, I could hear several cars start up, and I knew they'd be bearing down on me soon. Headlights flashed around the corner toward me, and I doubled my speed, feet flying as I raced across the street.

I could hear someone coming up behind me, breathing hard, and I cranked up my pace again. Images clicked through my brain like still photographs. Dark houses. No foot traffic. No help. A car had pulled up ahead of me at the corner, four doors hanging open now as the occupants ran toward me. I didn't have breath to waste on calling for help, but if somebody didn't come to my assistance soon, I was one dead chick. They'd pound me unconscious and toss me off a bridge, load me on a boat and dump me in the sea, hack me up and keep me in their freezers until they figured out what to do next. The whole street seemed to thunder with the sound of running feet. I caught a glimpse of Susie Grissom coming up on my right. I straight-armed her like a fullback and knocked her off balance. With an "ooomph!" she went down, but two more women took her place, and I sensed a third angling in from the rear.

My lungs were hot and I was gasping for air, but I was beginning to recognize the area and a plan was taking shape. I turned the corner, cutting left. I poured on the speed, heading for the lights I could see straight ahead. My brain felt disconnected, processing information at a leisurely rate while I ran for dear life. I was on Floresta now, a street I knew well. Just ahead, I could see four matching cars parked at the curb. Black-and-whites. Hot damn, I thought. The building behind them, which blazed now with lights, belonged to my beloved Santa Teresa Police. The members of the Santa Teresa Mystery Readers must have realized it, too, because I sensed that my pursuers were peeling away. By the time I reached the station house, there was no one left, and I flew up the front steps on winged feet, uncertain if I was laughing or crying when I finally burst through the doors.

a poison
that leaves no trace

THE WOMAN WAS waiting outside my office when I arrived that
morning. She was short and quite plump, wearing jeans in a size I've
never seen on the rack. Her blouse was tunic-length, ostensibly to
disguise her considerable rear end. Someone must have told her
never to wear horizontal stripes, so the bold red-and-blue bands ran
diagonally across her torso with a dizzying effect. Big red canvas
tote, matching canvas wedgies. Her face was round, seamless, and
smooth, her hair a uniformly dark shade that suggested a rinse. She
might have been any age between forty and sixty. "You're not Kinsey
Millhone," she said as I approached.

"Actually, I am. Would you like to come in?" I unlocked the door
and stepped back so she could pass in front of me. She was giving
me the once-over, as if my appearance was as remarkable to her as
hers was to me.

She took a seat, keeping her tote squarely on her lap. I went around to my side of the desk, pausing to open the French doors before I sat down. "What can I help you with?"

She stared at me openly. "Well, I don't know. I thought you'd be a man. What kind of name is Kinsey? I never heard such a thing."

"My mother's maiden name. I take it you're in the market for a private investigator."

"I guess you could say that. I'm Shirese Dunaway, but everybody calls me Sis. Exactly how long have you been doing this?" Her tone was a perfect mating of skepticism and distrust.

"Six years in May. I was with the police department for two years before that. If my being a woman bothers you, I can recommend another agency. It won't offend me in the least."

"Well, I might as well talk to you as long as I'm here. I drove all the way up from Orange County. You don't charge for a consultation, I hope."

"Not at all. My regular fee is thirty dollars an hour plus expenses, but only if I believe I can be of help. What sort of problem are you dealing with?"

"Thirty dollars an hour! My stars. I had no idea it would cost so *much*."

"Lawyers charge a hundred and twenty," I said with a shrug.

"I know, but that's in case of a lawsuit. Contingency, or whatever they call that. Thirty dollars an *hour* . . ."

I closed my mouth and let her work it out for herself. I didn't want to get into an argument with the woman in the first five minutes of our relationship. I tuned her out, watching her lips move while she decided what to do.

"The problem is my sister," she said at long last. "Here, look at this." She handed me a little clipping from the Santa Teresa newspaper. The death notice read: "Crispin, Margery, beloved mother of Justine, passed away on December 10. Private arrangements. Wynington-Blake Mortuary."

"Nearly two months ago," I remarked.

"Nobody even told me she was sick! That's the point," Sis Dunaway snapped. "I wouldn't know to this day if a former neighbor hadn't spotted this and cut it out." She tended to speak in an indignant tone regardless of the subject.

"You just received this?"

"Well, no. It came back in January, but of course I couldn't drop everything and rush right up. This is the first chance I've had. You can probably appreciate that, upset as I was."

"Absolutely," I said. "When did you last talk to Margery?"

"I don't remember the exact date. It had to be eight or ten years back. You can imagine my shock! To get something like this out of a clear blue sky."

I shook my head. "Terrible," I murmured. "Have you talked to your niece?"

She gestured dismissively. "That Justine's a mess. Marge had her hands full with that one," she said. "I stopped over to her place and you should have seen the look I got. I said, 'Justine, whatever in the world did Margery die of?' And you know what she said? Said, 'Aunt Sis, her heart give out.' Well, I knew that was bull the minute she said it. We have never had heart trouble in our family. . . ."

She went on for a while about what everybody'd died of: Mom, Dad, Uncle Buster, Rita Sue. We're talking cancer, lung disorder, an aneurysm or two. Sure enough, no heart trouble. I was making sympathetic noises, just to keep the tale afloat until she got to the point. I jotted down a few notes, though I never did quite understand how Rita Sue was related. Finally, I said, "Is it your feeling there was something unusual in your sister's death?"

She pursed her lips and lowered her gaze. "Let's put it this way. I can smell a rat. I'd be willing to *bet* Justine had a hand in it."

"Why would she do that?"

"Well, Marge had that big insurance policy. The one Harley took out in 1966. If that's not a motive for murder, I don't know what is." She sat back in her chair, content that she'd made her case.

"Harley?"

"Her husband—until he passed on, of course. They took out policies on each other and after he went, she kept up the premiums on hers. Justine was made the beneficiary. Marge never remarried and with Justine on the policy, I guess she'll get all the money and do I don't know what. It just doesn't seem right. She's been a sneak all her natural life. A regular con artist. She's been in jail four times! My sister talked till she was blue in the face, but she never could get Justine to straighten up her act."

"How much money are we talking about?"

"A hundred thousand dollars," she said. "Furthermore, them two never did get along. Fought like cats and dogs since the day Justine was born. Competitive? My God. Always trying to get the better of each other. Justine as good as told me they had a falling-out not two months before her mother died! The two had not exchanged a word since the day Marge got mad and stomped off."

"They lived together?"

"Well, yes, until this big fight. Next thing you know, Marge is dead. You tell me there's not something funny going on."

"Have you talked to the police?"

"How can I do that? I don't have any *proof.*"

"What about the insurance company? Surely, if there were something irregular about Marge's death, the claims investigator would have picked up on it."

"Oh, honey, you'd think so, but you know how it is. Once a claim's been paid, the insurance company doesn't want to hear. Admit they made a mistake? Un-uhn, no thanks. Too much trouble going back through all the paperwork. Besides, Justine would probably turn around and sue 'em within an inch of their life. They'd rather turn a deaf ear and write the money off."

"When was the claim paid?"

"A week ago, they said."

I stared at her for a moment, considering. "I don't know what to tell you, Ms. Dunaway—"

"Call me Sis. I don't go for that Ms. bull."

"All right, Sis. If you're really convinced Justine's implicated in her mother's death, of course I'll try to help. I just don't want to waste your time."

"I can appreciate that," she said.

I stirred in my seat. "Look, I'll tell you what let's do. Why don't you pay me for two hours of my time. If I don't come up with any-thing concrete in that period, we can have another conversation and you can decide then if you want me to proceed."

"Sixty dollars," she said.

"That's right. Two hours."

"Well, all right. I guess I can do that." She opened her tote and peeled six tens off a roll of bills she'd secured with a rubber band. I wrote out an abbreviated version of a standard contract. She said she'd be staying in town overnight and gave me the telephone number at the motel where she'd checked in. She handed me the death notice. I made sure I had her sister's full name and the exact date of her death and told her I'd be in touch.

My first stop was the Hall of Records at the Santa Teresa County Courthouse, two and a half blocks away. I filled out a copy order, supplying the necessary information, and paid seven bucks in cash. An hour later, I returned to pick up the certified copy of Margery Crispin's death certificate. Cause of death was listed as a "myocardial infarction." The certificate was signed by Dr. Yee, one of the contract pathologists out at the county morgue. If Marge Crispin had been the victim of foul play, it was hard to believe Dr. Yee wouldn't have spotted it.

I swung back by the office, picked up my car, and drove over to Wynington-Blake, the mortuary listed in the newspaper clipping. I asked for Mr. Sharonson, whom I'd met when I was working on another case. He was wearing a somber charcoal-gray suit, his tone of voice carefully modulated to reflect the solemnity of his work. When I mentioned Marge Crispin, a shadow crossed his face.

"You remember the woman?"

"Oh, yes," he said. He closed his mouth then, but the look he gave me was eloquent.

I wondered if funeral home employees took a loyalty oath, vowing never to divulge a single fact about the dead. I thought I'd prime the pump a bit. Men are worse gossips than women once you get 'em going. "Mrs. Crispin's sister was in my office a little while ago and she seems to think there was something . . . uh, irregular about the woman's death."

I could see Mr. Sharonson formulate his response. "I wouldn't say there was anything 'irregular' about the woman's death, but there was certainly something sordid about the circumstances."

"Oh?" said I.

He lowered his voice, glancing around to make certain we couldn't be overheard. "The two were estranged. Hadn't spoken for months as I understand it. The woman died alone in a seedy hotel on lower State Street. She drank."

"Nooo," I said, conveying disapproval and disbelief.

"Oh, yes," he said. "The police picked up the body, but she wasn't identified for weeks. If it hadn't been for the article in the paper, her daughter might not have ever known."

"What article?"

"Oh, you know the one. There's that columnist for the local paper who does all those articles about the homeless. He did a write-up about the poor woman. 'Alone in Death' I think it was called. He talked about how pathetic this woman was. Apparently, when Ms. Crispin read the article, she began to suspect it might be her mother. That's when she went out there to take a look."

"Must have been a shock," I said. "The woman did die of natural causes?"

"Oh, yes."

"No evidence of trauma, foul play, anything like that?"

"No, no, no. I tended her myself and I know they ran toxicology tests. I guess at first they thought it might be acute alcohol poisoning, but it turned out to be her heart."

I quizzed him on a number of possibilities, but I couldn't come up with anything out of the ordinary. I thanked him for his time, got back in my car, and drove over to the trailer park where Justine Crispin lived.

The trailer itself had seen better days. It was moored in a dirt patch with a wooden crate for an outside step. I knocked on the door, which opened about an inch to show a short strip of round face peering out at me. "Yes?"

"Are you Justine Crispin?"

"Yes."

"I hope I'm not bothering you. My name is Kinsey Millhone. I'm an old friend of your mother's and I just heard she passed away."

The silence was cautious. "Who'd you hear that from?"

I showed her the clipping. "Someone sent me this. I couldn't believe my eyes. I didn't even know she was sick."

Justine's eyes darkened with suspicion. "When did you see her last?"

I did my best to imitate Sis Dunaway's folksy tone. "Oh, gee. Must have been last summer. I moved away in June and it was probably sometime around then because I remember giving her my address. It was awfully sudden, wasn't it?"

"Her heart give out."

"Well, the poor thing, and she was such a love." I wondered if I'd laid it on too thick. Justine was staring at me like I'd come to the wrong place. "Would you happen to know if she got my last note?" I asked.

"I wouldn't know anything about that."

"Because I wasn't sure what to do about the money."

"She owed you money?"

"No, no. I owed *her*—which is why I wrote."

Justine hesitated. "Are you sure?"

"Your mother is Marge Crispin, isn't she?"

Justine blinked. "How much money did you owe her?"

"Well, it wasn't much," I said, with embarrassment. "Six hundred dollars, but she was such a doll to lend it to me and then I felt so bad when I couldn't pay her back right away. I asked her if I could wait and pay her this month, but then I never heard. Now I don't know what to do."

I could sense the shift in her attitude. Greed seems to do that in record time. "You could pay it to me and I could see it went into her estate," she said helpfully.

"Oh, I don't want to put you to any trouble."

"I don't mind," she said. "You want to come in?"

"I shouldn't. You're probably busy and you've already been so nice. . . ."

"I can take a few minutes."

Justine held the door open and I stepped into the trailer, where I got my first clear look at her. This girl was probably thirty pounds overweight with listless brown hair pulled into an oily ponytail. Like Sis, she was decked out in a pair of jeans, with an oversize T-shirt hanging almost to her knees. It was clear big butts ran in the family. She shoved some junk aside so I could sit down on the banquette, a fancy word for the ripped plastic seat that extended along one wall in the kitchenette.

"Did she suffer much?" I asked.

"Doctor said not. He said it was quick, as far as he could tell. Her heart probably seized up and she fell down dead before she could draw a breath."

"It must have been terrible for you."

Her cheeks flushed with guilt. "You know, her and me had a falling-out."

"Really? Well, I'm sorry to hear that. Of course, she always said you two had your differences. I hope it wasn't anything serious."

"She drank. I begged her and begged her to give it up, but she wouldn't pay me no mind," Justine said.

"Did she 'go' here at home?"

She shook her head. "In a welfare hotel. Down on her luck. Drink had done her in. If only I'd known . . . if only she'd reached out."

I thought she was going to weep, but she couldn't quite manage it. I clutched her hand. "She was too proud," I said.

"I guess that's what it was. I've been thinking to make some kind of contribution to AA, or something like that. You know, in her name."

"A Marge Crispin Memorial Fund," I suggested.

"Like that, yes. I was thinking this money you're talking about might be a start."

"That's a beautiful thought. I'm going right out to the car for my checkbook so I can write you a check."

It was a relief to get out into the fresh air again. I'd never heard so much horsepuckey in all my life. Still, it hardly constituted proof she was a murderess.

I hopped in my car and headed for a pay phone, spotting one in a gas station half a block away. I pulled change out of the bottom of my handbag and dialed Sis Dunaway's motel room. She was not very happy to hear my report.

"You didn't find anything?" she said. "Are you positive?"

"Well, of course I'm not positive. All I'm saying is that so far, there's no evidence that anything's amiss. If Justine contributed to her mother's death, she was damned clever about it. The autopsy didn't show a thing."

"Maybe it was some kind of poison that leaves no trace."

"Uh, Sis? I hate to tell you this, but there really isn't such a poison that I ever heard of. I know it's a common fantasy, but there's just no such thing."

Her tone turned stubborn. "But it's possible. You have to admit that. There could be such a thing. It might be from South America . . . darkest Africa, someplace like that."

Oh, boy. We were really tripping out on this one. I squinted at the receiver. "How would Justine acquire the stuff?"

"How do I know? I'm not going to set here and solve the whole case for you! You're the one gets paid thirty dollars an hour, not me."

"Do you want me to pursue it?"

"Not if you mean to charge me an arm and a leg!" she said. "Listen here, I'll pay sixty dollars more, but you better come up with something or I want this sixty-dollar payment back."

She hung up before I could protest. How could she get money back when she hadn't paid it yet? I stood in the phone booth and thought about things. In spite of myself, I'll admit that I was hooked. Sis Dunaway might harbor a lot of foolish ideas, but her conviction was unshakable. Add to that the fact that Justine was lying about *something* and you have the kind of situation I can't walk away from.

I drove back to the trailer park and eased my car into a shady spot just across the street. Within moments, Justine appeared in a banged-up white Pinto, trailing smoke out of the tailpipe. Following her wasn't hard. I just hung my nose out the window and kept an eye on the haze. She drove over to Milagro Street to the branch office of a savings and loan. I pulled into a parking spot a few doors down and followed her in, keeping well out of sight. She was dealing with the branch manager, who eventually walked her over to a teller and authorized the cashing of a quite large check, judging from the number of bills the teller counted out.

Justine departed moments later, clutching her handbag protectively. I would have been willing to bet she'd been cashing that insurance check. She drove back to the trailer, where she made a brief stop, probably to drop the money off.

She got back in her car and drove out of the trailer park. I followed discreetly as she headed into town. She pulled into a public parking lot and I eased in after her, finding an empty slot far enough away to disguise my purposes. So far, she didn't seem to have any idea she was being tailed. I kept my distance as she cut through to State Street and walked up a block to Santa Teresa Travel. I pretended to peruse the posters in the window while I watched her chat with the travel agent sitting at a desk just inside the front door. The two transacted business, the agent handing over what apparently were prearranged tickets. Justine wrote out a check. I busied myself at a newspaper rack, extracting a paper as she came out again. She walked down State Street half a block to a hobby shop, where she purchased one of life's ugliest plastic floral wreaths. Busy little lady, this one, I thought.

She emerged from the hobby shop and headed down a side street, moving into the front entrance of a beauty salon. A surreptitious glance through the window showed her, moments later, in a green plastic cape, having a long conversation with the stylist about a cut. I checked my watch. It was almost twelve-thirty. I scooted back to the travel agency and waited until I saw Justine's travel agent leave the premises for lunch. As soon as she was out of sight, I went in, glancing at the nameplate on the edge of her desk.

The blond agent across the aisle caught my eye and smiled.

"What happened to Kathleen?" I asked.

"She went out to lunch. You just missed her. Is there something I can help you with?"

"Gee, I hope so. I picked up some tickets a little while ago and now I can't find the itinerary she tucked in the envelope. Is there any way you could run me a copy real quick? I'm in a hurry and I really can't afford to wait until she gets back."

"Sure, no problem. What's the name?"

"Justine Crispin," I said.

I FOUND THE NEAREST public phone and dialed Sis's motel room again. "Catch this," I said. "At four o'clock, Justine takes off for Los Angeles. From there, she flies to Mexico City."

"Well, that little shit."

"It gets worse. It's one-way."

"I knew it! I just knew she was up to no good. Where is she now?"

"Getting her hair done. She went to the bank first and cashed a big check—"

"I bet it was the insurance."

"That'd be my guess."

"She's got all that money *on* her?"

"Well, no. She stopped by the trailer first and then went and picked up her plane ticket. I think she intends to stop by the cemetery and put a wreath on Marge's grave—"

"I can't stand this. I just can't stand it. She's going to take all that money and make a mockery of Marge's death."

"Hey, Sis, come on. If Justine's listed as the beneficiary, there's nothing you can do."

"That's what you think. I'll make her pay for this, I swear to God I will!" Sis slammed the phone down.

I could feel my heart sink. Uh-oh. I tried to think whether I'd mentioned the name of the beauty salon. I had visions of Sis descending on Justine with a tommy gun. I loitered uneasily outside the shop, watching traffic in both directions. There was no sign of Sis. Maybe she was going to wait until Justine went out to the grave site before she mowed her down.

At two-fifteen, Justine came out of the beauty shop and passed me on the street. She was nearly unrecognizable. Her hair had been cut and permed and it fell in soft curls around her freshly made-up face. The beautician had found ways to bring out her eyes, subtly heightening her coloring with a touch of blusher on her cheeks. She looked like a million bucks—or a hundred thousand, at any rate. She was in a jaunty mood, paying more attention to her own reflection in the passing store windows than she was to me, hovering half a block behind.

She returned to the parking lot and retrieved her Pinto, easing into the flow of traffic as it moved up State. I tucked in a few cars back, all the while scanning for some sign of Sis. I couldn't imagine what she'd try to do, but as mad as she was, I had to guess she had some scheme in the works.

Fifteen minutes later, we were turning into the trailer park, Justine leading while I lollygagged along behind. I had already used up the money Sis had authorized, but by this time I had my own stake in the outcome. For all I knew, I was going to end up protecting Justine from an assassination attempt. She stopped by the trailer just long enough to load her bags in the car and then she drove out to the Santa Teresa Memorial Park, which was out by the airport.

The cemetery was deserted, a sunny field of gravestones among flowering shrubs. When the road forked, I watched Justine wind up the lane to the right while I headed left, keeping an eye on her car, which I could see across a wide patch of grass. She parked and got out, carrying the wreath to an oblong depression in the ground where a temporary marker had been set, awaiting the permanent monument. She rested the wreath against the marker and stood there looking down. She seemed awfully exposed and I couldn't help but wish she'd duck down some to grieve. Sis was probably crouched somewhere with a knife between her teeth, ready to leap out and stab Justine in the neck.

Respects paid, Justine got back into her car and drove to the airport, where she checked in for her flight. By now, I was feeling baffled. She had less than an hour before her plane was scheduled to depart and there was still no sign of Sis. If there was going to be a showdown, it was bound to happen soon. I ambled into the gift shop and inserted myself between the wall and a book rack, watching Justine through windows nearly obscured by a display of Santa Teresa T-shirts. She sat on a bench and calmly read a paperback.

What was going on here?

Sis Dunaway had seemed hell-bent on avenging Marge's death, but where was she? Had she gone to the cops? I kept one eye on the clock and one eye on Justine. Whatever Sis was up to, she had better do it quick. Finally, mere minutes before the flight was due to be called, I left the newsstand, crossed the gate area, and took a seat beside Justine. "Hi," I said. "Nice permanent. Looks good."

She glanced at me and then did a classic double take.

"What are you doing here?"

"Keeping an eye on you."

"What for?"

"I thought someone should see you off. I suspect your aunt Sis is en route, so I decided to keep you company until she gets here."

"Aunt *Sis*?" she said, incredulously.

"I gotta warn you, she's not convinced your mother had a heart attack."

"What are you talking about? Aunt Sis is dead."

I could feel myself smirk. "Yeah, sure. Since when?"

"Five years ago."

"Bullshit."

"It's not bullshit. An aneurysm burst and she dropped in her tracks."

"Come on," I scoffed.

"It's the truth," she said emphatically. By that time, she'd recovered her composure and she went on the offensive. "Where's my money? You said you'd write a check for six hundred bucks."

"Completely dead?" I asked.

The loudspeaker came on. "May I have your attention, please. United Flight 3440 for Los Angeles is now ready for boarding at Gate Five. Please have your boarding pass available and prepare for security check."

Justine began to gather up her belongings. I'd been wondering how she was going to get all the cash through the security checkpoint, but one look at her lumpy waistline and it was obvious she'd strapped on a money belt. She picked up her carry-on, her shoulder bag, her jacket, and her paperback and clopped, in spike heels, over to the line of waiting passengers.

I followed, befuddled, reviewing the entire sequence of events. It had all happened today. Within hours. It wasn't like I was suffering brain damage or memory loss. And I hadn't seen a ghost. Sis had come to my office and laid out the whole tale about Marge and Justine. She'd told me all about their relationship, Justine's history as a con, the way the two women tried to outdo each other, the insurance, Marge's death. How could a murder have gotten past Dr. Yee? Unless the woman wasn't murdered, I thought suddenly.

Oh.

Once I saw it in *that* light, it was obvious.

Justine got in line between a young man with a duffel bag and a woman toting a cranky baby. There was some delay up ahead while the ticket agent got set. The line started to move and Justine advanced a step with me right beside her.

"I understand you and your mother had quite a competitive relationship."

"What's it to you?" she said. She kept her eyes averted, facing dead ahead, willing the line to move so she could get away from me.

"I understand you were always trying to get the better of each other."

"What's your point?" she said, annoyed.

I shrugged. "I figure you read the article about the unidentified dead woman in the welfare hotel. You went out to the morgue and claimed the body as your mom's. The two of you agreed to split the insurance money, but your mother got worried about a double cross, which is exactly what this is."

"You don't know what you're talking about."

The line moved up again and I stayed right next to her. "She hired me to keep an eye on you, so when I realized you were leaving town, I called her and told her what was going on. She really hit the roof and I thought she'd charge right out, but so far there's been no sign of her. . . ."

Justine showed her ticket to the agent and he motioned her on. She moved through the metal detector without setting it off.

I gave the agent a smile. "Saying good-bye to a friend," I said, and passed through the wooden arch right after she did. She was picking up the pace, anxious to reach the plane.

I was still talking, nearly jogging to keep up with her. "I couldn't figure out why she wasn't trying to stop you and then I realized what she must have done—"

"Get away from me. I don't want to talk to you."

"She took the money, Justine. There's probably nothing in that money belt of yours but old papers. She had plenty of time to make the switch while you were getting your hair done."

"Ha, ha," she said sarcastically. "Tell me another one."

I stopped in my tracks. "All right. That's all I'm gonna say. I just didn't want you to reach Mexico City and find yourself flat broke."

"Blow it out your buns," she hissed. She showed her boarding pass to the woman at the gate and passed on through. I could hear her spike heels tip-tapping out of ear range.

I reversed myself, walked back through the gate area and out to the walled exterior courtyard, where I could see the planes through a windbreak of protective glass. Justine crossed the tarmac to the waiting plane, her shoulders set. I didn't think she'd heard me, but then I saw her hand stray to her waist. She walked a few more steps and then halted, dumping her belongings in a pile at her feet. She pulled her shirt up and checked the money belt. At that distance, I saw her mouth open, but it took a second for the shrieks of outrage to reach me.

Ah, well, I thought. Sometimes a mother's love is like a poison that leaves no trace. You bop along through life, thinking you've got it made, and next thing you know, you're dead.

full circle

THE ACCIDENT SEEMED to happen in slow motion—one of those stop-action sequences that seem to go on forever though in truth no more than a few seconds have elapsed. It was Friday afternoon, rush hour, Santa Teresa traffic moving at a lively pace, my little VW holding its own despite the fact that it's fifteen years out of date. I was feeling good. I'd just wrapped up a case and I had a check in my handbag for four thousand bucks, not bad considering the fact that I'm a female private eye, self-employed, and subject to the feast-or-famine vagaries of any other freelance work.

I glanced to my left as a young woman, driving a white compact, appeared in my driver's-side mirror. A bright red Porsche was bearing down on her in the fast lane. I adjusted my speed, making room for her, sensing that she meant to cut in front of me. A navy blue pickup truck was coming up on my right, each of us jockeying for position as the late afternoon sun washed down out of a cloudless

California spring sky. I had glanced in my rearview mirror, checking traffic behind me, when I heard a loud popping noise. I snapped my attention back to the road in front of me. The white compact veered abruptly back into the fast lane, clipped the rear of the red Porsche, then hit the center divider and careened directly into my path. I slammed on my brakes, adrenaline shooting through me as I fought to control the VW's fishtailing rear end.

Suddenly, a dark green Mercedes appeared out of nowhere and caught the girl's car broadside, flipping the vehicle with all the expertise of a movie stunt. Brakes squealed all around me like a chorus of squawking birds and I could hear the successive thumps of colliding cars piling up behind me in a drumroll of destruction. It was over in an instant, a cloud of dust roiling up from the shoulder where the girl's car had finally come to rest, right-side up, half buried in the shrubbery. She had sheared off one of the support posts for the exit sign, which now leaned crazily across her car roof. The ensuing silence was profound.

I pulled over and was out of my car like a shot, the fellow from the navy blue pickup truck right behind me. There must have been five of us running toward the wreckage. The white car was accordion-folded, the door on the driver's side jammed shut. Steam billowed out from under the hood with an alarming hiss. The impact had rammed the girl headfirst into the windshield, which had cracked in a starburst effect. She was unconscious, her face bathed in blood. I willed myself to move toward her though my instinct was to turn away in horror.

The guy from the pickup truck nearly wrenched the car door off its hinges in one of those emergency-generated bursts of strength that can't be duplicated under ordinary circumstances. As he reached for her, I caught his arm.

"Don't move her," I said. "Let the paramedics handle this."

He gave me a startled look, but drew back as he was told. I shed my windbreaker and we used it to form a compress, staunching the flow of blood from the worst of her cuts. The guy was in his twenties, with dark curly hair and dark eyes filled with anxiety. Over my shoulder, someone was asking me if I knew first aid and I realized that others had been hurt in the accident as well. The driver from the green Mercedes was already using the roadside emergency phone, presumably calling police and ambulance. I looked back at the guy from the pickup truck, who was pressing the girl's neck, looking for a pulse.

"Is she alive?" I asked.

"Looks like it."

I jerked my head at the people on the berm behind me. "Let me see what I can do down there until the ambulance comes," I said. "Holler if you need me."

He nodded in reply.

I left him with the girl and moved along the shoulder toward a writhing man whose leg was visibly broken. A woman was sobbing hysterically somewhere close by and her cries added an eerie counterpoint to the moans of those in pain. The fellow from the red Porsche simply stood there numbly, immobilized by shock.

Meanwhile, traffic had slowed to a crawl and commuters were rubbernecking as if freeway accidents were some sort of spectator sport and this was the main event. Sirens approached. The next hour was a blur of police and emergency vehicles. I spotted my friend John Birkett, a photographer from the local paper, who'd reached the scene moments behind the paramedics. I remember marveling at the speed with which news of the pileup had spread. I watched as the girl was loaded into the ambulance. While flash-bulbs went off, several of us gave our accounts of the accident to the highway patrol officer, conferring with one another compul-sively as if repetition might relieve us of tension and distress. I didn't get home until nearly seven and my hands were still shaking. The jumble of images made sleep a torment of sudden awakenings, my foot jerking in a dream sequence as I slammed on my brakes again and again.

When I read in the morning paper that the girl had died, I felt sick with regret. The article was brief. Caroline Spurrier was twenty-two, a senior psychology major at the University of Califor-nia, Santa Teresa. She was a native of Denver, Colorado, just two months short of graduation at the time of her death. The photo-graph showed shoulder-length blond hair, bright eyes, and an impish grin. According to the paper, six other people had suffered injuries, none fatal. The weight of the young woman's death set-tled in my chest like a cold I couldn't shake.

My office in town was being repainted, so I worked at home that next week, catching up on reports. On Thursday, when the knock came, I'd just broken for lunch. I opened the door. At first glance, I thought the dead girl was miraculously alive, restored to health and standing on my doorstep with all the solemnity of a ghost. The illu-sion was dispelled. A close look showed a blond woman in her mid-forties, her face etched with weariness.

"I'm Michelle Spurrier," she said. "I understand you were a

witness to my daughter's accident. I saw your name and home address on a copy of the police report."

I stepped back. "Please come in. I'm sorry for your loss, Mrs. Spurrier. That was terrible."

She moved past me like a sleepwalker as I closed the door.

"Please sit down. Can I get you anything?"

She shook her head, looking around with bewilderment as if she couldn't quite remember what had brought her here. She set her purse aside and sank down on my couch, placing her cupped hands across her nose and mouth like an oxygen mask.

I sat down beside her, watching as she breathed deeply, struggling to speak. "Take your time," I said.

When the words came, her voice was so low I had to lean close to hear her. "The police examined Caroline's car at the impound lot and found a bullet hole in the window on the passenger side. My daughter was shot." She burst into tears.

I sat beside her while she poured out a grief tinged with rage and frustration. I brought her a glass of water and a fistful of tissues, small comfort, but all I could think to do. "What are the police telling you?" I asked when she'd composed herself.

She blew her nose and then took another deep breath. "The case has been transferred from Traffic detail to Homicide. The officer I talked to this morning says it looks like a random freeway shooting, but I don't believe it."

"God knows they've had enough of those down in Los Angeles," I remarked.

"Well, I can't accept that. For one thing, what was she doing speeding down the highway at that hour of the day? She was supposed to be at work, but they tell me she left abruptly without a word to anyone."

"Where was she employed?"

"A restaurant out in Colgate. She'd been waiting tables there for a year. The shift manager told me a man had been harassing her. He thinks she might have left to try to get away from him."

"Did he know who the guy was?"

She shook her head. "He wasn't sure. Some fellow she'd been dating. Apparently, he kept stopping by the restaurant, calling her at all hours, making a terrible pest of himself. Lieutenant Dolan tells me you're a private detective, which is why I'm here. I want you to find out who's responsible for this."

"Mrs. Spurrier, the police here are very competent. I'm sure they're doing everything possible."

"Skip the public relations message," she said with bitterness. "I have to fly back to Denver. Caroline's stepfather is very ill and I need to get home, but I can't go unless I know someone here is looking into this. Please."

I thought about it briefly, but it didn't take much to persuade me. As a witness to the accident, I felt more than a professional interest in the case. "I'll need the names of her friends," I said.

I made a note of Mrs. Spurrier's address and phone number, along with the name of Caroline's roommate and the restaurant where she'd worked. I drew up a standard contract, waiving the advance. I'd bill her later for whatever time I put in. Ordinarily I bypass police business in an attempt to stay out of Lieutenant Dolan's way. As the officer in charge of Homicide, he's not crazy about private eyes. Though he's fairly tolerant of me, I couldn't imagine what she'd had to threaten to warrant the recommendation.

As soon as she left, I grabbed a jacket and my handbag and drove over to the police station, where I paid six dollars for a copy of the police report. Lieutenant Dolan wasn't in, but I spent a few minutes chatting with Emerald, the clerk in Identification and Records. She's a heavy black woman in her fifties, usually wary of my questions, but a sucker for gossip.

"I hear Jasper's wife caught him with Rowena Hairston," I said, throwing out some bait. Jasper Sax is one of Emerald's interdepartmental foes.

"Why tell me?" she said. She was pretending uninterest, but I could tell the rumor cheered her. Jasper, from the crime lab, is forever lifting files from Emerald's desk, which only gets her in trouble when Lieutenant Dolan comes around.

"I was hoping you'd fill me in on the Spurrier accident. I know you've memorized all the paperwork."

She grumbled something about flattery that implied she felt flattered, so I pressed for specifics. "Anybody see where the shot was fired from?" I asked.

"No, ma'am."

I thought about the fellow in the red Porsche. He'd been in the lane to my left, just a few yards ahead of me when the accident occurred. The man in the pickup might be a help as well. "What about the other witnesses? There must have been half a dozen of us at the scene. Who's been interviewed?"

Emerald gave me an indignant look. "What's the matter with you? You know I'm not allowed to give out information like that!"

"Worth a try," I said equably. "What about the girl's professors from the university? Has Dolan talked to them?"

"Check it out yourself if you're so interested," she snapped.

"Come on, Emerald. Dolan knows I'm doing this. He was the one who told Mrs. Spurrier about me in the first place. I'll make it easy for you. Just one name."

She squinted at me suspiciously. "Which one's that?"

I took a flier, describing the guy in the pickup, figuring she could identify him from the list by age. Grudgingly, she checked the list and her expression changed.

"Uh-oh," she said. "I might know you'd zero in on this one. Fellow in the pickup gave a phony name and address. Benny Seco was the name, but he must have made that up. Telephone was a fake, too. Looks like he took off and nobody's seen him since. Might have been a warrant out against him he was trying to duck."

"How about the guy in the Porsche?"

I heard a voice behind me. "Well, well, well. Kinsey Millhone. Hard at work, I see."

Emerald faded into the background with all the practice of a spy. I turned to find Lieutenant Dolan standing in the hallway in his habitual pose, hands shoved down in his pants pockets, rocking on his heels. He'd recently celebrated a birthday, his baggy face reflecting every one of his sixty years.

I folded the police report and tucked it in my bag. "Mrs. Spurrier got in touch with me and asked me to follow up on this business of her daughter's death. I feel bad about the girl."

His manner shifted. "I do, too," he said.

"What's the story on the missing witness?"

Dolan shrugged. "He must have had some reason to give out a phony name. Did you talk to him at the scene?"

"Just briefly, but I'd know him if I saw him again. Do you think he could be of help?"

Dolan ran a hand across his balding pate. "I'd sure like to hear what the fellow has to say. Nobody else was aware that the girl was shot. I gather he was close enough to have done it himself."

"There's gotta be a way to track him down, don't you think?"

"Maybe," he said. "No one remembers much about the man except the truck he drove. Toyota, dark blue, maybe four or five years old from what they say."

"Would you object if I checked back with the other witnesses? I might get more out of them since I was there."

He studied me for a moment, then reached over to the file and removed the list of witnesses, which he handed to me without a word.

"Don't you need this?" I said, surprised.

"I have a copy."

"Thanks. This is great. I'll let you know what I find out."

Dolan pointed a finger. "Keep in touch with the department. I don't want you going off half cocked."

I DROVE OUT TO the campus area to the restaurant where Caroline Spurrier had worked. The place had changed hands recently, the decor downgraded from real plants to fake as the nationality of the food changed from Mexican to Thai. The shift manager, David Cole, was just a kid himself, barely twenty-one, tall, skinny, with a nose that belonged on a much larger face.

I introduced myself and told him I was looking into Caroline's death.

"Oh yeah, that was awful. I talked to her mom."

"She says you mentioned some guy who'd been bugging her. What else can you tell me?"

"That's about all I know. I mean, I never saw the guy myself. She was working nights for the last couple months and just switched back to days to see if she could get away from him."

"She ever mention his name?"

"Terry something, I think. He used to follow her around in this green van he drove. She really thought the dude was bent."

"Bent?"

"You know . . . twisted." He twiddled an index finger beside his head to indicate his craziness.

"Why'd she go out with him?"

"She said he seemed like a real nice guy at first, but then he got real possessive, all jealous and like that. In the end, I guess he was totally nuts. He must have showed up on Friday, which is why she took off."

I quizzed him, but couldn't glean much more from his account. I thanked him and drove over to the block of university housing where Caroline had lived. The apartment was typical of student digs—faintly shabby, furnished with mismatched items that had probably been languishing in someone's garage. Her roommate was a young woman named Judy Layton, who chatted despondently as she emptied kitchen cabinets and packed assorted cardboard boxes. I kept the questions light at first, asking her about herself as she wrapped some dinner plates in newspaper, shoving each in a box. She was twenty-three, a senior English major with family living in town.

"How long did you know Caroline?"

"About a year," she said. "I had another roommate, but Alice graduated last year. Caroline and I connected up through one of those roommate-referral services."

"How come you're moving out?"

She shrugged. "Going back to my folks'. It's too late in the school year to find someone else and I can't afford this place on my own. My brother's on his way over to help me move."

According to her, Caroline was a "party-hearty" who somehow managed to keep her grades up and still have a good time.

"Did she have a boyfriend?"

"She dated lots of guys."

"But no one in particular?"

She shook her head, intent on her work.

I tried again. "She told her mom about some guy harassing her at work. Apparently she'd dated him and they'd just broken up. Do you have any idea who she might have been talking about?"

"Not really. I didn't keep track of the guys in her life."

"She must have mentioned this guy if he was causing such a fuss."

"Look. She and I were not close. We were roommates and that was it. She went her way and I went mine. If some guy was bugging her, she didn't say a word to me."

"She wasn't in any trouble that you knew about?"

"No."

Her manner seemed sullen and it was getting on my nerves. I stared at her. "Judy, I could use a little help. People get murdered for a reason. It might seem stupid or insignificant to the rest of us, but there was *something* going on. What gives?"

"You don't know it was murder. The policeman I talked to said it might have been some bozo in a passing car."

"Her mother disagrees."

"Well, I can't help you. I already told you everything I know."

I nailed her with a look and let a silence fall, hoping her discomfort would generate further comment. No such luck. If she knew more, she was determined to keep it to herself. I left a business card, asking her to phone me if she remembered anything.

I spent the next two days talking to Caroline Spurrier's professors and friends. From the portrait that emerged, she seemed like a likable kid—funny, good-natured, popular, and sweet. She'd complained of the harassment to a couple of classmates without giving any indication who the fellow was. I went back to the list of witnesses at the scene of the accident, talking to each in turn. I was still tantalized by the guy in the pickup. What reason could he have to falsify his identity?

I'd clipped out the news account of Caroline Spurrier's death, pinning her picture on the bulletin board above my desk. She looked down at me with a smile that seemed more enigmatic with the passing days. I couldn't bear the idea of having to tell her mother my investigation was at an impasse, but I knew I owed her a report.

I was sitting at my typewriter when an idea came to me, quite literally, in a flash. I was staring at the newspaper picture of the wreckage when I spotted the photo credit. I suddenly remembered John Birkett at the scene, his flash going off as he shot pictures of the wreck. If he'd inadvertently snapped one of the guy in the pickup, at least I'd have something to show the cops. Maybe we could get a lead on the fellow that way. I gave Birkett a call. Twenty minutes later, I was in his cubbyhole at the Santa Teresa *Dispatch*, our heads bent together while we scanned the contact sheets.

"No good," John said. "This one's not bad, but the focus is off. Damn. I never really got a clear shot of him."

"What about the truck?"

John pulled out another contact sheet that showed various views of the wrecked compact, the pickup visible on the berm behind. "Well, you can see it in the background, if that's any help."

"Can we get an enlargement?"

"You looking for anything in particular?"

"The license plate," I said.

The California plate bore a seven-place combination of numbers and letters that we finally discerned in the grainy haze of two blow-ups. I should have called Lieutenant Dolan and had him run the license number, but I confess to an egotistical streak that sometimes overrides common sense. I didn't want to give the lead back to him just yet. I called a pal of mine at the Department of Motor Vehicles and asked him to check it out instead.

The license plate was registered to a 1984 Toyota pickup, navy blue, the owner listed as Ron Cagle with an address on McClatchy Way.

The house was stucco, dark gray, with the trim done in white. My heart was pounding as I rang the bell. The fellow's face was printed so indelibly in memory that when the door was finally opened, I just stood there and stared. Wrong man. This guy was probably six-foot-seven, over two hundred pounds, with a strong chin, ruddy complexion, blue eyes, auburn hair, red mustache. "Yes?"

"I'm looking for Ron Cagle."

"I'm Ron Cagle."

"You are?" My voice broke in astonishment like a kid reaching puberty. "You're the owner of a navy blue Toyota pickup?" I read off the number of the license plate.

He looked at me quizzically. "Yes. Is something wrong?"

"Well, I don't know. Has someone else been driving it?"

"Not for the last six months."

"Are you sure?"

He half laughed. "See for yourself. It's sitting on the parking pad just behind the house."

He pulled the door shut behind him, leading the way as the two of us moved off the porch and down the driveway to the rear. There sat the navy blue Toyota pickup, without wheels, up on blocks. The hood was open and there was empty space where the engine should have been. "What's going on?" he asked.

"That's what I'm about to ask you. This truck was at the scene of a recent accident where a girl was killed."

"Not this one," he said. "This has been right here."

Without another word, I pulled out the photographs. "Isn't that your license plate?"

He studied the photos with a frown. "Well, yes, but the truck isn't mine. It couldn't be." He glanced back at his pickup, spotting the discrepancy. "There's the problem. . . ." He pointed to the license. The plate on the truck was an altogether different set of numbers.

It took me about thirty seconds before the light finally dawned. "Somebody must have lifted your plates and substituted these."

"What would be the point?"

I shrugged. "Maybe someone stole a navy blue Toyota truck and wanted plates that would clear a license check if he was stopped by the cops. Can I use your telephone?"

I called Lieutenant Dolan and told him what I'd found. He ran a check on the plates for the pickup sitting in the drive, which turned out to match the numbers on a vehicle reported stolen two weeks before. An APB was issued for the truck with Cagle's plates. Dolan's guess was that the guy had left the state, or abandoned the pickup shortly after the accident. It was also possible that even if we found the guy, he might not have any real connection with the shooting death. Somehow I doubted it.

A week passed with no results. The silence was discouraging. I was right back where I started from with no appreciable progress. If a case is going to break, it usually happens fast and the chances of cracking this one were diminishing with every passing day. Caroline Spurrier's photograph was still pinned to the bulletin board above my desk, her smile nearly mocking. In situations like this, all I know to do is go back to the beginning and start again.

Doggedly, I went through the list of witnesses, calling everybody in turn. Most tried to be helpful, but there was really nothing new to add. I drove back to the campus to look for Caroline's roommate.

Judy Layton had to know something more than she'd told me at first. Maybe I could find a way to worm some information out of her.

The apartment was locked and a quick peek in the front window showed that all the furniture was gone. I picked up her forwarding address from the manager on the premises and headed over to her parents' house in Colgate, the little suburb to the north.

The house was pleasant, a story and a half of stucco and frame, an attached three-car garage visible at the right. I rang the bell and waited, idly scanning the neighborhood from my vantage point on the porch. It was a nice street, wide and tree-lined, with a grassy divider down the center planted with pink and white flowering shrubs. I rang the bell again. Apparently, no one was home.

I went down the porch steps and paused in the driveway, intending to return to my car, which was parked at the curb. I hesitated where I stood. There are times in this business when a hunch is a hunch—when a little voice in your gut tells you something's amiss. I turned with curiosity toward the three-car garage at the rear. I cupped my hands, shading my eyes so I could peer through the side window. In the shadowy interior, I saw a pickup, stripped of paint.

I tried the garage's side entrance. The door was unlocked and I pushed my way in. The space smelled of dust, motor oil, and primer. The pickup's license plates were gone. This had to be the same truck, though I couldn't think why it hadn't been dumped. Maybe it was too perilous to attempt at this point. Heart thumping, I did a quick search of the cab's interior. Under the front seat, on the driver's side, I saw a handgun, a .45. I left it where it was, eased the cab door shut, and backed away from the truck. Clearly, someone in the Layton household had been at the murder scene.

I left the garage at a quick clip, trotting toward the street. I had
to find a telephone and call the cops. I had just started my car, shoving it into gear, when I saw a dark green VW van pass on the far side
of the divider and circle back in my direction, headed toward the
Laytons' drive. The fellow driving was the man I'd seen at the accident. Judy's brother? The similarities were obvious now that I
thought of it. No wonder she'd been unwilling to tell me what was
going on! He slowed for the turn and that's when he spotted me.

If I'd had any doubts about his guilt, they vanished the minute he
and I locked eyes. His surprise was replaced by panic and he gunned
his engine, taking off. I peeled after him, flooring it. At the corner,
he skidded sideways and recovered, speeding out of sight. I went
after him, zigzagging crazily through a residential area that was laid
out like a maze. Ahead of me, I could almost chart his course by the
whine of his transmission. He was heading toward the freeway.

At the overpass, I caught a glimpse of him in the southbound
lane. He wasn't hard to track, the boxy shape of the van clearly visible as we tore toward town. The traffic began to slow, massing in
one of those inexplicable logjams on the road. I couldn't tell if the
problem was a fender bender in the northbound lane or a bottleneck
in ours, but it gave me the advantage I needed. I was catching him.

As I eased up on his left, I saw him lean on the accelerator, cutting to his right. He hit the shoulder of the road, his tires spewing
out gravel as he widened the gap between us. He was bypassing
stalled cars, hugging the shrubbery as he flew down the berm. I was
right behind him, keeping as close to him as I dared. My car wasn't
very swift, but then neither was his van. I jammed my accelerator to
the floor and pinned myself to his tail. He was watching me steadily

in his rearview mirror, our eyes meeting in a deadlock of determination and grit.

I spotted the maintenance crew just seconds before he did; guys in bright orange vests working with a crane, which was parked squarely in his path. There was no way for him to slow in time and no place else to go. His van plowed into the rear of the crane with a crash that made my blood freeze as I slammed on my brakes. I was luckier than he. My VW came to a stop just a kiss away from death.

Like a nightmare, we repeated all the horror of the first wreck. Police and paramedics, the wailing of the ambulance. When I finally stopped shaking, I realized where I was. The road crew was replacing the big green highway sign sheared in half when Caroline Spurrier's car had smashed into it. Terry Layton died at the very spot where he killed her.

Caroline's smile has shifted back to impishness in the photograph above my desk. I keep it there as a reminder, but of what I couldn't say. The brevity of life perhaps, the finality of death—the irony of events that sometimes connect the two.

a little
missionary work

SOMETIMES YOU HAVE to take on a job that constitutes pure missionary work. You accept an assignment not for pay, or for any hope
of tangible reward, but simply to help another human being in distress. My name is Kinsey Millhone. I'm a licensed private eye, in
business for myself, so I can't really afford professional charity, but
now and then somebody gets into trouble and I just can't turn my
back.

I was standing in line one Friday at the bank, waiting to make a
deposit. It was almost lunchtime and there were eleven people in
front of me, so I had some time to kill. As usual, in the teller's line,
I was thinking about Harry Hovey, my bank-robber friend, who'd
once been arrested for holding up this very branch. I'd met him
when I was investigating a bad-check case. He was introduced to me
by another crook as an unofficial "expert" and ended up giving me a

crash course in the methods and practices of passing bad paper. Poor Harry. I couldn't remember how many times he'd been in the can. He was skilled enough for a life of crime, but given to self-sabotage. Harry was always trying to go straight, always trying to clean up his act, but honest employment never seemed to have much appeal. He'd get out of prison, find a job, and be doing pretty well for himself. Then, something would come along and he'd succumb to temptation—forge a check, rob a bank, God only knows what. Harry was hooked on crime the way some people are addicted to cocaine, alcohol, chocolate, and unrequited love. He was currently doing time in the Federal Correctional Institution in Lompoc, California, with all the other racketeers, bank robbers, counterfeiters, and former White House staff bad boys.

I had reached the teller's window and was finishing my transaction when Lacy Alisal, the assistant bank manager, approached. "Miss Millhone? I wonder if you could step this way. Mr. Chamberlain would like a word with you."

"Who?"

"The branch vice president," she said. "It shouldn't take long."

"Oh. Sure."

I followed the woman toward Mr. Chamberlain's glass-walled enclosure, wondering the whole time what I'd done to deserve this. Well, okay. Let's be honest. I'd been thinking about switching my account to First Interstate for the free checking privileges, but I didn't see how he could have found out about *that*. As for my balances, I'd only been overdrawn by the teensiest amount and what's a line of credit for?

I was introduced to Jack Chamberlain, who turned out to be someone I recognized from the gym, a tall, lanky fellow in his early forties, whose workouts overlapped mine three mornings a week. We'd exchange occasional small talk if we happened to be doing reps on adjacent machines. It was odd to see him here in a conservative business suit after months of sweat-darkened shorts and T-shirts. His hair was cropped close, the color a wiry mixture of copper and silver. He wore steel-rimmed glasses and his teeth were endearingly crooked in front. Somehow, he looked more like a high school basketball coach than a banking exec. A trophy sitting on his desk attested to his athletic achievements, but the engraving was small and I couldn't quite make out the print. He caught my look and a smile creased his face. "Varsity basketball. We were state champs," he said, as he shook my hand formally and invited me to take a seat.

He sat down himself and picked up a fountain pen, which he capped and recapped as he talked. "I appreciate your time. I know you do your banking on Fridays and I took the liberty," he said. "Someone told me at the gym that you're a private investigator."

"That's right. Are you in the market for one?"

"This is for an old friend of mine. My former high school sweetheart, if you want the truth," he said. "I probably could have called you at your office, but the circumstances are unusual and this seemed more discreet. Are you free tonight by any chance?"

"Tonight? That depends," I said. "What's going on?"

"I'd rather have her explain it. This is probably going to seem paranoid, but she insists on secrecy, which is why she didn't want to make contact herself. She has reason to believe her phone is tapped.

I hope you can bear with us. Believe me, I don't ordinarily do business this way."

"Glad to hear that," I said. "Can you be a bit more specific? So far, I haven't really heard what I'm being asked to do."

Jack set the pen aside. "She'll explain the situation as soon as it seems wise. She and her husband are having a big party tonight and she asked me to bring you. They don't want you appearing in any professional capacity. Time is of the essence, or we might go about this some other way. You'll understand when you meet her."

I studied him briefly, trying to figure out what was going on. If this was a dating ploy, it was the weirdest one I'd ever heard. "Are you married?"

He smiled slightly. "Divorced. I understand you are, too. I assure you, this is not a hustle."

"What kind of party?"

"Oh, yes. Glad you reminded me." He removed an envelope from his top drawer and pushed it across the desk. "Cocktails. Five to seven. Black tie, I'm afraid. This check should cover your expenses in the way of formal dress. If you try the rental shop around the corner, Roberta Linderman will see that you're outfitted properly. She knows these people well."

"What people? You haven't even told me their names."

"Karen Waterston and Kevin McCall. They have a little weekend retreat up here."

"Ah," I said, nodding. This was beginning to make more sense. Karen Waterston and Kevin McCall were actors who'd just experienced a resurgence in their careers, starring in a new television series called *Shamus, P.I.*, an hour-long spoof of every detective series that's ever aired. I don't watch much TV, but I'd heard about the show and after seeing it once, I'd found myself hooked. The stories were fresh, the writing was superb, and the format was perfect for their considerable acting talents. Possibly because they were married in "real" life, the two brought a wicked chemistry to the screen. As with many new shows, the ratings hadn't yet caught up with the rave reviews, but things looked promising. Whatever their problem, I could understand the desire to keep their difficulties hidden from public scrutiny.

Jack was saying, "You're in no way obligated, but I hope you'll say yes. She really needs your help."

"Well. I guess I've had stranger requests in my day. I better give you my address."

He held up the signature card I'd completed when I opened my account. "I have that."

I soon learned what "cocktails five to seven" means to the very rich. Everybody showed up at seven and stayed until they were dead drunk. Jack Chamberlain, in a tux, picked me up at my apartment at six forty-five. I was decked out in a slinky beaded black dress with long sleeves, a high collar, and no back—not my usual apparel of choice. When Jack helped me into the front seat of his Mercedes, I shrieked at the shock of cold leather against my bare skin.

Once at the party, I regained my composure and managed to conduct myself (for the most part) without embarrassment or disgrace. The "little weekend retreat" turned out to be a sprawling six-bedroom estate, decorated with a confident blend of the avant-garde and the minimalist: unadorned white walls, wide, bare, gleaming expanses of polished hardwood floor. The few pieces of furniture were draped with white canvas, like those in a palatial summer residence being closed up for the season. Aside from a dazzling crystal chandelier, all the dining room contained was a plant, a mirror, and a bentwood chair covered with an antique paisley shawl. Très chic. They'd probably paid thousands for some interior designer to come in and haul all the knickknacks away.

As the party picked up momentum, the noise level rose, people spilling out onto all the terraces. Six young men, in black pants and pleated white shirts, circulated with silver platters of tasty hot and cold morsels. The champagne was exquisite, the supply apparently endless so that I was fairly giddy by the time Jack took me by the arm and eased me out of the living room. "Karen wants to see you upstairs," he murmured.

"Great," I said. I'd hardly laid eyes on her except as a glittering wraith along the party's perimeters. I hadn't seen Kevin at all, but I'd overheard someone say he was off scouting locations for the show coming up. Jack and I drifted up the spiral stairs together, me hoping that in my half-inebriated state, I wouldn't pitch over the railing and land with a splat. As I reached the landing, I looked down and was startled to see my friend Vera in the foyer below. She caught sight of me and did a double take, apparently surprised to see me in such elegant surroundings, especially dressed to the teeth. We exchanged a quick wave.

The nearly darkened master suite was carpeted to a hush, but again, it was nearly empty. The room was probably fifty feet by thirty, furnished dead-center with a king-sized bed, a wicker hamper, two ficus trees, and a silver lamp with a twenty-five-watt bulb on a long, curving neck.

As Jack ushered me into the master bathroom, where the meeting was to take place, he flicked me an apologetic look. "I hope this doesn't seem too odd."

"Not at all," I said, politely—like a lot of my business meetings take place in the WC.

Candles flickered from every surface. Sound was dampened by thick white carpeting and a profusion of plants. Karen Waterston sat on the middle riser of three wide, beige marble steps leading up to the Jacuzzi. Beside her, chocolate brown bath towels were rolled and stacked like a cord of firewood. She was wearing a halter-style dress of white chiffon, which emphasized the dark, even tan of her slender shoulders and arms. Her hair was silver-blond, coiled around her head in a twist of satin ropes. She was probably forty-two, but her face had been cosmetically backdated to the age of twenty-five, a process that would require ever more surgical ingenuity as the years went by. Jack introduced us and we shook hands. Hers were ice cold and I could have sworn she wasn't happy to have me there.

Jack pulled out a wicker stool and sat down with his back to Karen's makeup table, his eyes never leaving her face. My guess was that being an ex–high school sweetheart of hers was as much a part of his identity as being a former basketball champ. I leaned a hip against the marble counter. There was a silver-framed photograph of Kevin McCall propped up beside me, the mirror reflecting endless reproductions of his perfect profile. To all appearances, he'd been allowed to retain the face he was born with, but the uniform darkness of his hair, with its picturesque dusting of silver at the temples, suggested that nature was being tampered with, at least superficially. Still, it was hard to imagine that either he or Karen had a problem more pressing than an occasional loose dental cap.

"I appreciate your coming, Miss Millhone. It means a lot to us under the circumstances." Her voice was throaty and low, with the merest hint of tremolo. Even by candlelight, I could see the tension in her face. "I wasn't in favor of bringing anyone else into this, but Jack insisted. Has he explained the situation?" She glanced from me to Jack, who said, "I told her you preferred to do that yourself."

She seemed to hug herself for warmth and her mouth suddenly looked pinched. Tears welled in her eyes and she placed two fingers on the bridge of her nose as if to quell their flow. "You'll have to forgive me . . ."

I didn't think she'd be able to continue, but she managed to collect herself.

"Kevin's been kidnapped. . . ." Her voice cracked with emotion and she lifted her dark eyes to mine. I'd never seen such a depth of pain and suffering.

At first, I didn't even know what to say to her. "When was this?"

"Last night. We're very private people. We've never let anyone get remotely close to us. . . ." She broke off again.

"Take your time," I said.

Jack moved over to the stair and sat down beside her, putting an arm protectively around her shoulders. The smile she offered him was wan and she couldn't sustain it.

He handed her his handkerchief and I waited while she blew

her nose and dabbed at her eyes. "Sorry. I'm just so frightened. This is horrible."

"I hope you've called the police," I said.

"She doesn't want to take the risk," Jack said.

Karen shook her head. "They said they'd kill him if I called in the police."

"Who said?"

"The bastards who snatched him. I was given this note. Here. You can see for yourself. It's too much like the Bender case to take any chances." She extracted a piece of paper from the folds of her long dress and held it out to me.

I took the note by one corner so I wouldn't smudge any prints, probably a useless precaution. If this was truly like the Bender case, there wouldn't be any prints to smudge. The paper was plain, the printing in ball-point pen and done with a ruler.

FIVE HUNDRED THOU IN SMALL BILLS BUYS YOUR HUSBAND BACK. GO TO THE COPS OR THE FEDS AND HE'S DEAD MEAT FOR SURE. WE'LL CALL SOON WITH INSTRUCTIONS. KEEP YOUR MOUTH SHUT OR YOU'LL REGRET IT. THAT'S A PROMISE, BABY CAKES.

She was right. Both the format and the use of language bore an uncanny similarity to the note delivered to a woman named Corey Bender, whose husband had been a kidnapped about a year ago. Dan Bender was the CEO of a local manufacturing company, a man who'd made millions with a line of auto parts called Fender-Benders. In that situation, the kidnappers had asked for five hundred thousand dollars in tens and twenties. Mrs. Bender had contacted both the police and the FBI, who had stage-managed the whole transaction, arranging for a suitcase full of blank paper to be dropped according to the kidnappers' elaborate telephone instructions. The drop site had been staked out, everyone assuring Mrs. Bender that nothing could possibly go wrong. The drop went as planned except the suitcase was never picked up and Dan Bender was never seen alive again. His body—or what was left of it—washed up on the Santa Teresa beach two months later.

"Tell me what happened," I said.

She got up and began to pace, describing in halting detail the circumstances of Kevin McCall's abduction. The couple had been working on a four-day shooting schedule at the studio down in Hollywood. They'd been picked up from the set by limousine at seven P.M. on Thursday and had been driven straight to Santa Teresa, arriving for the long weekend at nine o'clock that night. The housekeeper usually fixed supper for them and left it in the oven, departing shortly before they were due home. At the end of a week of shooting, the couple preferred all the solitude they could get.

Nothing seemed amiss when they arrived at the house. Both interior and exterior lights were on as usual. Karen emerged from the limo with Kevin right behind her. She chatted briefly with the driver and then waved good-bye while Kevin unlocked the front door and disarmed the alarm system. The limo driver had already turned out of the gate when two men in ski masks stepped out of the shadows armed with automatics. Neither Karen nor Kevin had much opportunity to react. A dark sedan pulled into the driveway and Kevin was hustled into the backseat at gunpoint. Not a word was said. The note was thrust into Karen's hand as the gunmen left. She raced after the sedan as it sped away, but no license plates were visible. She had no real hope of catching up and no clear idea what she meant to do anyway. In a panic, she returned to the house and locked herself in. Once the shock wore off, she called Jack Chamberlain, their local banker, a former high school classmate—the only person in Santa Teresa she felt she could trust. Her first thought was to cancel tonight's party altogether, but Jack suggested she proceed.

"I thought it would look more natural," he filled in. "Especially if she's being watched."

"They did call with instructions?" I asked.

Again she nodded, her face pale. "They want the money by midnight tomorrow or that's the last I'll see of him."

"Can you *raise* five hundred thousand on such short notice?"

"Not without help," she said, and turned a pleading look to Jack.

He was shaking his head and I gathered this was a subject they'd already discussed at length. "The bank doesn't keep large reservoirs of cash on hand," he said to me. "There's no way I'd have access to a sum like that, particularly on a weekend. The best I can do is bleed the cash from all the branch ATMs—"

"Surely you can do better than that," she said. "You're a bank vice president."

He turned to her, with a faintly defensive air, trying to persuade her the failing wasn't his. "I might be able to put together the full amount by Monday, but even then, you'd have to fill out an application and go through the loan committee—"

She said, "Oh, for God's sake, Jack. Don't give me that bureaucratic bullshit when Kevin's life is at stake! There has to be a way."

"Karen, be reasonable—"

"Forget it. This is hopeless. I'm sorry I ever brought you into this. . . ."

I watched them bicker for a moment and then broke in. "All right, wait a minute. Hold on. Let's back off the money question, for the time being."

"Back *off*?" she said.

"Look. Let's assume there's a way to get the ransom money. Now what?"

Her brow was furrowed and she seemed to have trouble concentrating on the question at hand. "I'm sorry. What?"

"Fill me in on the rest of it. I need to know what happened last night after you got in touch with Jack."

"Oh. I see, yes. He came over to the house and we sat here for hours, waiting for the phone to ring. The kidnappers—one of them—finally called at two A.M."

"You didn't recognize the voice?"

"Not at all."

"Did the guy seem to know Jack was with you?"

"He didn't mention it, but he swore they were watching the house and he said the phone was tapped."

"I wouldn't bet on it, but it's probably smart to proceed as though it's true. It's possible they didn't have the house staked out last night, but they may have put a man on it since. Hard to know. Did they tell you how to deliver the cash once you got it?"

"That part was simple. I'm to pack the money in a big canvas duffel. At eleven-thirty tomorrow night, they want me to leave the house on my bicycle with the duffel in the basket."

"On a bike? That's a new one."

"Kev and I often bike together on weekends, which they seemed aware of. As a matter of fact, they seemed to know quite a lot. It was very creepy."

Jack spoke up. "They must have cased the place to begin with. They knew the whole routine, from what she's told me."

"Stands to reason," I remarked. And then to her, "Go on."

"They told me to wear my yellow jumpsuit—I guess so they can identify me—and that's all there was."

"They didn't tell you which way to ride?"

"I asked about that and they told me I could head in any direction I wanted. They said they'd follow at a distance and intercept when it suited them. Obviously, they want to make sure I'm unaccompanied."

"Then what?"

"When they blink the car lights, I'm to toss the canvas duffel to the side of the road and ride on. They'll release Kevin as soon as the money's been picked up and counted."

"Shoot. It rules out any fudging if they count the money first. Did they let you talk to Kevin?"

"Briefly. He sounded fine. Worried about me . . ."

"And you're sure it was him."

"Positive. I'm so scared. . . ."

The whole time we'd been talking, my mind was racing ahead. She had to call the cops. There was no doubt in my mind she was a fool to tackle this without the experts, but she was dead set against it. I said, "Karen, you can't handle something like this without the cops. You'd be crazy to try to manage on your own."

She was adamant.

Jack and I took turns arguing the point and I could see his frustration surface. "For God's sake, you've got to listen to us. You're way out of your element. If these guys are the same ones who kidnapped Dan Bender, you're putting Kevin's life at risk. They're absolutely ruthless."

"Jack, I'm not the one putting Kevin's life at risk. *You* are. That's exactly what you're doing when you propose calling the police."

"How are you going to get the money?" he said, exasperated.

"Goddamn it, how do I know? You're the banker. You tell me."

"Karen, I *am* telling you. There's no way to do this. You're making a big mistake."

"Corey Bender was the one who made a mistake," she snapped.

We were getting nowhere. Time was short and the pressures were mounting every minute. If Jack and I didn't come up with *some* plan, Kevin McCall was going to end up dead. If the cash could be assembled, the obvious move was to have me take Karen's place during the actual delivery, which would at least eliminate the possibility of her being picked up as well. Oddly enough, I thought I had an inkling how to get the bucks, though it might well take me the better part of the next day.

"All right," I said, breaking in for the umpteenth time. "We can argue this all night and it's not going to get us anyplace. Suppose I find a way to get the money, will you at least consent to my taking your place for the drop?"

She studied me for a moment. "That's awfully risky, isn't it? What if they realize the substitution?"

"How could they? They'll be following in a car. In the dark and at a distance, I can easily pass for you. A wig and a jumpsuit and who'd know the difference?"

She hesitated. "I do have a wig, but why not just do what they say? I don't like the idea of disobeying their instructions."

"Because these guys are way too dangerous for you to deal with yourself. Suppose you deliver the money as specified. What's to prevent their picking you up and making Kevin pay additional ransom for *your* return?"

I could see her debate the point. Her uneasiness was obvious, but she finally agreed. "I don't understand what you intend to do about the ransom. If Jack can't manage to get the money, how can you?"

"I know a guy who has access to a large sum of cash. I can't promise anything, but I can always ask."

Karen's gaze came to rest on my face with puzzlement.

"Look," I said in response to her unspoken question, "I'll explain if I get it. And if not, you have to promise me you'll call the police."

Jack prodded. "It's your only chance."

She was silent for a moment and then spoke slowly. "All right. Maybe so. We'll do it your way. What other choice do I have?"

Before we left, we made arrangements for her to leave a wig, the yellow jumpsuit, and the bicycle on the service porch the next night. I'd return to the house on foot sometime after dark, leaving my car parked a few discreet blocks away. At eleven-thirty, as instructed, I'd pedal down the drive with the canvas duffel and ride around until the kidnappers caught up with me. While I was gone, Jack could swing by and pick Karen up in his car. I wanted her off the premises in the event anything went wrong. If I was snatched and the kidnappers realized they had the wrong person, at least they couldn't storm back to the house and get her. We went over the details until we were all in accord. In the end, she seemed satisfied with the plan and so did Jack. I was the only one with any lingering doubts. I thought she was a fool, but I kept that to myself. . . .

I hit the road the next morning early and headed north on Highway 101. Visiting hours at the Federal Correctional Institution at Lompoc run from eight to four on Saturdays. The drive took about an hour with a brief stop at a supermarket in Buellton, where I picked up an assortment of picnic supplies. By ten, I was seated at one of the four sheltered picnic tables with my friend Harry Hovey. If Harry was surprised to see me, he didn't complain. "It's not like my social calendar's all that full," he said. "To what do I owe the pleasure?"

"Let's eat first," I said. "Then I got something I need to talk to you about."

I'd brought cold chicken and potato salad, assorted cheeses, fruit, and cookies—anything I could grab that didn't look like institutional fare. Personally, I wasn't hungry, but it was gratifying to watch Harry chow down with such enthusiasm. He was not looking well. He was a man in his fifties, maybe five-five, heavyset, with thinning gray hair and glasses cloudy with fingerprints. He didn't take good care of himself under the best of circumstances, and the stress of prison living had aged him ten years. His color was bad. He was smoking way too much. He'd lost weight in a manner that looked neither healthful nor flattering.

"How're you doing?" I asked. "You look tired."

"I'm okay, I guess. I been better in my day, but what the hell," he said. He'd paused in the middle of his meal for a cigarette. He seemed distracted, his attention flicking from the other tables to the playground equipment, where a noisy batch of kids were twirling round and round on the swings. It was November and the sun was shining, but the air was chilly and the grass was dead.

"How much time you have to serve yet?"

"Sixteen months," he said. "You ever been in the can?"

I shook my head.

He pointed at me with his cigarette. "Word of advice. Never admit nothin'. Always claim you're innocent. I learned that from the politicians. You ever watch those guys? They get caught takin' bribes and they assume this injured air. Like it's all a mistake, but the truth will out. They're confident they'll be vindicated and bullshit like that. They welcome the investigation so their names can be cleared. They always say that, you know? Whole time I'm in prison, I been saying that myself. I was framed. It's all a setup. I don't know nothin' about the money. I was just doing a favor for an old friend, a big-wig. A Very Big Wig. Like I'm implying the governor or the chief of police."

"Has it done you any good?"

"Well, not yet, but who knows? My lawyer's still trying to find a basis for appeal. If I get outta this one, I'm going into therapy, get my head straight, I swear to God. Speaking of which, I may get 'born again,' you know? It looks good. Lends a little credibility, which is something all the money in the world can't buy."

I took a deep breath. "Actually, it's the money I need to talk to you about." I took a few minutes to fill him in on the kidnapping without mentioning any names. Some of Karen Waterston's paranoia had filtered into my psyche and I thought the less I said about the "victim," the better off he'd be. "I know you've got a big cache of money somewhere. I'm hoping you'll contribute some of it to pay the ransom demands."

His look was blank with disbelief. "Ransom?"

"Harry, don't put me through this. You know what ransom is."

"Yeah, it's money you give to guys you never see again. Why not throw it out the window? Why not blow it at the track—"

"Are you finished yet?"

He smiled and a dimple formed. "How much you talking about?"

"Five hundred thousand."

His eyebrows went up. "What makes you think I got money like that?"

"Harry," I said patiently, "an informant told the cops you had over a million bucks. That's how you got caught."

Harry slapped the table. "Bobby Urquhart. That fuck. I should have known it was him. I run into the guy in a bar sitting at this table full of bums. He buys a round of tequila shooters. Next thing I know, everybody else is gone. I'm drunk as a skunk and flappin' my mouth." He dropped his cigarette butt on the concrete and crushed it underfoot. "Word of warning. Never confide in a guy wearing Brut. I must have been nuts to give that little faggot the time of day. The money's gone. I blew it. I got nothin' left."

"I don't believe you. That's bullshit. You didn't have time to blow that much. When you were busted, all you had were a few lousy bucks. Where's the rest of it?"

"Un-uhn. No way."

"Come on, Harry. It isn't going to do you any good in here. Why not help these people out? They've got tons of money. They can pay you back."

"They got money, how come they don't pay the shit themselves?"

"Because it's Saturday and the banks are closed. The branch VP couldn't even come up with the cash that fast. A man's life is at stake."

"Hey, so's mine and so what? You ever try life in the pen? I worked hard for that money so why should I do for some guy I never seen before?"

"Once in a while you just gotta help people out."

"Maybe you do. I don't."

"Harry, please. Be a prince . . ."

I could see him begin to waver. Who can resist a good deed now and then?

He put his hand on his chest. "This is giving me angina." He wagged his head back and forth. "Jesus. What if the cops get wind of it? How's it gonna look?"

"The cops are never going to know. Believe me, this woman's never going to breathe a word of it. If she trusted the cops, she'd have called them in the first place."

"Who are these people? At least tell me that. I'm not giving up half a million bucks without some ID."

I thought about it swiftly. I was reluctant to trade on their celebrity status. On the other hand, she was desperate and there wasn't time to spare. "Swear you won't tell."

"Who'm I gonna tell? I'm a con. Nobody believes me anyway," he said.

"Kevin McCall and Karen Waterston."

He seemed startled at first. "You're kidding me. No shit? You're talking *Shamus, P.I.*? Them two?"

"That's right."

"Why'n't you say so? That's my favorite show. All the guys watch that. What a gas. Karen Waterston is a fox."

"Then you'll help?"

"For that chick, of course," he said. He gave me a stern look. "Get me her autograph or the deal's off."

"Trust me. You'll have it. You're a doll. I owe you one."

We took a walk around the yard while he told me where the money was. Harry had nearly two million in cash hidden in a canvas duffel of his own, concealed in the false back of a big upholstered sofa, which was locked up, with a lot of other furniture, in a commercial self-storage facility.

Harry said, "On the off chance I don't get my money back, I can think of another way I might benefit. I've been worried the cops would figure out where my stash is hidden. Certain other evidence might come to light, in which case I'd be in more trouble than I'm in now. If you can do me this one thing, I'd consider us square."

"As long as it doesn't put delivery of the ransom money in jeopardy, I'll listen to anything you have to say."

He told me his idea, which I pondered briefly. I couldn't see how any harm would come of doing what he suggested.

I headed back to Santa Teresa with the key in my hand. Unearthing the money took the balance of the afternoon. The couch was at the bottom of an eight-by-eight-foot storage locker crammed with goods. Tables, chairs, cardboard boxes, a desk—a hundred or more items, which I removed one by one, stacking them behind me in the narrow aisle between bins. The facility was hot and airless and I could hardly ask for help. By the time I laid my hands on the canvas tote hidden in the couch, there was barely room in the passageway to turn around. By six o'clock, feeling harried, I had taken all but half a million out of Harry's tote. The rest of the stash, I stuffed back into the couch, piling furniture and boxes helter-skelter on top of it. I'd have to return at some point—when the whole ordeal was over— and pack the bin properly.

THE DROP PLAYED out according to the numbers, without the slightest hitch. At ten that night, I eased through a gap in the hedge on the north side of the Waterston-McCall property and made my way to the house with Harry's canvas bag in tow. I slipped into the darkened service entry, where Karen was waiting. Once the door shut behind me, I shoved Harry's canvas tote into the larger duffel she provided. We chatted nervously while I changed into the wig and yellow jumpsuit. It was just then ten-thirty and the remaining wait was long and tense. By eleven-thirty, both of us were strung out on pure adrenaline and I was glad to be on the move.

Before I took off on the bicycle, Karen gave me a quick hug. "You're wonderful. I can't believe you did this."

"I'm not as wonderful as all that," I said, uncomfortably. "We need to talk the minute Kevin's home safe. Be sure to call me."

"Of course. Absolutely. We'll call you first thing."

I pedaled down the drive and took a right on West Glen. The cash-heavy duffel threw the bike out of balance, but I corrected and rode on. It was chilly at that hour and traffic was almost nonexistent. For two miles, almost randomly, I bicycled through the dark, cursing my own foolishness for thinking I could pull this off. Eventually, I became aware that a sedan had fallen in behind me. In the glare of the headlights, I couldn't tell the make or the model, only that the vehicle was dark blue and the front license plate was missing. The sedan followed me for what felt like an hour, while I pedaled on, feeling anxious, winded, and frightened beyond belief. Finally, the headlights blinked twice. Front wheel wobbling, I hauled the duffel from the basket and tossed it out onto the shoulder of the road. It landed with a thump near a cluster of bushes and I pedaled away. I glanced back only once as the vehicle behind me slowed to a stop.

I returned to the big house, left the bicycle in the service porch, and made my way back across the blackness of the rear lawn to my car. My heart was still thudding as I pulled away. Home again, in my apartment, I changed into a nightie and robe, and huddled on the couch with a cup of brandy-laced hot tea. I knew I should try to sleep, but I was too wired to bother. I glanced at my watch. It was nearly two A.M. I figured I probably wouldn't get word from Karen for another hour at best. It takes time to count half a million dollars in small bills. I flipped on the TV and watched a mind-numbing rerun of an old black-and-white film.

I waited through the night, but the phone didn't ring. Around five, I must have dozed because the next thing I knew, it was 8:35. What was going on? The kidnappers had ample time to effect Kevin's release. *If* he's getting out alive, I thought. I stared at the phone, afraid to call Karen in case the line was still tapped. I pulled out the phone book, looked up Jack Chamberlain, and tried his home number. The phone rang five times and his machine picked up. I left a cryptic message and then tried Karen at the house. No answer there. I was stumped. Mixed with my uneasiness was a touch of irritation. Even if they'd heard nothing, they could have let me know.

Without much hope of success, I called the bank and asked for Jack. Surprisingly, Lacy Alisal put me through.

"Jack Chamberlain," he said.

"Jack? This is Kinsey. Have you heard from Karen Waterston?"

"Of course. Haven't you?"

"Not a word," I said. "Is Kevin okay?"

"He's fine. Everything's terrific."

"Would you kindly tell me what's going on?"

"Well, sure. I can tell you as much as I know. I drove her back over to the house about two this morning and we waited it out. Kevin got home at six. He's shaken up, as you might imagine, but otherwise, he's in good shape. I talked to both of them again a little while ago. She said she was going to call you as soon as we hung up. She didn't get in touch?"

"Jack, that's what I just said. I've been sitting here for hours without a word from anyone. I tried the house and got no answer—"

"Hey, relax. Don't worry. I can see where you'd be ticked, but everything's fine. I know they were going back to Los Angeles. She might have just forgotten."

I could hear a little warning. Something was off here. "What about the kidnappers? Does Kevin have any way to identify them?"

"That's what I asked. He says, not a chance. He was tied up and blindfolded while they had him in the car. He says they drove into a garage and kept him there until the ransom money was picked up and brought back. Next thing he knew, someone got in the car, backed out of the garage, drove him around for a while, and finally set him out in his own driveway. He's going to see a doctor once they get to Los Angeles, but they never really laid a hand on him."

"I can't believe they didn't call to let me know he was safe. I need to talk to her." I knew I was being repetitive, but I was really bugged. I'd promised Harry her autograph, among other things, and while he'd pretended to make a joke of it, I knew he was serious.

"Maybe they thought I'd be doing that. I know they were both very grateful for your help. Maybe she's planning to drop you a note."

"Well, I guess I'll just wait until I hear from them," I said and hung up.

I showered and got dressed, sucked down some coffee and drove over to my office in downtown Santa Teresa. My irritation was beginning to wear off and exhaustion was trickling into my body in its wake. I went through my mail, paid a bill, tidied up my desk. I found myself laying my little head down, catching a quick nap while I drooled on my Month-At-A-Glance. There was a knock on the door and I woke with a start.

Vera Lipton, the claims manager for the insurance company next door, was standing on my threshold. "You must have had a better time than I did Friday night. You hungover or still drunk?" she said.

"Neither. I got a lousy night's sleep."

She lifted her right brow. "Sounds like fun. You and that guy from the bank?"

"Not exactly."

"So what'd you think of the glitzy twosome—Karen and Kev."

"I don't even want to talk about them," I said. I then proceeded to pour out the whole harrowing tale, including a big dose of outrage at the way I'd been treated.

Vera started smirking about halfway through. By the end of my recital, she was shaking her head.

"What's the matter?" I asked.

"Well, that's the biggest bunch of horsepuckey I ever heard. You've been taken, Kinsey. Most royally had."

"*I* have?"

"They're flat broke. They don't have a dime—"

"They do, too!"

She shook her head emphatically. "Dead broke. They're busted."

"They couldn't be," I said.

"Yes, they are," she said. "I bet you dollars to doughnuts they put the whole scam together to pick up some cash."

"How could they be broke with a house like that? They have a hot new series on the air!"

"The show was canceled. It hasn't hit the papers yet, but the network decided to yank 'em after six episodes. They sank everything they had into the house up here when they first heard they'd been picked up."

I squinted at her. "How do you know all this stuff?"

"Neil and I have been looking for a house for months. Our real estate agent's the one who sold 'em that place."

"They don't have *any* money?" I asked.

"Not a dime," she said. "Why do you think the house is so empty? They had to sell the furniture to make the mortgage payment this month."

"But what about the party? That must have cost a mint!"

"I'm sure it did. Their attorney advised them to max out their credit cards and then file for bankruptcy."

"Are you sure?"

"Sure I'm sure."

I looked at Vera blankly, doing an instant replay of events. I knew she was right because it suddenly made perfect sense. Karen Waterston and Kevin McCall had run a scam, that's all it was. No wonder the drop had gone without a hitch. I wasn't being followed by kidnappers—it was him. Those two had just successfully pocketed half a million bucks. And what was I going to do? At this point, even if I called the cops, all they had to do was maintain the kidnapping fiction and swear the bad guys were for real. They'd be very convincing. That's what acting is all about. The "kidnappers," meanwhile, would have disappeared without a trace and they'd make out like bandits, quite literally.

Vera watched me process the revelation. "You don't seem all that upset. I thought you'd be apoplectic, jumping up and down. Don't you feel like an ass?"

"I don't know yet. Maybe not."

She moved toward the door. "I gotta get back to work. Let me know when it hits. It's always entertaining to watch you blow your stack."

I sat down at my desk and thought about the situation and then put a call through to Harry Hovey at the prison.

"This is rare," Harry said when he'd heard me out. "I think we got a winner with this one. Holy shit."

"I thought you'd see the possibilities," I said.

"Holy shit!" he said again.

The rest of what I now refer to as my missionary work, I can only guess at until I see Harry again. According to the newspapers, Kevin McCall and Karen Waterston were arrested two days after they returned to Los Angeles. Allegedly (as they say), the two entered a bank and tried to open an account with nine thousand dollars in counterfeit tens and twenties. Amazingly, Harry Hovey saw God and had a crisis of conscience shortly before this in his prison cell up in Lompoc. Recanting his claims of innocence, he felt compelled to confess he'd been working for the two celebrities for years. In return for immunity, he told the feds where to find the counterfeit plates, hidden in a special zippered compartment at the bottom of a canvas tote, which turned up in their possession just as he said it would.

the lying game

THIS IS MY DEFINITION of misery. Pitch-black night. Cold. Hunger. Me in the wilderness . . . well, okay, a California state park, but the effect is the same. I was crouched in the bushes, peering at a campsite where identical twin brothers, alleged murderers, were rustling up supper: biscuits and a skillet full of eggs fried in bacon grease. The only bright note in all of this was my Lands' End Squall Parka with its advanced Thermolite Micro insulation. On a whim, I'd ordered the parka from a Lands' End catalog, little knowing that within weeks I'd be huddled in the woods, spying on fellows who cooked better than I did.

The surveillance threatened to be a long one and I was wondering how close to the temp rating of -10/-30°F the mountain air would get. My color choices had been Black, Field Khaki, or True Red. I'd chosen the black on the theory that at night I'd be rendered invisible, always a good thing in my line of work. I'm a skulker by nature and I prefer to be inconspicuous while doing it.

Not that you asked, but just for the record, I'd like to state my name is Kinsey Millhone. I'm a private investigator, female, thirty-seven years old, and twice divorced. I never made it through college, but I'm smart as a whip.

The Puckett twins, my subjects (which is what I call people when I'm spying on them), had been tried and convicted of whacking their wealthy parents, with an eye to inheriting their considerable estate. By one of those infuriating loopholes in the legal system, the verdict was overturned on appeal and "the boys" were now free. In two days, Doyle, the older twin, would be returning to his Ivy League college, where women would doubtless be fawning all over him. Before parting company, the two had retreated to this isolated spot, where I hoped they were searching their consciences, assuming either of them had one. In a tabloid tell-all, each lad had accused the other of masterminding the murder and accidentally pulling the trigger two dozen times, including reloads. One of the brothers had a reputation for truth-telling, while the other was a chronic liar. I'd been hired to keep an eye on them and, if possible, to persuade one twin to rat the other out, soliciting a confession, which would form the basis of a wrongful death suit being mounted by their only sister.

I refocused my attention on the campfire, realizing belatedly the skillet had been abandoned and neither twin was in sight.

"Can I help you?" someone asked. One of the two was standing right behind me, about a foot away.

I jumped and my shriek was as piercing as the one I emit when a mouse jumps out of my kitchen junk drawer. "You scared me!" I said, patting my chest to soothe my thundering heart.

He said, "Sorry, but we spotted you earlier and my brother and I would like to know what you're up to. Nice jacket, by the way. It looks warm."

"Thanks, it is. It's also machine washable. Speaking of which, I guess I might as well come clean. I know who you are. I've seen pictures of you and your brother plastered in the news everywhere. As it happens, the three of us have something in common. I'm a bit of a twisted sister, attracted to criminals of every size and kind. I also have a passion for dissembling."

"For doing what?"

"Fibbing. Telling lies. Of course, you don't have to fess up, but I've been wondering if you're the brother who tells the truth or the one who lies."

He hesitated and then said, "I'm the one who tells the truth."

I stared at him. "But wouldn't you say exactly the same thing if you were the twin who perpetually lied?"

He reached in his pocket and pulled out a .357 Magnum Colt Python I knew would rip right through my water-resistant Supplex nylon shell.

The other Puckett twin stepped out of the dark. He took the gun from his brother and pointed it at me. "That's right. Only one of us pulled the trigger when our parents went down. Ask him, if you don't believe me."

"I'll take your word for it," I said as I looked from one to the other. "Just taking a flier here, but which one of you did it?"

"You figure it out," the second brother said. "Tell you what we'll do. I'll put this loaded gun on the ground between us. If you come up with the right answer, the weapon is yours and you can make a citizen's arrest."

"Guess wrong and you're dead," the first brother inserted for the sake of clarity.

"Seems a bit severe, but why not?" I said. I thought about the situation for a moment and then turned to the first brother. "Let's try this. If I asked your brother who killed your mom and dad, what would he say?"

He shifted uneasily, avoiding his brother's eyes. After a moment's reflection he said, "He'd tell you I did it."

I said, "Ah. That's all I need to know." I leaned down and picked up the gun, pointing it at the second brother. "You're under arrest."

"Why me?" he said, insulted.

I smiled. "Well, if he told the truth that would mean that you're the brother who lies. He'd know you'd lie about the murder and you'd tell me he was the shooter. If he's the liar, that means he knows you'd tell the truth, so he'd twist the facts and reverse your answer. His claim would be that you'd admit to the shooting yourself thinking I'd be fooled. Therefore, since he accused himself the answer he gave is false, which is the only reason you'd agree. You killed them, right?"

The second brother smirked. "Sure, but what difference does it make? We can't be tried twice for the same crime. It's double jeopardy."

"But this time you won't be tried for murder, you'll be tried for perjury."

"Only if you manage to get out of here alive. As it happens I also lied about the weapon. That gun's not loaded," he said, indicating the .357 Magnum.

I tossed the .357 Magnum aside. "But mine is," I said. I reached into my exterior cargo pocket and removed my little semiautomatic and a pair of handcuffs that I snapped on his wrist. "Don't pull any funny business or I'll shoot to kill. I've done it before and that's the truth."

Later, I did wonder if the brother who lied had lied when he told me about the gun being loaded, but I never figured that one out.

entr'acte

An Eye for an I:
Justice, Morality, the Nature of the Hard-boiled Private Investigator, and All That Existential Stuff

I WAS RAISED ON a steady diet of mystery and detective fiction. During the forties, my father, C. W. Grafton, was himself a part-time mystery writer and it was he who introduced me to the wonders of the genre. In my early teens, on the occasions when my parents went out for the evening, I'd be left alone in the house with its tall, narrow windows and gloomy high ceilings. By day, surrounding maple trees kept the yard in shadow. By night, overhanging branches blocked out the pale of the moon. Usually, I sat downstairs in the living room in my mother's small upholstered rocking chair, reading countless mystery novels with a bone-handled butcher knife within easy reach. If I raised my head to listen, I could always hear the nearly imperceptible footsteps of someone coming up the basement stairs.

Mystery novels were the staple of every summer vacation when, released from the rigors of school days and homework, I was free to read as much as I liked. I remember long August nights when the darkness came slowly. Upstairs in my bedroom, I'd lie in a shortie nightgown with the sheets flung back, reading. The bed lamp threw out a heat of its own and humidity would press on the bed like a quilt. June bugs battled at the window, an occasional victor forcing its way through the screen. It was in this atmosphere of heightened awareness and beetle-induced suspense that I worked my way from Nancy Drew through Agatha Christie and on to Mickey Spillane. I can still remember the astonishment I felt the night I leapt from the familiarity of Miss Marple into the pagan sensibilities of *I, the Jury*. From Mickey Spillane, I turned to James M. Cain, then to Raymond Chandler, Dashiell Hammett, Ross Macdonald, Richard Prather, and John D. MacDonald, a baptism by immersion in the dark poetry of murder. I think I sensed even then that a detective novel offered the perfect blend of ingenuity and intellect, action and artifice.

During the thirties, hard-boiled private eyes seemed to be spontaneously generated in pulp fiction like mice in a pile of old rags. After World War II, the country was caught up in boom times, a bonanza of growth and cockeyed optimism. "Our boys" came home from overseas and took up their positions on assembly lines. Women surrendered their jobs at defense plants and (brainwashed by the media) returned to Home Sweet Home. In that postwar era of ticky-tack housing and backyard barbecues, the hard-boiled private eye was a cynical, wisecracking, two-fisted, gun-toting hero. We could identify with his machismo, admire his ruthless principles and his reckless way with a .45. He smoked too much, drank too much, screwed and punched his way through molls and mobsters with devastating effect. In short, he kicked ass. In his own way, he was a fictional extension of the jubilance of the times, a man who lived with excess and without regard for consequence. He embodied the exhilaration of the faraway battlefield brought back to home turf.

Through the forties and fifties, the hard-boiled private eye novel was escapist fare, reassuring us by its assertion that there was still danger and excitement, a place where treachery could threaten and heroism could emerge. Despite the mildly depressing lull of the postwar peace, detective fiction proved that adventure was still possible. The core of the hard-boiled private eye novel was a celebration of confrontation, as exotic as the blazing guns of the old West, as familiar as the streets beyond our white picket fences. In fictional terms, the hard-boiled private eye provided evidence that the courage of the individual could still make a difference.

Crime in those days had a tabloid quality. Murder was fraught with sensationalism and seemed to take place only in the big cities half a continent away. Justice was tangible and revenge was sweet.

With his flat affect, the hard-boiled private eye was the perfect emissary from the dark side of human nature. War had unleashed him. Peace had brought him home. Now he was free to roam the shadowy elements of society. He carried our rage. He championed matters of right and fair play while he violated the very rules the rest of us were forced to embrace. Onto his blank and cynical face, we projected our own repressed impulses, feeling both drawn to and repelled by his tough-guy stance.

There was something seductive about the primal power of the hard-boiled narrative, something invigorating about its crude literary style. For all its tone of disdain, the flat monotone of the narrator allowed us to "throw" our own voices with all the skill of ventriloquists. *I* was Mike Hammer. *I* was Sam Spade, Shell Scott, Philip Marlowe, and Lew Archer, strengthened and empowered by the writers' rawboned prose. Little wonder, years later, in a desire to liberate myself from the debilitating process of writing for television, I turned to the hard-boiled private eye novel for deliverance.

Times have changed. In the years since Mike Hammer's heyday, rage has broken loose in the streets. We live in darker times, where the nightmare has been made manifest. Violence is random, pointless, and pervasive. Passing motorists are gunned down for the vehicles they drive; teens are killed for their jackets and their running shoes. Homicide has erupted on every side of us in a wholesale slaughter of the innocent. Even small-town America has been painted by its bloody brush. The handgun is no longer a symbol of primitive law and order; it is the primogenitor of chaos. The bullet makes its daily rampage, leaving carnage in its wake. We are at the mercy of the lawless. While the cunning of fictional homicide continues to fascinate, its real-life counterpart has been reduced to senseless butchery. Murder is the beast howling in the basement, rustling unleashed in the faraway reaches of our souls.

In this atmosphere of anarchy, we are forced to revitalize and reinvent a mythology from which we can draw the comforts once offered to us by the law. The fictional adventures of the hard-boiled private eye are still escapist and reassuring, but from a topsy-turvy point of view. The hard-boiled private eye in current fiction represents a clarity and vigor, the immediacy of a justice no longer evident in the courts, an antidote to our confusion and our fearfulness.

In a country where violence is out of control, the hard-boiled private eye exemplifies containment, order, and hope, with the continuing, unspoken assertion that the individual can still make a difference. Here, resourcefulness, persistence, and determination prevail. The P.I. has been transformed from a projection of our vices to the mirror of our virtues. The hard-boiled private eye has come to represent and reinforce not our excess but our moderation. In the current hard-boiled private eye fiction, there is less alcohol, fewer cigarettes, fewer weapons, greater emphasis on fitness, humor, subtlety, maturity, and emotional restraint. It is no accident that women writers have tumbled onto the playing field, infusing the genre with a pervasive social conscience. Entering the game, too, are countless other private eye practitioners, writers representing the gay, the African American, the Native American, the Asian, an uncommon variety of voices now clamoring to be heard.

The hard-boiled private eye novel is still the classic struggle between good and evil played out against the backdrop of our social interactions. But now we are championed by the knight with a double gender, from talented writers who may be female, as well.

Women have moved from the role of "femme fatale" to that of prime mover, no longer relegated to the part of temptress, betrayer, or loyal office help. The foe is just as formidable, but the protagonist has become androgynous, multiracial, embracing complex values of balance and compassion. I do not necessarily maintain that today's hard-boiled hero/ine is cast of finer mettle, only that s/he is more diverse, more protean, a multifaceted arbiter of our desires in conflict. Because of this, the hard-boiled private eye novel is once more rising to the literary forefront, gaining renewed recognition. Now, as before, we are serving notice to the reading public that not only is the genre alive and well, but that we, as its creators, are still adapting, still reacting, and, with wit and perspicacity, we are still marching on.

part two

. . . and me

introduction

Du ring the course of an interview once, I was asked about the influence my father, a mystery writer himself, had on my writing. I talked about what he'd taught me of craft, about surviving rejection, coping with editorial criticism. When I finished, the journalist looked up from her notes and said briskly, "Well now, you've talked about your father, but what did you learn from your mother?" Without even pausing to consider, I said, "Ah, from my mother I learned all the lessons of the human heart."

One of the benefits of growing up as the child of two alcoholics was my lack of supervision. Every morning, my father downed two jiggers of whiskey and went to the office. My mother, similarly fortified, went to sleep on the couch. From the age of five onward, I was left to raise myself, which I did as well as I could, having had no formal training in parenthood. I lived in an atmosphere of apparent permissiveness. I read anything I liked, roamed the city at will, rode the bus lines from end to end, played out intense melodramas with the other kids in the neighborhood. (I was usually an Indian princess, tied to the stake.) I went to the movies on Friday night, Saturday afternoon, and again on Sunday. There were few, if any, limits placed on me.

My sister, three years older than me, spent a lot of time in her room. She and my mother clashed often. I was Little Mary Sunshine, tap-dancing my way through life just to the left of stage center, where the big battles took place. Discipline, when it came, was arbitrary and capricious. We had no allies, my sister and I. When life seemed unbearable, my father, to comfort me, would sit on the edge of my bed and recount in patient detail the occasion when the family doctor had told him he'd have to choose between her and us and he'd chosen her because she was weak and needed him and we were strong and could survive. In such moments, at the ages of eight and ten and twelve, I would reassure him so he wouldn't feel guilty at having left us to such a fate. My father was perfect. It was only later that I dared experience the rage I felt for *him*. Not surprisingly, I grew up confused, rebellious, fearful, independent, imaginative, curious, free-spirited, and anxious. I wanted to be good. I wanted to do everything right. I wanted to get out of that house.

By the time I was eighteen, I was obsessed with writing. I was also married for the first time—twin paths, leading in opposite directions. The writing was my journey into the self, the marriage a detour into a world I thought I could perfect if I were allowed to make all the choices myself. I was convinced I could construct a "normal" household, unaware that I possessed only the clumsiest of tools. I was determined to have a picture-book life, and was dismayed to discover my efforts were as amateurish as a child's. How could I have known I hadn't yet finished growing up when it *felt* like I'd been running my own life since I was five?

In the years between eighteen and thirty-seven, when I began to fashion the "personhood" of Kinsey Millhone, writing was my salvation—the means by which I learned to support myself, to face the truth, to take responsibility for my future. I have often said that Kinsey Millhone is the person I might have been had I not married young and had children. She is more than that. She is a stripped-down version of my "self"—my shadow, my projection—a celebration of my own freedom, independence, and courage. It is no accident that Kinsey's parents were killed when she was five. My father went into the army when I was three. He came back when I was five and that's when the safety of my childhood began to unravel. Through Kinsey, I tell the truth, sometimes bitter, sometimes amusing. Through her, I look at the world with a "mean" eye, exploring the dark side of human nature—my own in particular.

If Kinsey Millhone is my alter ego, Kit Blue is simply a younger version of me. The following thirteen stories were written in the decade following my mother's death, my way of coming to terms with my grief for her. I realized early in the process of the writing that I could take any moment I remembered and cut straight to the heart of our relationship. It was as if all moments—any moment, every moment—were the same. Every incident I had access to seemed connected at the core; that rage, that pain, all the scalding tears I wept, both during her life and afterward. All of it is part of the riddle I think of now as love.

a woman capable
of anything

Kɪᴛ sᴀᴛ ɪɴ her mother's rocking chair, watching her mother smoke. Her mother lay on the couch with a paperback novel which she'd put facedown on her chest so that she could light her cigarette without losing her place. From where Kit sat, she could see the top of her mother's head, the pale hair disarranged, the length of her mother's body, wasted and thin. Her feet were bare except for the nylon peds she wore and her toes occasionally made a lazy circle, idle movement in that otherwise still frame. The hand which rested on the rim of the coffee table made the journey from the ashtray to her mother's mouth and back, cigarette glowing, ash increasing until Kit strained at the sight, expecting at any moment, cigarette, ash and ember would tumble. There were already ridges burned into the table, black scars on the rug where fallen cigarettes had eaten away the fibers. Her mother's hands were bony, fingers long and thin, the fingernails as tough as horn. Kit bit her own nails. Her fingernails were soft and ragged and she needed to work them with her teeth, gnawing at the skin at the tips until they were raw. She was fascinated by her mother's nails, gnawed at them sometimes, taking her mother's bony fingers, testing their mettle against that anxious hunger of hers. She had sucked her thumb as a child until her mother painted her thumb with something fiery hot. Her mother had even tried painting her own fingertips to keep Kit from putting them in her mouth but Kit had a taste by then for that acid heat that ate into her tongue like liquid ice.

Her mother's cigarette went out, but the hand remained, resting on the edge of the table, poised while her mother drifted into sleep. Her breathing slowed until Kit, watching, wondered if she were dead. Often she sat and stared at her mother that way, wondering if she would die like that, on the couch in the cool of the day. Maybe alcoholics died from never waking up or died from lying down too long. Kit hated her with a kind of resignation, patience, servitude. Kit sat with her mother, talked to her, fixed toast for her or a cup of tea, and all the while, she felt like some ancient doctor with a dying thing, a zombie lady or a skeleton. How could she love what was not even alive?

Kit had seen other mothers in the world. She had seen women who were sober all day long, bright-eyed and talkative, who dressed up in high-heeled shoes and went to country clubs, who cleaned their houses, cooked meals, drank coffee in the afternoons and laughed, women who joined the PTA and took their daughters to department stores to buy them bras. Kit's mother could hardly go anywhere. She drove the car from time to time, a black 1940 Oldsmobile with Hydra-Matic drive, perched on a cushion and even so, not tall enough to see with ease. Her mother drove slowly, hugging the right side of the street and sometimes Kit caught her breath at how close her mother came to skinning parked cars. Her mother ordered groceries from the corner store, ordered liquor from the drugstore four blocks down and in that manner managed to live most of her life in the living room, stretched out on the couch. In the kitchen, colored women would iron for hours and in the yard, the grass was mowed by colored men. And all the time, Vanessa lay there, saying nothing, moving not at all except to smoke. What went on inside that head? What could her mother think of hour after hour, day after day? Kit could remember that her mother had once played the piano and when she was angry, she'd sit there pounding the keys, the thunderous chords announcing her displeasure to the rooms upstairs. What was the woman angry about? In those days, they had at least known, that she felt *something*. Now, no one was sure. The anger had been sealed off and burned in silence now: frustration, defeat, whatever it was she felt. Kit had seen that veil come down across her mother's face. When she was angry now, she just withdrew, her facial expression fading, lids coming down to shield those telling eyes. No one would know if there was pain or tears. She was like a secretive child, stealing away to a world she had locked up inside, like an animal nibbling from some secret store. It was hard to love a lady who couldn't cry. It made Kit feel too much power, too little care. Kit wept bitterly, scalded at times by the loathing that welled up like tears. There were times too when she felt a great rush of pity, of shame and love and regret. Whatever else she was, Vanessa was the only mother Kit had, the only place Kit knew that was really home, however silent, tortured, and chill.

Sometimes Vanessa's condition deteriorated to the level of disease and then an ambulance came, attendants lifting her mother from the couch to the stretcher, wheeling her out to the street, where the neighbors would stand, full of sympathy. They liked her mother, who in her better days had been their friend, who'd listened to their aging ills when she called them up on the phone. Now in silence they watched her ride away and they would question Kit afterward about how Vanessa was getting along. Within a week or ten days she'd be home, that miraculous change having taken place. Vanessa would be back on her feet, exuberant, energetic, and gay, and each time, Kit's heart would fill with hope. Vanessa would plan the meals, would chat in the kitchen with Jessie or Della while they ironed, would supervise the black men in the yard, make cheery phone calls to everyone. Maybe they'd go out to dinner again on Sunday nights, the four of them, Vanessa and Daddy, Kit and her older sister, Del. Maybe they'd go to some basketball games or to *Holiday on Ice* or maybe they'd walk to the drugstore at night to buy comic books. The burden would lift and the world would puff up like a colored balloon and even though it wasn't perfect, it would be all right.

And then she would see it again in her mother's face, the first signs of defeat, the faint slur, exaggerated walk, the little silent trips to the pantry, where the bourbon bottles were. Vanessa would sink back down to her day-long dream and Kit, when the time came, would sit in her mother's chair, keeping that vigil of hate and hope, wishing her mother would die or that she'd go down again far enough so that someone would come and take her away and make her right.

Kit had seen it there, the evidence of the woman who was, the light in the round face, quick bright eyes, something nervous and splendid pouring out of that body from her very bones. This was a woman capable of anything, the woman who had been Kit's perfect mother once but was no more. This was the woman whose life was failing her right before their eyes, whose year was made up of secret cycles which lifted her first and plunged her down again, full circle, beginning, middle, and end. And each time she rose and each time went down again until she could rise no more. And Kit sat in her mother's rocking chair, caught up in a cycle of her own, of love, of pity, of hate. And she knew that her mother was lost and strong and she knew that somewhere the thunder rang from chords still sounding inside. But how would this woman ever be free and how would she let Kit go? How would any of them be whole again when they'd gone down together so often into that little death?

that's not an
easy way to go

Later in my life when I'm asked what happened to
her, I think I'll just say, "Well, we don't know exactly
what it was. She may have fallen into enemy hands.
From the look of her, she was tortured to death, and
that's not an easy way to go."

SHE STANDS AT the foot of the stairs, one hand on the bannister,
swaying slightly, smelling of cigarettes and Early Times and Wrig-
ley's chewing gum. She has fallen near the telephone stand in the
front hall and her left arm is now cradled painfully against her
waist. Jessie stands on one side of her and I stand on the other and
together we pull a pale blue dress over her pale brown hair, easing it
gently down over the injured arm.

"Does that feel all right?" I say to her, buttoning the front of the dress to support her arm.

"Sure," she says. "It doesn't bother me at all."

THERE ARE QUESTIONS I could ask her, but I don't. I could ask, for instance, how many jiggers of Early Times she managed to drink while she stood in the pantry pretending to open a carton of cigarettes, but she would say "none" and then I would have the lie to accept or refute and at the moment, it doesn't seem that important. I know and she knows that she is drunk—though "drunk" of course is not the proper word to describe the condition she's in. She is simply beyond her tolerance for alcohol, a tolerance which has never been great because she is, herself, a tiny person, barely five feet tall, weighing not even a hundred pounds. If you took a delicate ten-year-old child and gave her even a sample of fine bourbon, the result would be the same, except that the child would not know enough, perhaps, to pretend otherwise.

My mother pretends that there is no pain when I know and she knows that we will shortly discover a hairline fracture near her left shoulder. At the moment, I don't even worry about the drive to the hospital or the X-ray or the doctor's confirmation. I worry about the buttons on her dress and the knee-length stockings which are rolled down around her frail ankles and the shoes which are fifteen years out of style. We dress her, Jessie and I, saying nothing much and I am thinking as I smooth her fine pale hair back into the hairpins that I am, in fact, being a mother to my mother. I am nineteen and I am remembering the years—two years? three?—that I have been changing places with her: taking her to the doctor's office, buying her clothes, helping her up to bed, giving her long, self-righteous lectures about her "drinking problem," which I had decided, at the age of fifteen, needed to be brought out in the open and dispensed with once and for all. For three years I have been lecturing to her in this manner, sitting in the living room in her small gray rocker, rocking as I speak, and for three years she has been lying there on the couch, her eyes closed, a lighted cigarette in her fingers, saying nothing. From time to time, I have extracted weighty promises from her, promises which she seems utterly incapable of keeping especially in the light of her constant denials of any such problem at all. The contradictions are apparent but we choose, both of us, to ignore them so that we can get on with the business at hand.

I have given up praying for her. I have given up even praying for myself and I've taken instead to pouring hidden bottles of bourbon down the bathroom sink and filling the bottles up with tepid tea. This is insidious, of course, because she discovers the ruse almost at once but cannot admit it or acknowledge it, cannot even defend the loss of so much expensive whiskey into the sewer systems of the world. And so we continue, this woman and I, she feigning sleep, I intoning almost without conviction the terrible price she will have to pay for her secret sins.

In the moment that I discover that I'm the mother to my mother, dressing her there at the foot of the stairs, I feel both a sense of loss and resentment. It's as though in the very act of perceiving this, I have given something away which I will never be able to retrieve. And at the same time, I know that whatever it is I've lost—whether innocence or childhood or a simple illusion about the nature of our relationship—whatever the loss, it's something I gave away a long time ago, something I've merely retained by default for some years.

I look at her closely: small round face, faded blue eyes, a shade of lipstick (far too dark for her fair coloring), fragile skeleton, faintly fleshed out into the form of a woman, aging and underfed. We have conversations, this woman and I, about what she's eaten in any given day which is never much. A piece of toast, she says, or soda crackers broken up in a glass of milk. She's burning up bourbon and she has no need for food. Her bewildered body shrinks away from her, failing, failing, surrendering up to malnutrition, pneumonia, some grief in her bones. From this pale remnant of a person, I can work backward in my mind to a time when she was nineteen, too. There's a picture of her taken at Virginia Beach that year. She's standing on the other side of a pair of swinging doors, her legs visible beneath, her arms resting along the top. The face is the same, small and round, and her hair is pale. She wears it in long thin braids wrapped around her head in fine ropes. She is very tanned and her smile is broad and free, her legs very shapely and firm. She remembers this time as a good time in her life and she returns to it in her talking, rambling talk, as out of fashion as her shoes. I have no notion in the world what has happened to her between that time and this; only that some battle must have raged somewhere to take such a toll from that once sturdy frame.

I know, as a matter of course and without dismay, that she's attempted suicide twice but she seems to be insincere in this and no one pays much attention. She might drink. She might smoke forty cigarettes a day, eat little, scarcely stir from the place where she lies all day long in the long dream of her life, but we cannot seem to understand among us that she has no use for her life, lives with no joy at all, suffers some secret silent anguish which is draining away, drop by drop, any reason of hers to go on. She is simply with us and our collective acceptance of this fact will have to serve as her motive for life. She is living because she hasn't yet managed to die. She has come one step closer now. She has fallen again, her body announcing with a faint snap that it cannot go on much longer under the regimen of abuse and deprivation which she has imposed upon it. She is winning a fifteen-year battle and she knows it. Only the rest of us are not yet informed. We can see the evidence but the sight has been before us for so long that we no longer register pity or amazement or despair. I will understand in a year, or maybe five, that she is one of the loneliest women in the world, this mother, but for now there is only this job to be done, the dressing of her brittle body so that we may take it to the body mender to be fixed—bandaged and glued and wrapped all around with gauze and adhesive tape. She suffers this to be done though it seems to matter little to her. We insist that she go on living, so she does, but only until the moment when she can outwit us—which she will—soon—in her way.

In the meantime, she is ready and I help her out to the car. I forget now what we talk about because it doesn't matter much. She knows and I know that we will never get around to the conversation we should really have and probably neither of us will ever understand just why that is so. I take her to Norton's Infirmary, to the parking lot around in back where I always park when she's been hospitalized, usually twice a year. The sun is shining though it's bitterly cold and I walk with her up the emergency ramp, down the broad corridor with its mottled marble floor polished to a soft gleam, to the elevator with its doors which shush us in and shush us out again on the fifth floor, X-ray department.

Dr. Belton has called in advance and they take her in to be X-rayed, she denying any pain, denying even the existence of her own soul if she could. The X-ray will show it. One soul, sadly cracked in a way that no one can mend. Perhaps the doctor will prescribe lots of alcohol, who knows? I sit in the hallway and smoke and stare out at the window, where the branches of the trees are bitter and bare. Later in my life, though I know nothing of it now, I will like hospitals. They will seem familiar to me, a little like my mother, who has lived so many disconnected fragments under doctors' care. Hospitals will always seem a little like the holiday they were when I was young and she went in and my sister Del and I were at home, free for a little while of the burden of caring for her. Hours and hours of my life have been spent in hospital corridors. Hours and hours of my life have been spent waiting for her to come home.

After a day or two in the hospital, the difference in her is remarkable. Sober, she is cheerful, as bright as a bird, roaming up and down the hall, into other patients' rooms, where she visits with them. The nurses joke with her, hide in her room to smoke. She is a favorite on the floor and when she leaves, they gather around her and wish her luck, kiss her cheek, and bundle her warmly into her coat. And when she comes home again, she begins to drink almost at once. Now and then to frighten her into good behavior, we threaten to commit her to an institution—the doctors, my father, and I. I think now we should really have done that, for her sake. She might have found protection there, some peace, some sense of purpose in an otherwise pointless life. Instead, ironically, she stays at home and suffers whatever it is she suffers: boredom, frustration, loneliness, defeat, the worst diseases of mankind and she with some inherited tendency for each.

We put her in. They fix her up and then we take her home again and none of us understand what she's dying of, what's killing her one-two-three. It's us. It's me. It's Del, my father, and that house. It's time; the past that looms up like a phantom, the future rising up like a blank bare wall. She is a haunted lady whom nobody will abandon. We stick by her. Loyal. True. And we are killing her with our misdirected virtues, the apparitions of love instead of its flesh and blood. We are weighing her down with our devotion and we cannot let her go. We will discover later, though we never admit it among us, that it was she holding *us* together in her way. And I will know much later that I loved her. And I'll know much later that she loved me, too.

For the moment, I am sitting in this corridor, staring out at the bitter trees beyond, while the medics declare her broken again and set about to mending her with plaster and dry sticks. How will I tell her, driving home again, what has broken in me and how will I make her understand that in the scheme of things, it is she who was meant to mother me and I meant to receive?

lost people

IN THE PANTRY, there was a wide shelf of mahogany which smelled perpetually of bourbon. Above it was a cabinet where the china plates were kept, cups and saucers, glasses, bowls, and serving pieces. There were two drawers filled with cocktail napkins, sticky swizzle sticks, corkscrews, pencils and a strange array of coasters, matches, chewing gum, and string. My mother drank her bourbon there with her back turned, tossing down jiggers of Old Crow and Early Times when she went to get a pack of cigarettes from one of the cartons of Camels kept there on the shelf. My father drank his bourbon from the same jigger glass, two every morning before he brushed his teeth. He told me once that there was a time when he drank a fifth of Old Crow a day and still practiced law, still argued his cases in court, wrote briefs and letters and legal opinions. I can remember how proud I was that he could accomplish such a feat. All of my life, my father did amazing things and the fact that he might become an accomplished alcoholic came as no surprise to me. His drinking was a part of his daily routine and attracted no notice from me. My mother's drinking was another thing. I suppose I resented as much as anything the fact that she did not handle herself as well as he did . . . as though they might be in some competition between them for who might out-drink whom. In the end she won . . . or perhaps he did because she's dead and he still drinks. For a while he quit. His drinking had triggered some peculiar malady that caused him to lose half a day at a time. He drove a great deal through the state, try-ing legal cases in obscure Kentucky towns, and every time he lost one, he would buy a pint of bourbon. One night he drove his car into a muddy field in the rain and a carload of teenaged boys found him standing amid the furrows, the rain beating down on his head. He never knew why he had gone there or what he had done in the hours before and after he was found. He had a gasoline receipt from a fill-ing station in the town nearby. He had driven a hundred miles on that tank of gas and at the end of it, he was standing in the field, his car parked at a jaunty angle near the road. It bothered him to lose that day and he curbed his drinking for a while. The doctor pre-scribed a medication which would make him sick if he drank and after a time, he drank again anyway. My mother never lost any time at all. She stood at the pantry shelf to drink and she lay on the couch when she was done. She seldom drove anywhere and never in the rain. There were no fields for her to find and no carloads of people coming after her to save her from the wind, to rescue her out of the dark rows where she stood. Whatever journey she took, she went by herself and in the course of her drinking, she never remarked about lost days, or hours which she could not identify, nor time that she could not find. Her intention, I think, was to give time away while his was to escape it and both of them ended up in front of the same pantry shelf.

They shared the bottles of Early Times. They shared the cartons of Camels and the swizzle sticks and chewing gum. They had shared more than that once upon a time and where the past disappeared to, neither of them could say. They bought a house and my mother swore she would never leave it until the day she died. And after she died, the house was torn down and he married somebody else. He isn't any happier now. Somehow his twenty-eight years with Vanessa conditioned him to misery and he married a woman who makes him suffer equally. She doesn't drink much, this new wife. She doesn't drive him out into the rain but she complains about him all the time, and rails and chides him for his frailties. Sometimes he smiles at me in a way I recognize. It is the smile of a man being taken away on a stretcher to surgery. It's probably the same smile he smiled when they found him that night in the dark of the field.

Whether my mother ever smiled that way I cannot say.

My father is a very gentle man. He is a man of great intelligence, a man who has known the law, and some of life and a little bit of the land where he grew up. He is a tall man, lean and soft and graying, and his memory fails him now and then. He is a tired man and he's been tired all his life, a weary, driven man who cannot sleep. Once he told me that he wanted written on his grave: Here lies the loneliest man who ever lived.

My parents were lost people, refugees, and not from any country that I've seen, not the victims of the known wars on this earth, but refugees in subtle battles fought somewhere inside and won and lost and borders crossed and flags laid down. My parents were the displaced . . . not of this world but from their lives, separated from themselves somehow when all those inner wars came to an end.

They never found between them any separate peace, no common enemy, no alien pain but only something savage, undefined and dread.

My inner child is like the sad-eyed waif in those paintings that used to be so popular. Time to grow up, I think.

clue

IN THE WINTER of 1959, my mother spent five days with me in Char-
ing Cross. Peter and I had moved into the little house on Carousel
Lane with all our matching Danish modern furniture and almost a
year of marriage behind us. We were waiting for the birth of our first
child, trapped for the Christmas holidays in a small southern college town emptied of students. It was a dreary season.

The snow had piled up silently in a patchwork of soot and dog
urine and the world plodded patiently through it. Nights came early
and the skies were pearl gray with clouds. We were bored with each
other, bored with the B-grade movies at the State, bored looking for
a bootlegger in a dry county, bored waiting for the baby, already one
week overdue. We talked, watched television, smoked, and thought
of home. I did not even know I was unhappy.

Vanessa came, with her birdlike energy and incessant chatter.
She'd stopped drinking the summer before. I don't remember now

what crisis precipitated the abrupt end to her long and intimate relationship with alcohol. She'd been hospitalized. There was an intervention of sorts—nothing formal or staged. Some combination of threats and dire warnings got through to her and she quit cold. During the six months she'd been sober, she'd begun to complain of pain on the left side of her jaw. The family doctor and an ear-nose-and-throat specialist found nothing and we wrote it off as hypochondria, a burgeoning need for attention that seemed like a small price to pay. The pain was, in point of fact, a smoldering ember of esophageal cancer catching fire in her throat, but the diagnosis wouldn't come for another month. For me, there were a few false labor pains. How irritable I was, grotesque and clumsy. It is the evenings I remember. The house was full of light, sealed off by the chill of December, isolated, close. We sat in the warm green of the living room, playing children's games. One was a Perry Mason detective game with little plastic cars, symbolic criminals, and dice. There was a maze of paper streets, cardboard city blocks through which we ran, inch by inch. And we played Clue with its secret list of suspects, the tiny plastic weapons and the floor plan of a house.

"I believe the murder was committed by Mr. Black in the billiard room with the . . . let me see, oh yes . . . the rope."

"Very clever, Peter. Your dice."

Over and over again, Clue and Perry Mason, television, the hands of gin rummy, naps and false contractions, the constant flow of conversations which had no beginning and no end, no rise, no fall, only words as level and as stale as the snow outside. The year dragged its feet like a sulky child and we could not escape the weight and pull of time.

We experimented with tea. It was the twilight ritual. There were
five different kinds in all: Jasmine, Formosa Oolong, Gunpowder
Green, Earl Grey, and English Breakfast tea. They came in metal cyl-
inders, probably only an ounce or so in each, given to me by Vanessa
as a Christmas gift. We prepared the tea in a squatty china pot,
white with a pattern of floral blue. The cups were thin and they sat
unevenly on hand-painted saucers. Boiling water, a strainer, one
rounded teaspoon of leaves. We debated them one by one. Jasmine
with its heady fragrance, its biting taste, a pale yellow tea with a
gentle debris in the bottom of the cup . . . Formosa Oolong with its
taste of curio shops and cheap silk . . . English Breakfast tea, flat to
the taste and tawny . . . Earl Grey with its smoky flavor, Gunpowder
Green, which was sharp and unpleasant.

She left before the week was ended. She had come to see me
through Christmas; she would return when the baby was born. I
remember her cheeks, downy, patterned with surface veins; the way
she closed her eyes when she laughed and the faded cap of hair. She
went home on the Greyhound bus, smiling at us through the window
in a pantomime of good-byes. She was wearing her gray fur coat and
a cotton scarf on her head, nodding and chatting to us through the
tinted glass . . . another of her endless stories . . . talking and smiling, talking and saying good-bye. And God! the guilt of the moment
afterward . . . that I was relieved to see her go.

night visit,
corridor a

At first, you think you're in the wrong room. You're nineteen and you've flown to New York to see your mother after her surgery. Your luggage has been lost, sent to La Guardia on the plane you missed, so that you arrive in the city strangely free. You check into the St. Regis Hotel and then you take a taxi to Memorial Hospital through streets grown dark, in a month that is bitterly cold in a city you love at once because it is vast and unknown to you. You pay the driver and you stand for a moment on the sidewalk. The hospital itself is massive and old. The concrete steps look ancient and drab and the lamps on either side are turn-of-the-century wrought iron with milky globes. It is a building alive with light and you view it with the same sense of mystery and excitement you feel for all hospitals. They represent a kind of freedom to you. Your mother has spent many hours there and so have you and by now, a bond has been formed between you and the sight of that concrete world with its miles of brown corridors.

You climb the steps and move into the lobby through revolving doors. The whole of it reminds you of some elegant hotel, a very exclusive club to which you have gained access through your mother's suffering. It seems odd to you that she's come so far to suffer when she suffered so well at home, but this, you learn, is a special kind of suffering in which you can only participate indirectly. You inquire at the desk and you're given the number of her room and the floor she's on. You go up in the elevator, feeling strangely that you're moving back in time. For a moment that puzzles you and then you remember that you've seen the city before, or a version of it anyway, in a book of Peter Arno cartoons depicting the war years in New York. That same feeling pervades, from the gray night outside to the charcoal lines of the building; a sense of simplicity, a sense that something somewhere is remotely funny if you only knew the reference points. The elevator is exactly like the ones in old, respectable department stores and you add that notion to the other notions in your head.

By the time you reach your mother's room, you feel disoriented so that you're not exactly surprised to see the stranger in her bed. You cannot immediately connect this woman with your mother though you notice, almost at once, that she's as thin as your mother is and lean in the aching way of alcoholics. This woman is sober though, with a long blank face and a cleft chin, a flap of gauze across her throat and a look in her eyes that chills you when she turns. It's Vanessa. The sight of her alarms you, like a nightmare, because so many parts of it are familiar that you have to struggle wildly with the rest. Trembling, she gets out of bed and reaches to embrace you, pantomiming joy, surprise. She has not known you were coming and she acts out her amazement. She reaches for her Magic Slate and scribbles a message to you—simple, angular writing more familiar to you than the sight of her face. You laugh and chatter, light up a cigarette and smoke and all the while you register what has been done to her.

The catalog of change is fearful, horrifying. They have cut down through her lower lip, through her chin, and across her throat, a razor-thin incision that curves up along her left cheek. They have taken away her vocal cords and most of her tongue. They have left her a hole in her throat through which she breathes. She motions to you that she wants a cigarette but when she tries to puff at yours, she can't even draw smoke. The flap of gauze at her throat moves ineffectually and she acts out her disgust. A pack and a half of cigarettes a day for twenty years are probably responsible for the cancer, but you can't help admiring her spunk. She has written you in a letter that she was angry that she survived the surgery and you can see why. She has no sensation in her lower lip, can taste nothing, and she tells you, as though it were a bother, that the stump of her tongue makes her feel that she's constantly chóking. Still that valiant little body of hers, after years of abuse, has resisted this staggering blow. The day after surgery, she was sitting up, watching television, writing notes on her Magic Slate, jokes about her "face-lift." She has learned since then how to change her own bandages, how to suction mucus from her windpipe, how to insert the tubes through her nose three times a day for her liquid meals. She tells you, in silent detail, how she's had a wisdom tooth removed on top of everything else and she's tickled about it, pantomiming *What next?* with a shrug.

It's odd to talk to her this way. Your own voice sounds loud and the messages you give her seem not to the point. You tell her about the flight, the loss of your luggage, of your room at the St. Regis which looks out on that blazing city. Her room is high up too, she says, but the view is different. She asks you about Peter Blue and your baby, a girl only eight weeks old, and together you think back to that January night, before all this, when she was whole and sat with you through labor. *You see?* you say to one another mutely with your eyes, all the best things have happened to us in places like this, all the best things have come to us just this way. And you know that the whole of your relationship probably has to do with holding hands in rooms no bigger than this, in cities no better known to you than the one where you now reside.

So you hold her hand and watch TV and you try not to think what it means, her life or yours. At ten, when you leave to go back to the hotel, her eyes fill with tears and you hug her briefly. Oddly enough, you try not to care because caring is too painful. The caring is made up of things you can't deal with yet, things you won't understand or accept for a long time to come. So you kiss her good night in a quick way and promise you'll be back by morning. She walks with you as far as the nurses' station where she introduces you, mutely and proudly, to the nurses sitting there.

The elevator doors slide open and you step inside, turning then to look at her once more as the doors slide shut. And you understand in that moment how like a prison this place is also, how like a prisoner she is, shut away now in the captive silence of her head. And you understand that she's always been this way, locked away from you, locked away from life. And you know that death is the only way she can ever be free.

You go out to the street, out through the glass revolving doors to the bitter cold beyond. An icy March wind whistles down the deserted street and the night stretches out before you, stark and chill. A taxi pulls up and you step inside, glancing back at the hospital once as you close the door.

april 24, 1960

THE PHONE RINGS and you say, "I'll get it," moving into the downstairs hall to the telephone stand. Peter Blue, who's been your husband for a year and a half, is sitting on the couch in the living room
watching a baseball game on TV. It's a Sunday afternoon and he's
drinking beer, bent forward slightly, elbows on his knees, chin
propped on one fist. From time to time, almost idly, he lights a cigarette. He's excited by baseball games, which he watches most weekends while you sit, not quite involved, but hoping to be.

The phone rings again and you take up the receiver, glancing as
you always do at the photograph of your older sister which hangs
there on the wall. The picture was taken when she was six. She
stands, smiling broadly, hands at her sides, wearing a light wool
coat. Her hair is arranged in long dark ringlets to her shoulders and
her two front teeth are missing. Whenever you see the picture, you
remember the story that goes with it, of how you were meant to be

there, too. You were three at the time and frightened of the photographer who'd been out hunting squirrels. When he came to the house with the gun, you believed he meant to shoot you, too, and you wept so hard you were not allowed to stand there with her on the steps.

"Hello?" you say, and your father's voice comes through the line.

"Hello, Kit?" he says, his voice tilting up with uncertainty. "This is Daddy. Oh," he says, and he sighs then before he goes on. "I just thought I better call and let you know. Vanessa died a little while ago."

"Are you all right?" you ask him, not knowing what else to say.

"Yes, I'm all right. I'm just waiting here for Dr. Belton."

"Do you want me to come down to the hospital?" you ask.

"Oh, no, that isn't necessary. He'll have to sign the death certificate and then I'll be home. It shouldn't take long. They've put in a call for him now."

"Do you want me to do anything?"

"No, just tell Del for me if you would. We'll talk more about it when I get home."

"All right, Daddy. We'll see you soon then."

"All right, that's fine. Bye now, sweetie," he says, and his voice holds ever so slightly the tremor of tears locked away.

Del stands at the head of the stairs and you see her now as you set down the phone. She's twenty-three and a long way from the girl in the photograph.

"Vanessa died a while ago," you say.

"Well," she says, "did Daddy say when he'd be home?"

"Pretty soon he said. He's waiting for Dr. Belton now to sign the death certificate."

"Well," she says again, "I'll be down in a minute."

You move back to the living room and tell Peter Blue that your mother has died and you sit down with him on the couch and watch TV for a while. It isn't that you don't care. It isn't that the death doesn't give you pain. You wished her dead many times and you'll have to deal with that in the years to come. For now, you simply don't know what to do with the death. And Peter Blue doesn't know. He tries a consoling pat to your shoulder but you haven't asked for that and you shrug him off. You don't even know, in that moment, how annoyed you will be with Peter Blue for offering all those wrong gestures and all those conventional sentiments when you're struggling so hard with the fact of Vanessa's death. His clichés are just a distraction, just an impediment to the pain which you reach for tentatively in your head. You can't even tell him why he's wrong to pat you that way and you have to pretend you're simply shifting positions on the couch.

By and by, your sister Del comes down and sits in Vanessa's rocker nearby and the baseball game goes on, a tableau of men on a field of gray. For a while you take refuge in the sight. Del lights a cigarette and so do you and the silence in the living room is peopled only with the sounds of shouting fans. The announcer tells you what is taking place but it's all the same to you. You don't even know which teams are playing and you doubt that you'll ever care anyway. You're twenty years old today, on this Sunday when Vanessa's elected to die. You add the fact of your birthday to the fact of her death and you think what a strange anniversary that will be next year, what an odd celebration, birth and death. Both have been a freedom to you—both have set you free but you won't understand the freedom any more than you'll understand your own life for a while yet.

Upstairs, there are two babies sleeping, your daughter and Del's son, and Del's husband, Andy, will be home later in the day from a visit with his mother, who lives next door. Your life is crowded with people upstairs and down and you'd like to get away from them. The need to be alone is the same need you felt when your daughter was being born and you lay on a hospital bed for two days, thinking, God, go away, just leave me alone to bear this pain in peace, just leave me alone to call out if I must, to cry. But you sit there on that couch with your sister and Peter Blue and you all avoid, at any cost, the mention of death as though it would be out of place. You're all pretending the baseball game is real, that Vanessa's death is the game you can shut off at will. And you wonder, sitting there, who won Vanessa's life and you feel a faint moment of relief, not knowing yet that the loss is yours, too.

After a while the babies wake, and you have to take care of that: the feeding, the bathing, the changing of diapers, feeling with your daughter just what you felt with Peter Blue, that hint of annoyance that she's intruded on your grief, a hint of dismay at finding your-self a mother to her when you haven't recovered yet from being a daughter to the one who died. It's very complex, this life of yours, full of strangers who make demands; a husband and baby who want you to be someone you're not ready for. And a nagging voice says, You did it—you chose this life and now you'll just have to bear it—you'll just have to bear what has to be borne. But you won't, of course. The fact of Vanessa's death will change all that in a way you never dream of, hugging your daughter tightly as you do.

In the meantime, your father comes home looking tired and he talks in a weary way about her death, about how he sat by her bed while the nurse left the room, about how she died in the space of a breath before the nurse returned. You had sat there too, by that bed, and you know what it was for him, to sit there with her, holding her pale white hand, the fingers as cold and as unresisting as the empty leather fingers of a glove. You know what it was to listen to her breathing, counting once and twice and then pause and counting once and twice again. Now and then her breath would come quite softly, like a sigh from someplace far away, a sleep too far down for her to come up again. She would die. You knew that then, when you sat with her, and in some ways you knew it better then than you do now. Now, in this house, with the babies to be fed, with dinner to be managed and the long-distance calls to be made, with Peter Blue smoking cigarettes, saying all the wrong things—now Vanessa's death seems less than real.

And later when you get in bed and the day is done, later when you think you'll have a moment to yourself, later Peter Blue is asking in that absolutely silent way of his if he can make love to you. And you think, Oh Peter Blue, you are so damn dumb, you are so insensitive. But you married the man because he was normal and now that burden is yours, too. And you say to yourself, He means well—he means to comfort me, and the same voice says, He's dumb anyway.

"Just leave me alone," you whisper harshly to him in the dark and he creeps away and you cry then to yourself without a sound, as much for his being dumb as for her death.

the closet

THIS IS A STORY about the contents of a closet. It's the only story of its kind and it will only be told once, so listen carefully.

There was a woman who died when she was fifty-one and after the funeral, it was necessary to clean out her closet, to dispose of her belongings. In her bedroom, there was a picture of her, taken when she was thirty-one or thirty-two. She had a round face, rather a pretty face, with light brown hair in two gleaming braids coiled around her head, a pleasant smile showing nice teeth, and eyes that must have been hazel or blue though the picture is in black and white. She's wearing a summer cotton, dotted swiss, and a necklace of white plastic beads—not beads, but buttons strung together in a double row, the sort of necklace children noticed when she held them.

The furniture in her bedroom hadn't changed since 1940, twenty years ago: a bed, a dressing table with a stool, a chest of drawers, all done in a wood veneer. It's the sort of furniture you see now at the Salvation Army stores. You could cut off the legs and antique the dresser but it would still be unattractive, spindly and cheap. The wallpaper was patterned with gloomy bouquets, gray and dusky rose, and the ceiling fixture was shaped like a shell in a shallow pool of light. She had rearranged the room only twice in all those years.

The closet door usually stood open and on it hung a shoe bag filled with her shoes. Most were size five, the last pair probably purchased in 1948; wedgies, white canvas wedgies with a strap that buckled behind the heel, toeless, not terribly worn; several pairs of slippers. There were two pairs of black leather shoes, toeless, with low square heels and black laces.

The clothes hung on a wooden rod to the left of the walk-in closet (the only closet in that massive house and hers, the only bedroom without a gas fireplace). Above the rod, on a shelf that never got much light, was a gray-and-white-striped hat box and an old water heater, looking ominous and out of place, dusty and ineffectual. On the right, six drawers and about as many shelves, containing very little—a few old hats, musty black straw hats with crumpled veils, a red felt hat with a big rhinestone buckle. In the drawers, she kept her stockings, some cotton slips, two empty fifths of Old Crow and half a fifth of King, a red patent leather purse made to look like a bound leather volume, another purse, black cloth with an old hand-kerchief wadded up in it, a diaphragm looking as ancient as a pair of wire-rimmed spectacles. She didn't have many clothes. Some of the dresses, like the black knit, were as dated as the shoes, and strangely cut, with plump shoulder pads, the fabric faintly powdered with dust. There was a gold satin blouse—somewhere there's a photograph taken of her in that blouse, at a party, maybe 1946— beside the blouse a black gabardine suit with black braid buttons and next to that, a gathered cotton skirt in a pastel blue, a red-and-white-checked blouse with long sleeves, and a white blouse with a lacy trim. She was buried in a blue wool suit, which was bought for her, as were the newer outfits, by her daughter Kit.

On the dressing table, there were boxes of loose powder in a ruddy hue, nail files and hairpins, bobby pins, astringent lotion, tortoiseshell combs which she fixed together with rubber bands to form the waves in her hair, some dark red lipsticks worn down at a slant, a brush with a wooden handle and a tangle of fine brown hair in the bristles. In the drawers, a jumble of junky costume jewelry: pins, earrings, and a necklace of white plastic buttons.

From this, you might draw a few conclusions about her. She was not a woman who cared much for her surroundings. She did not care for clothes. She cared for bourbon, Old Crow and King, and she wore wedgies once upon a time. She didn't go out much and her needs were few. She cared so little about most things she didn't even bother to throw them away, or maybe she simply preferred old things to emptiness. Someone bought a few things for her. Someone sorted through them when she died and piled them all up on the bed: shoes and stockings, hats, junky jewelry, and the clothes still on the hangers, dusty-smelling, out of style. Somehow, at some point, and for reasons unknown, the woman in the photograph, looking fresh and pleased with herself at thirty-two, became no more than a pile of rags on a dark green spread.

Now that her daughter is getting older, nearing thirty-two her-self, she does not see in it sadness as she once did, or tragedy or waste or ruin. She sees a kind of dignity, a kind of pride, something fierce and stubborn, something free. And even though the face is gone, and even though the house has been destroyed, some things remain the same. Life is as veiled, as elusive as death and there is no way to separate one from the other.

maple hill

KIT WALKED THROUGH the empty house, listening to her footsteps resounding against the pale dead floors. The strips of blue carpeting had been taken up from the hallway, ripped away from the stairs so that the sound of her walking was unfamiliar to her—she who had walked in that house for twenty years. Now the windows stood open to the summer heat and a wind that smelled of lilacs touched at the screens. From her bedroom, she could look out into the side yard, where the cherry tree had blossomed every April since time began, and beyond to the part of the yard they had always called the jungle, to the walnut tree, the lilac arbor, the maples which had shaded the front of the lot and drawn away the moisture so that no grass ever grew there by the front walk. She could remember climbing out onto the red tin roof outside her bedroom windows, watching her mother rake the maple leaves into two enormous piles. She and her sister, Del, had tumbled in that rustling ocean of dry brown year after year, had watched later while the leaves were burned, leaving two black circles like burial mounds on which the passing seasons were laid.

Between her room and Del's was a narrow room where the maid had slept early in their lives, a withered old colored woman named Pee Wee who later took care of Teddy Roosevelt the Fourth, she was told. All she could remember of Pee Wee was that she had no teeth. When Pee Wee left, she and Del had begun to use the little room for a playroom, an office, a grocery store where empty tins were bought and sold for a cardboard coin or two.

Kit crossed the hall to Del's room, marveling as she always did at how clearly the differences between them were spelled out. Both rooms had the same high ceilings, the same narrow windows, the same fireplaces which had been converted to gas and later stuffed with newspapers to keep bats and stray birds from flying down the chimneys. Both rooms had the same shallow shell fixture in the ceiling, throwing light down like some pale echo of the sea, far away, far away. The wallpaper in Kit's room was dark green sprinkled with pink rosebuds on a curving stem and the curtains had been frothy white from ceiling to floor, the rug a dusty pink, the bedspreads white. In Del's room the wallpaper had no pattern at all and the deep rose hue seemed stark and plain. Instead of curtains, Del had pasted Chinese rice paper on the glass, leaving the windows bare of ornament. The picture frames she had chosen were no more than two sheets of glass between which she had pressed magazine illustrations, all of it held in place by two metal clamps and a wire affixed to the strip of molding near the ceiling. The one picture Kit remembered was of a young man who sat squarely facing the camera. One hand rested on a table in front of him, fingers tucked out of sight, and near him was a single rose in a Coke bottle. Kit had never understood why her sister would select such a picture, all in black-and-white and tones of gray. Del had never kept a china figurine, had never collected dolls or stamps or shells or party invitations. Del was three years older than Kit and Del had collected books. It was one of the great frustrations in Kit's life that no matter how many books she read or how fast she read them or in what order, Del was always three years ahead of her. Del was ahead of her in everything. She heard all of the beautiful music first, knew Botticelli, Titian, and Renoir before Kit had given away her dolls.

And now the house was being sold and the land, their mother was dead, their father remarried: all of life, everything was breaking apart, breaking down, being leveled, destroyed, razed, rendered obsolete, that childhood, that life, that family as odd and unhappy as it had been.

Kit wandered down the hallway to her mother's room, bleak relic from the thirties with its grim bouquets of roses marching across the walls, its dark woodwork, the shades lowered, radiator peeling cream-colored paint. Gone was the dresser with its splintered veneer, gone was the dark plush dressing-table stool, the chest of drawers, the bed with its dark chenille spread. The closet drawers were empty now of the whiskey bottles which Kit had raided time after time, pouring five-dollar bourbon down the bathroom sink in some misguided attempt to save her mother from the doom of secret drinking. At some point in her life, Kit's mother had come in from raking leaves and had taken instead to the quiet life of an alcoholic. Kit thought of her mother always, stretched out in the cool of the living room on the couch, a cigarette burning in her fingers, a paperback novel laid facedown across her chest. Kit's mother had read Shell Scott, had smoked, had tottered out to the pantry for a jigger of Early Times, had tottered up to her bedroom for Old Crow and King. Kit's mother had been hauled off to the hospital several times a year suffering malnutrition, pneumonia, and broken bones. Kit's mother had been hauled off, toward the last, with cancer of the throat and finally suicide. After the funeral, Kit had slept in her mother's bed, wondering how her mother had felt on the last night of her life with a hundred phenobarbital burning in her belly. Ruined woman, wreck of a life. Her mother had been razed and the rest of them now followed, one by one, an oddly self-destructive lot, having learned that from the cradle.

Off her mother's room was the sleeping porch, screened-in, where she and Del had slept every summer, lulled by the tapping of green slatted shades which could be rolled down against the morning sun, rolled up at night to let in the sound of chill summer rain and the smell of drenched lilacs. Every spring there had been the ritual of the cleaning of that porch when the yard man, James or a black George Washington, would hose down the screens, scrub down the winter dirt, black soot and dust which collected with the snow. The rollaway beds were moved out onto the porch then and made up with fresh sheets, with cotton spreads which were pale brown and patterned with Navajo designs. There was a trap in the porch ceiling which led up to the attic. Kit had been told that the roof of the original farmhouse was still there, bent down, the new roof built over it after the first house had burned. Somehow she had always had a horror of that, of the old roof still intact and that part of the brick wall which remained. The farmland itself had been eaten away so that now there was only this one acre left like an island out of the past, floating among present houses and present neighborhoods. Even that last acre had been sold (thirty-five thousand dollars she'd heard) and once the house was torn down there'd be two or three apartment buildings instead.

Downstairs, she passed through the dining room to the tiny room where her father had slept for the last ten years on an old maroon daybed. The room had apparently been intended for the raising of house plants. The floor was of cold tile, smooth dark red stone with a drain in the middle and a faucet which no longer functioned. There were windows on two sides of the room and hooks in the ceiling for hanging pots. The room was scarcely large enough for the three pieces of old maple furniture which had been moved in: the daybed, a small coffee table, and a maple armchair. There was also a revolving drugstore rack that had been filled with the paperback books they bought and read. Kit's mother had marked each in pencil when she finished it—"dull" or "dirty" or "good"—so that Kit had at her disposal an endless supply of Mickey Spillane in that monk's cell where her father slept, without sheets, with his shoes on, covered by an ancient varicolored afghan which her mother had crocheted during pregnancy. How could she have known, that woman, that her needlework would only eventually warm his celibacy in the winter of their life? It was gone now, of course, maple furniture and dirty books, man and wife.

The living room looked the same to her, somewhat smaller with the furniture removed, somewhat colder with the rug taken out. The mirror had been taken down from its place above the mantel, leaving a dead blank space where once the hallway had been reflected. There was still on the pale green paper, the ghostly imprint of the lath and plaster behind it, shadowy ribs of the house showing through. In the hall where the upright piano had been, there was now a clean square of wallpaper, rimmed with fingerprints. All those years of piano lessons, what had they been for? Her parents had once had friends who came to the house and played during parties, George Gershwin tunes and Irving Berlin, and the neighbors up and down the block would remark the next morning how lovely it had been. Kit could hardly imagine such a thing. Kit's last recollection of the house was the wild summer after her father had remarried and moved out. She had lived there by herself with her infant son and the cook who came in days and the men who came in nights. There had been two men that summer and one of them she had now married. The neighbors had watched his sports car come and go and in the mornings, they made no remarks at all. Poor dears. The man across the street had shot himself one day; the two sisters down the block were dying. The big houses all around them were being converted into apartments. There was a pattern of death and decay and destruction, the old swallowed up by the new, bent down, built over, layers and layers of wallpaper in an empty room. Even the walls came down eventually when they could hold no more; even a life could tumble when its burden was past bearing.

She left the front door open, thinking surely there was nothing more to be locked in or out of that house. To the right of it, on the border of the yard above the alley, there was an old stone hitching post. She had watched it, through her life, being slowly engulfed by the trunk of a tree growing near it. That suffocation would be stopped at least when the bulldozers came; stone post and tree would go down together. In certain moments there were no distinctions made between host and parasite, begetter, begotten. In time, both fell prey to the passing of years, some new order which wiped away love and hate as though they were the same. They had struggled as a family and now it was done and whatever it meant, whatever it had done to them or they to each other simply had no meaning anymore. She could walk away from that house and still be haunted by it. Whatever time and distance she set between herself and the house and all that it had been to her, she would never be free of it. Those twenty years would be imprinted on her heart like the shadows of that lath and plaster in the wall, and she would act them all out over and over again, bending down, building over, house upon house, heart upon heart. She was a walking blueprint of those years, mind and memory, a habit of that world, repeating in every relationship the wrongs she had learned in that house. There was nothing more to be locked in or out of her. There was only summer and the smell of lilacs and a house called Maple Hill, and as she drove away, she knew how thoroughly the lessons of her life had all been learned.

a portable life

During that last summer I lived alone there with my infant son. I had made a nursery of the narrow room between my room and Del's and he slept there, tiny creature with his wobbly infant's head and his unfocused eyes. During the previous winter I had redone my room, stripped off the dark green wallpaper with its pattern of rosebuds, patched the cracks in the plaster, and taken away the faint glass fixture in the ceiling. For a while the room remained that way, quite bare, naked of paint and paper. Even the plaster was the color of cold flesh and the wind rattled at the empty windows. The glass was as chill and clear as the ice along the sills, and the snow, when it came, made the room glow with gray light. The few pieces of furniture were draped with sheets, and a narrow bed was set in the center of the room. The whole of it was as raw and as clean as a crater, a place bombed-out and abandoned except for me. Everything else in the house remained the same—the runners of dark blue carpeting in the hall, the tall oval mirror that stood just outside my bedroom door, my sister's room across the hall, my mother's room to the right, the landing to the stairs, the rooms below, laid out like a vast museum—all the relics of the life which everyone had left but me. My son was born in April. My father married again in May and by the time summer came, there were shutters at my windows, painted chocolate brown, and the walls were the color of mushroom soup in a can.

The windows were thrown open and the heat poured in, smelling of grass and earth and occasional summer rains. The record player stood between two windows and I played Respighi and Aaron Copland. When I listen to those records now I understand what that music was to me—distant and sweet; in one, the sound of scented waves on a tropical shore, in the other, the sound of the prairies, something wide and windy, full of sunshine and bending grasses; unpopulated music where no people walked at all. I lived in the music and it lived in me and tonight as I listen, I can remember exactly how it felt to be in that room. I can sense its dimensions, length and breadth, the pale floors, sanded down to a honeyed hue and varnished to a soft gloss, the new ceiling fixture like a hanging funnel enameled black so that the light by contrast was hot and white. The new rug was an oval of black plush, and the room seemed wonderfully empty, straight and simple, as though a hundred seasons could come and go and never set a mark upon those walls.

I don't know how I could have cared so much for a house. When Mildred came, of course, she had to tear it down. She was Daddy's new life and nothing could remain of the old. I understood and it was right, I suppose. For a long time I wouldn't go back, wouldn't look at the land where the house had been, where apartment buildings now stand. I couldn't give the sight away, the one in my mind's eye of that house, hung in shade where the maples threw pale green shadows on the walk and the weeping willow in the corner of the lot hid all my childhood games. I couldn't give away what that was to me, all the pleasure and pain, the visions and the fantasies; all the doors we slammed on one another in anger and the sound of piano music in the front hall, Del and me playing scales. The basement flooded in winter, water creeping up the basement stairs like a thief; bats came down the chimneys, and the walls in certain sections of the house were solid brick a foot thick so that the plumbing could never be improved. There would be occasions when my father would go up with a flashlight into the eaves of the house and the air up there must have been eighty-five years old. The house was made up of oddities and improvisations. The laundry chute between the two bathrooms was boarded up but stale wind still blew from the cabinet below. I would drop things into that darkness now and then, knowing there could never be a bottom to a pit like that, though there was, of course. One could run down to the basement and open the laundry bin to retrieve lost combs and doll shoes, old rags. When I was young, if I wet my pants I would toss them down that chute thinking that I would never be discovered in my sins. I hate to think, when the house was torn down, what the workmen uncovered in a day's destruction: messages I hid under loosened fireplace tiles in my bedroom hearth; old dreams boarded up in the walls. God, I'm glad I never saw the house torn down, rooms exposed when the walls were ripped away. I've seen houses like that, opened up like ripe fruit, and I always think I shouldn't look, that the rooms are meant only for the eyes of those who lived there. And what does it all mean, wallpaper and window shades, bare bulbs hanging down where the fixtures have all been auctioned off? What does it mean when there's nothing left but a hole where the basement was and a winding stairway that rises up out of nowhere and ends abruptly nowhere, too? And what does it mean to see those disconnected pipes like metal shoots, growing up out of plaster beds, powdered as fine as snow? I think it means that life is done and someone should let go. I think it means that no one can hang on to dreams like that, no matter how precious, no matter how full of pain. I think it means we should all escape while we can with our suitcases bumping our legs and our airplane tickets to the West Coast. Out there, they tell me, the houses are made of stucco instead of frame and the roofs are made out of rock instead of tin. There are no basements to flood, no icy winters to remind us of the other winters in our lives. And the music, when it comes again, might sound the same but the prairies are closer to home and the wide hills and the wind. In the West there is even an ocean like the one Respighi heard. You have to give the house away to have it, have to give away the trees, sign away the mortgage on your father who belongs to someone else now, sign away your mother's grave. When it's done and the papers are filed away in your heart, you can make a new life for yourself, take your infant son and your unborn daughter out of bondage. And it's all right, the trade you make, that transaction among trust deeds. You'll know that the music you heard in the summer of 1961 was only the song of the next decade drifting back at you, out of time, and that's all right, too. When you get there, when you make it safely, you can

look back on the old rooms and you'll understand then why they had
to go, why they had to be torn down. And you'll know she never can
destroy the structure in your head, the dream house you've resur-
rected in your mind. That's yours and you can furnish it as you like,
out of truth, out of memories, out of recollection and grief. You can
make of it a mausoleum too where all your lives are laid out like the
dead. On the West Coast there are graves with no headstones and the
funeral homes look like Howard Johnson restaurants in the East.
And for all you know, you'll end up there in the pastures of Forest
Lawn with no more to commemorate your life than a statue of Aph-
rodite in the nude. I think you'd best make your peace with the past
since you've come this far. I think you know by now that you won't go
back again.

the quarrel

THERE WAS A KNOCK at the bedroom door and Kit glanced up from her packing. "Come in," she said, hesitantly, and then she went on with what she was doing, folding a sweater, placing it neatly beside the folded skirt in the half-filled suitcase.

"Kit? Can I come in a minute?" It was her father, standing in the doorway, still in his robe and slippers.

"Yes, that's all right, Daddy," she said.

He was looking uncomfortable, his lean face lined with regret, his mouth creasing into a smile which hovered, hopefully, looking for one in return.

She smiled for him but not from any joy of her own. She smiled because she recognized the look on his face. He was being sent like an emissary from an enemy camp; the eternal diplomat, poor dear.

"Everything all ready to go?" he said.

"Just about. I have a few things more but it's mostly done."

He sat down on the twin bed and took a pack of cigarettes from the pocket of his robe. "Is there an ashtray in here?" he said, glancing around at the chest of drawers.

Kit took the blue one from the windowsill and handed it to him, watching while he lit his cigarette and offered one to her. She shook her head slightly.

"I just put one out," she said.

"Will you sit down and talk a minute?" he asked, and she nodded, knowing exactly what he would say but unable somehow to refuse him. It would be painful, she knew, because they would skirt the truth. It would be a conversation like a hundred others she could remember except that this one would deal with Mildred where the others had dealt with Vanessa. Vanessa was her first mother, her real mother, and Mildred was her second. Kit really didn't want to talk about either of them. In fact, she had assumed when Vanessa died that all the conversations between fathers and daughters about their mothers would end. But here was another mother to be discussed, circumstances to be justified, forgiveness rendered like a judgment in which Kit had already been condemned.

Mildred went to church. Mildred did good works. In the community at large, she was known for her tireless efforts in behalf of others. This charity did not extend to Kit or her sister.

Mildred was a partner in her father's law firm so Kit had known her for years. When she'd heard the two were getting married, she'd felt happy about it, not realizing what shrill surprises were waiting for her down the line. Mildred specialized in estate planning and wills. She told Kit in passing about the bequest of an elderly client who was leaving twelve thousand dollars for the care of her beloved dog in the event of her death. Mildred had the dog put down the same week the woman died.

The quarrel the night before had been a bitter one. Mildred was a fighter where Vanessa's tyranny had been the silent, sullen type. To Kit, in the moment, thinking back across all those other moments, it might have been one long quarrel springing out of the same relentless rage. It might even have been the same mother for all the good it did her. Mildred had a sharp tongue and an icy accuracy, plunging deep and hard and sometimes even wildly so that the wounds were all-encompassing and not easily healed. Without any conscious intent, Kit had begun trying to appease and placate the woman to no particular effect. Once in a while Kit blew, which she'd done the night before. And here was her father again, bright and early to patch things up, to smooth over an unsightly anger, explain away any excess emotion. Blessed are the peacemakers, she thought, except that she didn't consider her father blessed at all but damned because he was willing to pay any price. He was not a meek man but a beaten one. Vanessa, in twenty-eight years of marriage, had worn him down and now he had married Mildred and that would finish him off. He was a man strangely satisfied by grief.

"Mildred had to go over to her mother's this morning. She and Clara have to take turns, you know. The uh . . . old woman doesn't know them anymore of course . . . hardly knows anyone, but the nurses need relief one day a week so Mildred and the other sisters take turns. She said she was sorry she couldn't be here to see you off."

Kit didn't make much reply to that. Mildred, she knew, must have been delighted to go sailing off first thing, her martyrdom clearly visible, leaving Kit and her father to finish up whatever ugly business remained from the night before.

"Mildred really does have a lot on her mind," he said, and Kit felt a little pinch of pain. "She works awfully hard," he went on, "and you know how she is. She has a quick temper sometimes but she has a heart of gold and she's really a pretty good old gal."

Kit lit a cigarette and emptied her mind. It might have been Vanessa he was talking about, some stranger, a character in a book. It all seemed the same and what was he really saying? He was saying, "Kit, dear, do me this one thing . . . let's overlook the god-awful thing this woman has done and just be glad anyone would have us at all." He was saying, "You and I are the strong ones, Kit, so we'll have to be the ones who forgive, let bygones be bygones." He was saying, "Try, Kit, to get along on just this fantasy between us, that your mother means well but falters now and then."

And all the while whatever it was that they were overlooking, Kit and her father together in these little chats, whatever they were being so courtly about, was in truth some monstrous violation of the values he had taught her, some disastrous wrong which later, afterward, he carefully explained away. Sometimes Kit got so caught up in the make-believe forgiveness she couldn't remember what it was that did her in, what hellish thing had taken place the night before. Even now the details of her quarrel with Mildred were indistinct. Quarrels were like that. Quick and brutal and disconnected so that later it was nearly impossible to reconstruct the logic of those cruel accusations and cutting rebuffs. Mildred was an expert at it, of that she was certain, and maybe that's all the quarrel had been intended to be: a testing of weapons, of strength, of skills. Mildred was a paralyzing opponent because she stopped at nothing. Kit had been utterly vulnerable, caught off guard by some snide remark which then triggered that violent exchange. Kit had come off poorly and in retrospect could think of a thousand withering remarks when she had really only burst into tears and run upstairs. Mildred had cried then too, not to be outdone, and Kit's father had stayed downstairs playing diplomat to Mildred's hysterics so that Mildred had managed to win twice: once in the real arena and once offstage.

Kit got up and folded a pair of plaid wool slacks and placed them in the suitcase, listening idly while her father droned on about Mildred's goodness of heart which was only occasionally overlaid by venom, spite, and vituperation. Mildred was a big woman, angry and insecure, an abrasive woman who marched through life hoarding grudges like bad debts on which she could eventually collect. She was not all that bad, Kit thought to herself, even while she berated Mildred in her head, but the instinct to temper her judgment was something her father had taught her and even now she resented that peacemaker's tool. Her father amended and qualified and overlooked and understood and soothed and pacified until reality was not even recognizable. What he did, in effect, was to take all the blame for whatever went on and then humbly ask someone to forgive him.

"It was really my fault," he was saying gruffly. "I should have realized she was tired. She tried so hard to have everything just right for you. God, she cleaned house for weeks and cooked. I guess the holidays are pretty darned hard on her too with that bursitis acting up like it does. It's a nasty business, bursitis. . . ."

Kit tuned him out again. Medical problems, now what the hell did she care about Mildred's medical problems? She knew she was meant to understand from what he said that Mildred was suffering, staunchly, some terrible ill which was in fact responsible for whatever cruel things she had said. And Kit would buy it. She knew she would. It was like some incredible game they had played, these twenty years, being noble and long-suffering while first Vanessa and then Mildred went at them tooth and claw. What was she supposed to do with all that pain? What was she meant to do with the anger she felt? Eat it up, gulp it down? She had done that now for twenty years and she knew that it was anger that made her stomach cramp, burned the walls of her abdomen like cigarettes from inside. It was anger that perforated, eventually, and spilled out your guts, as his had spilled, leaving nothing of all that nobility but a scar a yard wide. It was anger too that cut away love so that angry people were numb to the core, uncaring and cut off from tenderness, cut off from tears.

He finished what he was saying and Kit chimed in with the usual clichés and comments, together manufacturing a plausible excuse for all that was inexcusable in the world. He patted her hand and kissed her cheek and when he had shuffled out again, she went right on packing, putting two blouses in with the sweater, her hosiery with the nightgown and slippers. She noticed she was crying into the suitcase as she worked and it seemed absurd somehow that whatever true tears she wept for him would only be packed away with her shoes and carried back with her to California. I could have cried on the West Coast, she thought. I could have wept without coming three thousand miles for more. But she couldn't, she knew, have completed that strange transaction of mercy, the last bond between them. Father and daughter, heads bent together, acting out rites that neither of them could identify. If Mildred died, some other lady would come along to do them in, to cut at them and whip them, giving them grace to forgive again and peace to indemnify.

jessie

"YOUR MOTHER WAS a wonderful person," Jessie says to me, her
forehead furrowing as she speaks. Her face is a warm coffee brown
and her cheeks are high, her teeth very white and her black hair
streaked with gray. She came to work for us when I was sixteen and
my father had just had his ulcer surgery. That was fifteen years ago
and now everything is different except Jessie and me. When I see
her, we talk about the house, about Daddy and Mildred, about my
mother too. Somehow Jessie is the only person in the world now who
remembers Vanessa as I do and we talk together about everything
that was, as though we can between us reconstruct some portion of
the past forever lost to us.

"I remember when Miss Mildred brung me out to the house for
an interview and your mother set on the couch in the living room
and ast me did I know how to make hot breads. And I don't know . . .
just something about her face and the way she spoke made me think

to myself, Now, Jessie, I believe this is where you should stay. I didn't have any idea in the world that I'd be with her that long but seems like it just worked out that way. Miss Mildred ast me some questions too but I never did care for her even then. I won't call her Mrs. Conway, you know. To me, your mother was the only Mrs. Conway."

"Oh, Jessie," I laugh, "what do you call her then?"

Jessie laughs too and her white teeth flash into view. "I try not to call her anything. Oh, sometimes I call her Mrs. C. but mostly I call her Miss Mildred. That bothers her some, I can tell, but she won't let on," she says, and then she goes on, talking almost to herself.

"I don't see much of your daddy since he married her. Miss Mildred, you know, she didn't like having me around once your mother was gone. It was too much reminder of everything that had gone before. I was just as glad when I started working for Del though she don't say a whole lot to me. Your sister don't say nothing to anyone. And I love Del, so don't get me wrong. It isn't that. But she and your daddy are kinda close-mouth, you know. Miss Mildred now, she'll say anything. Like she says to me one day, 'Jessie,' she said, 'Jessie, I want you to know how sorry Mr. Conway feels that he don't see more of you.' She didn't say she was sorry. Just him. So I didn't let on I noticed that and I said, 'Why, Miss Mildred, what do you mean? He comes down to visit with me now and then.'

" 'I mean, up to the house,' she says.

"And I said, 'Why, Miss Mildred, I love to go anywhere I'm invited.' She didn't mention any more 'up to the house' after that. Up to the house, my foot. You know she don't want me up there. If she want me to go 'up to the house' she knows where I am.

"You know, I went up there one day when I got off work from Del, and Miss Mildred she didn't like that much, I could tell, so I didn't go unannounced since then. Your mother would never have done me that way."

"Well," I say, "she was a good lady, I suppose."

"Yes, she was," Jessie says firmly. "She was just a real sweet person. I remember on the day she died . . . well, not the day she passed away, but the day she took them pills. She come out the back way when I went home from work that day. Followed me out to the porch and gave me a potted chrysanthemum. She'd already said she meant me to have it whenever the blooms were gone so I could plant it in my backyard, but she give it to me then and I remember thinking, Now why would she do such a thing? But it wasn't 'til later I knew. She hugged me real tight and waved good-bye and that was the last time I seen her alive."

death review

I AM SITTING IN Dr. Sherwood's office, typing on a Remington Twenty-Five electric machine, not even much amazed to find myself working again in a hospital atmosphere. Outside my office door, the patients walk up and down in their robes, reaching in occasionally to snitch a pastel mint from the blue glass bowl on my desk. Carts are rolled by with a rattle of breakfast trays and a bell pings relentlessly as the elevators go up and down. And the stretchers go by with their cargo wrapped in sheets and the nurses stroll past my door and the second hand on the big clock in the hall sweeps up and around as it nudges the minute hand. Across the hall, two attendants discuss a money-order chain letter presently making the rounds. For a twenty-dollar investment, the friend of one has made two hundred and forty dollars in four days.

I came to Pacific Coast Medical Center last Wednesday as a Western Girl but I'll be here a year or two. Somehow in a week of working, I've come to understand that this is true. And I don't much mind. I've worked in a hospital once before and I've worked in a doctor's office too. I know what it's like to share an elevator ride with a man on a stretcher going up to surgery and I know what it's like to see the same man come down and I know what it's like to catch sight of four tumors in bottles down in Pathology, formaldehyde like a tide pool in which they've been caught unwittingly. I know what it's like to hear Dr. Sherwood call down on the telephone and inquire if the doctor there has an interesting death to report for the monthly death review.

I review death too, sitting out here at my desk; at least I review the death I've known intimately . . . which was hers, my mother's, eleven years ago. The intern on the floor complained this morning that he'd been given a patient with cancer of the lungs, which he thought uninteresting. And for a moment I hoped to myself that I'd die of something smart. I don't resent his obsession with obscure disease, his desire for peculiar contagions and growths of an unknown sort. I don't even resent that death and the dying are commonplace to him. He'll go down someday with the rest of us, dying of something dull, and he'll pay just as much attention as we do. He's just young right now and caught up in the point of view that medical death shouldn't be a wasted event for a man with so much to learn.

My mother died of an overdose of sleeping pills after extensive surgery so that the cause of death was probably listed as Despair. I would list it, I think, as Fortitude or Courage or Hope or one of the other rare virtues she suffered from. She was a burning woman in a burning world and she drank herself down to death and she smoked until her throat caught fire and they had to douse the flame and excise the scorched tissue. After the surgery, what could she do but finish the job she'd begun? They had saved her when she didn't want to survive, rescued her life with their brand-new stainless steel tools when she was already done. After cancer, she did them one better with phenobarbital and from that, there was no salvation. They pumped medication into her arms and legs, filled her with blood and glucose and oxygen but she knew she had won and the silence of her death had a smug quality. And what was there left for me to say except "Good show."

So I'm back in a hospital job again, maybe looking for her in the files or looking for her on the carts rolling by or hoping for word of her in the medical journals on Dr. Sherwood's desk. I've even thought of asking him to send for her medical records in New York as though in the cataloging of heart, lungs, and temperature, I might learn something new about who she was and how she's related to me. Instead, I sit out here and type and smile at the patients in the hall and hope that some medical secretary years ago smiled at her and offered her a pastel mint for all her pain.

a letter
from my father

A FEW DAYS BEFORE your twenty-ninth birthday, he writes you a letter, this father of yours, and in it, he tells you what he remembers of you.

"In the course of thinking back over your twenty-nine years," he says, "I called to mind many charming memories (and some distressing ones as well); and among the highest ranking of them all was when you were three, just before I went into military service. I sat on your bed and you knelt to say your prayers, and after praying for all the regular and proper people, and thanking God for all the regular and proper things . . . you concluded with 'And God bless Santa Claus and the Easter Bunny and the Easter Bunny's Helper.' I don't know where the helper came from, and I didn't want to laugh at your prayers, but I nearly exploded in an effort to contain my laughter until you were in bed, had got kissed good night, and I could get downstairs.

"And in the same year, when the day came for me to put on my uniform and leave for Fort Knox, I didn't see how I could possibly say good-bye without crying all over the place, so I had to think up something. You won't remember, but what I suggested to you and Del was that instead of saying good-bye, I would come to attention, and so would you and Del—and then we would salute each other, as I had taught you to do. Del burst into tears and ran upstairs to her room, but you came to a very exaggerated state of attention, with your chest out and belly in, and chin very straight—and we saluted—and then I went out to the taxi, scarcely able to see what I was doing. I looked back and waved, and you waved too; and then I looked up at Del's window, and she was standing there, with a handkerchief against her mouth, and she waved finally. A memory that is very sweet, and very upsetting and almost unbearable all at the same time.

"Then when I came back from military service, I remember the warm evenings, sitting on the front steps, when you and Del would beg me to tell a story. And in those evenings I made up Silly Mongoose, and the story about the little white dog and the blind horse that the French family had to leave behind when they fled in front of the German armies in 1940—and other rambling tales I can't remember anymore. Sometimes I would start one without the foggiest notion of where it was going, or how it would end . . . and those seemed to be the ones you liked best. Both you and Del liked the sad stories best (but with a happy ending just in the nick of time) so I invented sad ones, and more of them. One time I got so engrossed in my own story that I was crying with you! Doesn't seem possible but it's true. I had to find a happy ending for that one and in a hurry. Then I blew my nose and felt better.

"Another bittersweet memory is when they brought you down from the operating room after your tonsils were removed. You were groggy with sedation and kept urping up frightening amounts of blood and with your eyes still closed, the first thing you said was 'I want my daddy.' So I sat by your bed and you hung on to the index finger of my right hand forever, and I would not have moved away for any amount of money."

That letter is the story of your life, all the stuff of which you are made, so that reading it again, a year later, you are amazed to see how carefully your character has been described in the course of those paragraphs. Twenty-five years are missing in his recollection of you and in those twenty-five years you have lived out all the consequences of the first four or five. There was a time in your life when you didn't believe in psychology, when you didn't believe that intelligent, rational people were the product of anything more than their own intelligence and their own rationality. Now you believe in everything; past, present, and future. You believe in memories. You believe in the suffering of truth and all that it requires. You believe that you are exactly the life-sized projection of that child sitting on the front steps of that house, listening to stories that were rescued, always, at the brink of truth.

You do remember the day your father went away. You remember your own confusion about your sister's sudden tears and her running to her room. That was not what your father had asked you to do. Your father had told you to salute and so you saluted proudly and you knew, even at the age of three, that you would do anything he asked, at whatever the cost.

Now that you are nearly thirty, you are writing letters to him and what you say to him is this: we did, yes, fail in our lives, the four of us; you and Vanessa, Del and me. We died of all the unwept tears and all the things we never understood.

You talk to him about your mother's death, about her need to die, about the ways in which her death has set you free, and how her death has bound you, broken you, and mended you again. You tell him, as a mother would, that you have loved him, whatever his failings, that you forgive him, that you have failures, too, which require forgiveness of him. You tell him that you have loved your life, that you are at peace with the person you have become and that he may have that peace too in your behalf. "We none of us die of grief," you say, "but only of not grieving quite enough."

And what you want for him is that he may weep too, for himself, for the ruin of all those years. You want to say to him, "Oh, my father, don't you see that we are healed, all of us, by being exactly what we are, by loving, by remembering, by opening up the wounded places in our lives and letting go?"

You want to tell him you treasure all the relics of the past. You know now that you are a living museum, full of rooms and crooked corridors that repeat themselves at every turn. And you want to tell him that by loving you, he can love himself too, that he can choose again rightly for every cloudy choice he's made, that he can learn to have his life instead of giving it away.

And you wonder if he'll hear you, years and years away, across the wide far country of your life, across the sins and resurrections of your soul. You wonder if he'll understand that, groggy in your life and full of pain, you call to him before you have even opened your eyes, that his presence there when you were four has reached across the world to you and touches you where you are now.

acknowledgments

Kinsey and Me (Bench Press, 1991), © 1991 Sue Grafton.

The following stories from *Kinsey and Me* first appeared as noted:

"Between the Sheets," © 1986 The Hearst Corporation. First published in *Redbook*. Reprinted by permission of the author.

"Long Gone," © 1986 The Hearst Corporation. First published in *Redbook* as "She Didn't Come Home." Reprinted by permission of the author.

"The Parker Shotgun," © 1986 Sue Grafton. First published in *Mean Streets*, an anthology.

"Non Sung Smoke," © 1988 Sue Grafton. First published in *An Eye for Justice*, an anthology.

"Falling off the Roof," © 1989 Sue Grafton. First published in *Sisters in Crime*, an anthology.

"A Poison That Leaves No Trace," © 1990 Sue Grafton. First published in *Sisters in Crime 2*, an anthology.

"Full Circle," © 1991 Sue Grafton. First published in *A Woman's Eye*, an anthology.